ALL WOUND UP

JACI BURTON

BERKLEY BOOKS, NEW YORK

BERKLEY

An imprint of Penguin Random House LLC
375 Hudson Street, New York, New York 10014

This book is an original publication of Penguin Random House LLC.

BERKLEY® and the "B" design are registered trademarks of Penguin Random House LLC.
For more information, visit penguin.com.

Burton, Jaci.
All wound up / Jaci Burton.—Berkley trade paperback edition.
pages ; cm.—(A play-by-play novel)
ISBN 978-0-425-27680-8 (trade)
I. Title.
PS3602.U776A79 2015
813'.6—dc23
2015013060

PUBLISHING HISTORY
Berkley trade paperback edition / August 2015

PRINTED IN THE UNITED STATES OF AMERICA

10 9 8 7 6 5 4 3 2 1

Cover photo by Claudio Marinesco.
Cover design by Rita Frangie.
Interior text design by Kristin del Rosario.

Penguin
Random
House

ACKNOWLEDGMENTS

There are so many people who make a book shine and who help me behind the scenes so I have the time to write. So to Telisa and Kati, thank you for your pinpoint proofing and beta reading. You make my books better, and I'm so grateful. To Lillie, I couldn't survive without you wrangling my incredibly unwieldy series bible and advising me when my timeline is off. And to Fatin, without you managing the day to day, I'd never finish a book.

I could not do this job without all your help. Thank you all so much.

ONE

IT WAS COOL, DARK AND—MOST IMPORTANTLY— private in Clyde Ross's wine cellar, which was why Tucker Cassidy had brought Laura, his girlfriend, down here.

She'd had a lot to drink today, and when she drank, she got loud and obnoxious.

She was also pissed at him at the moment.

Laura angry, drunk and loud? Not a good combination, especially not while they were at the house of the owner of the St. Louis Rivers. Clyde Ross was Tucker's boss, and the last thing he needed was his girlfriend making a scene. He had enough of a bad boy image without Laura making things worse by screaming at him in the middle of Clyde's very nice, very fancy party.

"I don't think there's anything more to discuss, Tucker, about why you keep dragging your feet about the two of us moving in together."

Yeah that so wasn't happening. "We can talk about this when I take you home tonight, Laura."

He'd brought her to the wine cellar in the hopes of cooling her down. Plus, they were alone here and no one could hear them. Okay, mainly no one could hear Laura, since she was the one who was doing all the talking. Loud talking. She was like a dog with a favorite bone once she got on a topic.

"We've been dating two whole months, Tucker. Don't you think it's time we make it official?"

It had been the most awful *two whole months* of his entire life. Okay, maybe not at the beginning. Laura was a knockout. Tall, with long dark hair, curves that just didn't quit and the best ass he'd ever seen. She was a cocktail waitress and they'd met one night when he'd been having drinks in the bar where she worked. They hit it off right away and had gone out, had a night of hot sex and had started dating. She'd been fun, adventurous, great in the sack and they had a lot in common.

Plus, she liked baseball, and he played for the Rivers. Not that it was a deal breaker if a woman he dated wasn't a baseball fan, but it didn't hurt if she was. She'd come to watch him play and she actually knew the game, as opposed to other women he'd dated who claimed to but in fact didn't know balls from strikes or a curve from a fastball. In his mind, that was a goddamned crime.

But as the weeks progressed, he'd noticed she didn't hold her liquor well, and when she drank, she was not a fun drunk. She was loud, obnoxious and she insulted his friends. Whenever she allowed him to be around his friends. Which lately wasn't often because she'd also grown more demanding of his time. Whenever they weren't together, she wanted to know where he was and how soon he was coming over. In other words, when he wasn't playing ball, she wanted him with her. *Only* with her. And she wanted him to account for every minute of his time.

He didn't need a mother—he had a pretty great one already.

And now the past few times they'd been together she'd thrown down hints about the two of them moving in together. He was so not ready for that.

So now he had to redirect her and calm her down before things got out of hand.

"How about we check out Clyde's awesome wine collection?"

She pushed at his chest. "I don't give a shit about Clyde or his wine. I want you to make a commitment to me."

He sighed and raked his fingers through his hair. He didn't want to do this here, but she hadn't left him much of a choice. "That's not gonna happen. We've only been dating two months and I'm not ready to live together."

She poked at his chest. "You know what? You're a sonofabitch. I thought we were heading somewhere. You led me to believe—"

He was going to have to stop her there. "I never made promises to you, Laura."

And now the tears. He'd seen a lot of those lately, too. Especially when she'd been drinking.

"I thought we were in love, Tucker."

"I never said that, either."

She broke down then and sobbed.

Well, shit. He walked over to her and pulled her into his arms. "I'm sorry."

"Sorry my ass. You're not sorry at all."

He didn't know how a woman could be so drunk, yet so accurate, but her knee hit his crotch at just the right angle, and he went down like a fighter who'd just been blasted by a perfect punch.

Lights out. Only instead of a hit to his jaw, she'd KO'd him right in the balls.

He vaguely registered her slurred words. "You're a prick. We're done, Tucker. I'm calling a taxi to take me home."

He heard the click of her heels on the stone floor as she walked away.

He couldn't even breathe, let alone care that she'd just fucking left him on the ground.

Jesus Christ, that had hurt. His balls throbbed like someone had—

Well, someone *had* shoved a knee into them.

He lay there for what seemed like hours, but he knew it was only minutes before he managed to stagger to his knees. He found the wall, still struggling to catch his breath.

In a minute. He'd be able to stand in just a minute.

"Oh, my God. Are you okay?"

He heard a female voice.

Great. Just what he needed. A witness to his humiliation.

Then cool, soft hands swept across his forehead.

"Are you hurt? Did you fall?"

He shook his head. "I'm fine."

"You are not fine. You're sweating and practically hyperventilating. Tell me what happened."

His eyes were still closed and he concentrated all his effort on trying to determine if his balls were still attached to his body. He did not want some woman being nice to him.

Actually, he wanted nothing to do with any female. Possibly ever again.

He managed to stand—with the woman's help, unfortunately.

"Tell me where you're hurt," she said.

He shook his head. "I'm not hurt. Just go away."

"I am not going to go away. I'm a doctor and I can help you."

Awesome. This night was getting worse by the second. "I don't need a doctor."

"How about you let me be the judge of that?"

He opened his eyes and looked over at his unwanted savior.

She was, of course, gorgeous. Which made her immediately untrustworthy, since he'd just vowed to never again fall for a beautiful woman.

She was average height, with short blond hair and the most intense blue eyes he'd ever seen. She also had the most perfect mouth—

Not that he was ever going to think about a woman in a sexual way again. Thoughts like that only led to trouble, and crushed testicles.

He leaned against the cool wall and tried to think about anything but this humiliating situation.

She slipped her fingers around his wrist.

"What are you doing?" he asked.

"Shhh."

Fine with him. Maybe if he didn't say anything, or look at her, she'd disappear.

But she didn't. She kept holding on to him.

"Your pulse rate is a little high."

He opened his eyes and looked down at her. "Not surprising since I just got kicked in the balls."

She pursed her lips as she met his gaze. "Literally or figuratively?"

"Literally."

"Ouch. I can't speak from experience, of course, but that must have been painful. What did you do to deserve that?"

Figures she'd think he was deserving of a knee to the groin. "Nothing. I had a drunk girlfriend who had it in her head we were supposed to move in together. When I tried to let her down easy, that was her response."

"Ouch again. Sorry."

He shrugged. "Not your fault."

She rubbed her hands together. "I should examine you."

He let out a laugh. "Honey, no offense, but the last thing I want is any woman near my balls tonight. Or possibly ever again."

She smiled. "You say that now. You'll change your mind once they feel better. And you need to let me take a look and feel them to make sure your girlfriend—"

"Ex-girlfriend."

"Okay. To make sure your ex-girlfriend didn't seriously injure you."

"Uh, no. I'm okay."

She put her hands on her hips. She had nice hips, showcased in a white lacy sundress, which was attached to one very cute figure. Not that he was into noticing that kind of thing at the moment. "Who's the doctor here? Me or you?"

"You. Or so you say. This could be some conspiracy. You could be a friend of Laura's setting me up for round two of let's-destroy-Tucker-Cassidy's-manhood night."

Now it was her turn to laugh. "I can assure you I have no idea who your girlfriend—"

"Ex-girlfriend."

"Right. I can assure you I am not in league with your nefarious ex-girlfriend."

"I like that." He finally had something to smile about.

"Like what?"

"Nefarious. It fits her. But you're still not getting in my pants."

"Playing hard to get, Tucker?"

He looked her over. "I'll show you mine if you show me yours."

"I see you're starting to feel better. That's a very good sign. But no, I'm not showing you mine. I am going to look at yours, though. And in your weakened condition, I'm pretty sure I can get into your pants."

His balls still throbbed. What if Laura had broken them? What if he was unable to have kids? Not that he wanted any—right now. But someday . . .

"Okay. Fine. You're really a doctor?"

"I really am. So drop 'em and let's take a look at the goods."

He reached for the zipper of his pants. "If I had a dollar for every time a woman said that to me . . ."

She snickered, moved in closer, and he caught a light citrusy scent. He breathed it in, the best thing he'd smelled all night. It smelled like renewal, like starting over.

Which was ridiculous because he didn't even know the doctor's name. But if she fixed him, she'd be his savior.

She cradled his ball sac in her hand, then examined his dick. There was something about having a woman so close to his goods that should be exciting as hell. But he wasn't getting hard. He hurt too damn bad.

"It's inflamed, but she didn't break your penis."

"Well, hallelujah."

She tilted her head to the side and gave him a wry smile. "Right? She hit you pretty hard, though. Your testicles are swollen and red."

She took a step back. "You can pull your pants up now. You'll be sore for a couple of days, but you're going to be fine."

"Thanks."

"You're welcome."

He zipped up. "I hope your husband or boyfriend doesn't mind you inspecting my stuff down here in the wine cellar."

"No husband. No boyfriend. I'm a resident at Washington University here in St. Louis, and way too busy for that."

"I see. So who are you here with?"

"Oh, my father is Clyde Ross. I'm Aubry."

Shit. Shit, shit, shit. The boss's daughter. This night couldn't get any worse.

"I didn't know that. I mean, I knew he had a daughter in medical school or something. I don't know why I didn't make the connection."

"No reason for you to. Nice to meet you, Tucker. I've seen you pitch. You're pretty damn good."

"So are you, Doc. Thanks for the once-over."

"You're welcome. I actually came down here to grab a bottle of wine for my dad." She obviously knew what she wanted, because she made a direct beeline for a spot on the far wall and plucked a bottle from the rack before turning to face him. "Got it. Shall we go upstairs, or do you need more time to reflect on your evening?"

"No, I think I've spent enough time . . . reflecting down here."

He led her toward the stairs, hoping like hell Aubry was discreet enough not to tell her father what had happened to him.

Still, he stopped and turned to face her. "One question."

"Sure."

"Did you make me drop trou because it was medically necessary, or because you wanted to get a good look at my dick?"

One side of her mouth curved up in a sexy-as-hell smile. "Tucker. I'm surprised you'd ask that question. I am a doctor, after all."

She turned and headed up the stairs.

Which wasn't an answer at all.

The night was starting to look up.

But his balls still hurt like hell. After the debacle with Laura, and given the fact that the doc was Clyde's daughter, he should definitely avoid Aubry Ross.

Or . . . maybe not.

TWO

AFTER GRABBING A COLD BEER AND MAKING MINIMAL rounds at the party, Tucker determined that Laura was, in fact, gone.

He should have been ashamed to feel relief about that, but he wasn't. Not after the episode in the wine cellar. As far as he was concerned, they were over. More than over. If he was lucky, he'd never hear from her again.

Now he needed to find somewhere out of the way to sit so he could nestle the beer in his crotch like an ice pack. It was too early to leave without a good explanation, and he sure as hell didn't want to call attention to himself. Laura had done enough of that by getting drunk as hell within the first hour. He hoped he could lie low for a bit, then leave without anyone noticing.

He found a perfect spot outside in Clyde and Helen Ross's backyard. Clyde's property was expansive, and since the team party included family and friends, there was enough of a crowd that

Tucker could disappear for a while without anyone noticing. He intended to get lost in one of the many winding garden areas, and he finally found a gazebo that was fortunately deserted. He laid his head back in one of the very comfortable cushioned chairs, nestling his beer between his thighs.

Hell of a night. He could enjoy this solitude for—

"I would have been happy to get you an ice pack for your testicles."

That could only be one person. He peeked one eye open. "My balls are fine, Aubry. This is just where I rest my beer."

"Between your legs, which is one of the warmest areas on your body? What man in his right mind wants warm beer?"

He sighed, opened both eyes and set his beer on the table next to the chair. "Are you following me?"

She laughed, then stepped inside the gazebo. "No. I was on my way to the guesthouse to check on . . . something."

He cocked a brow. "Something? Or someone?"

She shrugged. "Maybe both."

She gave a quick glance to the house in the distance.

"Searching for your boyfriend?" he asked.

She quirked a smile. "Uh, no. My uncle. He has a tendency to wander off with inappropriate people. People who aren't my aunt."

"Oh."

"My mom asked me to check and see if he was in the guesthouse."

He stood, trying not to wince as he did. "I'll go with you."

"That's not necessary."

"Still, I'll go with you."

She looked him over. "Are you sure you can walk that far, given your . . . condition?"

"Funny. Let's go."

He stepped off the gazebo and walked next to her as she made her way around the gardens and toward the house.

"So your uncle? Related to your mom or your dad?"

"He's my mom's brother."

"Do you like him?"

She shrugged. "I tolerate him because he's married to my aunt, whom I love, and he's the father of my cousins, whom I also love. My uncle has an unfortunate wandering eye, according to my mother."

"And does your aunt know about this?"

"Apparently she does, and she looks the other way because they've been married a long time and have three kids—my cousins. My aunt, according to my mother, is . . ."

He waited, but she didn't finish, so he glanced over at her. "Comfortable?"

Aubry shrugged. "I guess so."

"And what do you think?"

"I think it's none of my business."

He stopped. "Surely you have an opinion."

"I don't want to get involved in their marriage. And if it works for both of them, then why should I get in the middle of it?"

He looked over at the guesthouse. "Isn't that what you're doing right now?"

"No. I'm doing a favor for my mother, who doesn't want Aunt Farrah to be publicly embarrassed if someone else wanders into the guesthouse and finds Uncle Davis in flagrante delicto with some bimbo."

He wanted to cringe at her use of the word "bimbo." He didn't know the relationship dynamics between Aubry's aunt and uncle, but apparently they weren't good.

She stopped at the entrance to the house. "Lights are off."

"Which means nothing."

She sighed. "True."

She dug the keys out of the pocket of her dress, stared at the house and hesitated. Not that he blamed her. If it were his family member, he wasn't sure he'd want to know, either.

"Would he be able to get in there without keys?" he asked.

"He knows where the spare set is kept. He's stayed in the guesthouse before when he and my aunt have had . . . tiffs."

"I see. Would you like me to go in there?"

She frowned. "Why?"

"You know, that way if your uncle—"

"Davis."

"Right. If your Uncle Davis is in there, then you don't have to see anything, and he won't know you were the one to find him."

"You make valid points." She handed him the keys.

"I'll be right back."

As Tucker headed off, Aubry inhaled a deep breath, then let it out slowly, hoping Tucker wouldn't find anyone at all inside the guesthouse, let alone Uncle Davis, who shouldn't be with anyone but Aunt Farrah.

She did not understand relationships. Or marriage. Her mother tried to explain the nuances of Uncle Davis and Aunt Farrah's, but she'd always held up her hands and told her she didn't want to know. It wasn't her business. She loved her aunt and stood by her decision to stay with Uncle Davis, but this cat-and-mouse game the two of them played was ridiculous.

You either loved someone or you didn't. You were either committed to them or you weren't. And if you didn't want to be with that person anymore, then why not get out of the relationship, before someone got hurt?

She'd seen her Aunt Farrah watch her uncle tonight, had seen the way her uncle flirted with some young woman. She'd seen the pain in her aunt's eyes before she'd masked it with a laugh and a flip of her gorgeous hair.

Aunt Farrah might tell her mom that everything was fine, but clearly it wasn't.

Her Uncle Davis confused her. He'd always been nice to her, and he absolutely adored his children. And when he was side by side with Aunt Farrah? The adoration he showed her was so loving.

But sometimes men were douchebags. Why was it so hard to be faithful? Her aunt, who'd just turned fifty, was still stunning, had an amazing figure, was an incredibly successful businesswoman and had raised three amazing children. And if Davis couldn't see and appreciate that, then—

Tucker came back outside, shut and locked the door.

She hadn't heard any voices, no yelling or embarrassed female screams, and the lights hadn't come on.

A hopeful sign.

He dropped the keys in her hand. "No one was inside. I even checked the closets. Nice guesthouse."

"Thanks. And thank you for looking around."

"Not a problem."

She stood there for a minute, gathering her bearings.

"Are you ready to go back to the house?"

"I suppose."

He studied her, and she, in turn, studied him. She'd been in full doctor mode earlier, so she hadn't taken the time to fully appreciate Tucker's good looks. He was tall and lean, with thick, dark hair and amazing green eyes. The dark glasses he wore only added to his appeal. He wore a blue button-down shirt, untucked, and dark jeans.

And she'd already seen the package, which had been quite impressive. Though she'd only admit that to herself.

Not that she had any intention of seeing it again. After finding out about Uncle Davis, she'd decided all men were pigs.

Even men with impressive packages.

Besides, she had no time in her life for men. Residency was overwhelming. She was lucky she had a night off tonight to spend with her parents. Too bad it had to coincide with a team party to celebrate the start of the Rivers season, which meant her parents' house was filled with men.

When they made it back to the house, she stopped and turned to Tucker. "Well, thanks again."

"Thank *you*. You know, for helping me out earlier."

Her lips curved. "You're welcome. Take care of your testicles."

He laughed. "I think you might be the first woman who's ever said good-bye to me by telling me to look out for my balls."

She lifted her gaze to his. "They are important. And delicate. Try not to piss off any more women."

"I'll try. Thanks again, Aubry."

"You're welcome, Tucker."

He opened the back door for her and she went inside, the loudness of the party reminiscent of the emergency room at the hospital.

Tucker disappeared into the throng, and, after taking a moment to admire his very fine ass, she dropped the keys on the hook inside the door, then grabbed a glass of wine from the island in the kitchen.

She'd been hoping to steal some quiet time, visit with her parents and catch up. Since medical school, she hadn't seen them often enough.

But she wasn't going to get to see them much tonight, either. She went in search of her mother, found her with her usual group of friends, Aunt Farrah among them. Her mom spotted her, excused herself, and grasped Aubry around the arm.

"Anything?"

She shook her head. "The guesthouse was dark and closed up. No sign of Uncle Davis or anyone there."

"That's good, I guess. Though I haven't seen him anywhere."

"Maybe he's in the den reading a book or watching TV."

Her mother slanted her a look. "And miss a party? Davis never misses a good party. Besides, I already checked the den, and the pool house. He's not there. I didn't check the wine cellar, though."

"I was down there earlier. He's not there."

"Okay."

"I'll take another look around, Mom. And stop worrying. I'm sure everything's okay."

Her mom patted her arm. "You're probably right. Thanks for checking out the guesthouse, Bree."

"Not a problem."

"I'm going to stop worrying about Davis. Let's go have some fun." Instead of rejoining her friends, her mother led them over to the padded window seat, where it was just the two of them. She motioned to a crowd of guys, one of which was Tucker. "Why don't you go chat up some of the very available single men here?"

Aubry laughed. "Mom. Seriously. You know I'm not dating anyone. Or looking to date anyone."

Her mother graced her with a benevolent smile. "I know. That's why I want you to go talk to some of the single men here."

She linked her arm with her mother's. "How about I hang out with you instead?"

Her mother sighed. "At this rate, I'll never have grandchildren."

Aubry laughed. "I'm only twenty-eight, Mom, and still in my residency. That's a lot of stress. I don't have time for men."

"Oh, honey. There's always time for men. Besides, great sex is good for stress."

"Not having the sex conversation with you again, Mom." She

loved her mother, but sometimes the things that fell out of her mouth were appalling. And so embarrassing.

Maybe some daughters didn't mind being frank with their mothers about relationships and sex. Aubry was not that daughter. She preferred to keep their discussions light and easy and about topics like television and fashion.

Not sex.

"I don't know why not," her mother said. "You're a doctor for heaven's sake, Aubry. You've talked about the most disgusting medical anomalies during dinner. Yet we can't be open about your sex life?"

"There's a big difference between my talking about what I do at work and what I do . . ."

Her mother graced her with a knowing smile. "At play?"

She rolled her eyes. "Something like that. Which I don't, by the way."

"Don't what?"

"Play."

"And that's your problem. You're not having enough sex, which is why you're so tense all the time."

Since when did her mother think she was tense? Which she wasn't at all. "I'm not tense. I'm busy."

Her mother arched a brow. "There's a difference?"

"Yes."

"I don't think so. Anyway, look at those men over there. I know Gavin Riley is married, and so is Dedrick Coleman. Garrett Scott is engaged. I think Jack Sanchez is single, though he has a very cute date with him tonight. But how about that hot one with the glasses? He is so attractive. Tucker Cassidy, isn't it?"

Of all the men her mother pointed out, it had to be Tucker Cassidy. "Yes, he's very nice looking."

"I know he's single. He's only been with the Rivers for about a year, but oh, Aubry, he's looking your way. And smiling. You should go over and talk to him."

It was like the sixth grade dance all over again, when her mother chaperoned. Aubry wasn't the least bit interested in the boys back then. Not because she didn't like boys. She did. But she was way more interested in her math teacher, Mr. Griffin, who of course had been way too old for her—and married.

But she'd been twelve and more interested in math—and Mr. Griffin—than twelve-year-old boys who smelled bad and thought making fart jokes was hilarious.

Her mother hadn't understood then any more than she'd understand now. She should tell her mom now about her infatuation with Mr. Griffin. Wouldn't she be horrified? The thought of it amused her. Then again, probably not a good idea. Right now she had to dissuade her mother from trying to fix her up with any baseball players. And especially with Tucker Cassidy.

"No, Mom."

"Would you like me to introduce you to Tucker Cassidy?"

"Uh, no. We've already met."

Her mother shifted sideways. "Really. When and how?"

Now, that she wouldn't explain. "I ran into him earlier tonight."

"Is he nice?"

"Yes. He's very nice."

"Good." Her mother stood, grabbed her hand and lifted Aubry out of the seat. "Let's go talk to him."

Aubry tugged at her hand. "Let's not."

But it was too late, and the one thing she'd known all her life was that Helen Ross had a very strong grip.

God, this night couldn't get any more complicated.

THREE

TUCKER HAD SEEN AUBRY TALKING TO HER MOTHER. He saw her mother stand and take Aubry by the hand, and then the horrified look on Aubry's face as they made their way over to him.

"Tucker Cassidy," Mrs. Ross said.

"Mrs. Ross. How are you doing this evening?"

"I'm doing fine. My daughter here tells me the two of you met earlier."

Uh-oh. Surely she wouldn't . . .

He shot a quick look over at Aubry, who shook her head back and forth very fast.

"We did."

"Before you dragged me over here, Mom, I was going to tell you I met Tucker outside by the gardens."

"That's right," Tucker said. "Your property is beautiful, by the way."

Mrs. Ross smiled. "Thank you so much. We've done extensive work to the place over the years. And I do love my flowers."

"It shows. I'm a big fan of the outdoors, so I had to take a walk out there. That's where I ran into Aubry—near the gazebo."

Aubry's mom turned to her. "Of course. Well, I'm so glad you two met. I'll leave you to talk, because I see someone I should say hello to. Nice to see you again, Tucker."

He nodded. "Mrs. Ross."

After she left, Aubry laid her hand on his arm. "I am so sorry about that. My mother is in matchmaking mode tonight."

Tucker's lips curved. "And she thought you and I—"

Aubry shrugged. "Apparently. Again, I'm really sorry. I saw that look of panic on your face and you can rest assured the incident in the wine cellar will stay between us."

"Thanks for that. But really, quit apologizing. It's not like you're hideous, Aubry. Any guy would be happy to be fixed up with you."

"Thank you, but I'm not looking to get fixed up. Especially not by my mother."

He laughed. "I can understand that. Parents seem to have that need to see their kids settled."

She seemed to relax after that. "Yours too?"

"My mother texts me all the time whenever she sees pictures of me with women."

"And?"

"She mostly disapproves. And then she tells me that she knows this really nice girl . . ."

Aubry laughed. "Thank you. That makes me feel better."

He led her away from the middle of the living room, toward the open French doors leading out back. They walked outside where it was quieter. "Though in the case of Laura—"

"The ex from the wine cellar?" Aubry asked.

"Yes. In the case of Laura, my mom might have been right to disapprove."

"I can't say I blame her. Was this now ex-girlfriend of yours always so . . . angry?"

"No. In the beginning she was fun and easygoing, always up for anything. She didn't show her true colors until recently. Then it was all demands and heavy drinking." He turned to face her. "Laura is not a fun drunk."

Aubry wrinkled her nose. "We see a lot of 'not fun drunks' in the ER."

"You're doing a rotation in the ER?"

"Actually, I've changed my specialty. At first I wanted to go into obstetrics. One rotation in the ER changed all that."

He took a seat in one of the Adirondack chairs and motioned for her to do the same. She didn't hesitate. "There's a big difference between delivering babies and working in emergency medicine. Why the switch?"

She liked that he took an interest in her work. "There's such a thrill about working emergency medicine. The immediacy of it, the chance to really do some good for people who are injured or sick. It hit me in the gut when I did my first rotation in there, and I knew right then that I had to make it my career."

"I can see how it would suit you."

She cocked her head to the side. "You don't even know me."

"You helped me earlier, during my . . . issue."

"Oh. Right. Well, you were definitely hurting."

"You can say that again."

"How are you feeling by the way? Down there."

"Better. Thanks. I don't think I'll be up for sex anytime soon, but I'm sure I'll recover."

"Good to know." She stood. "I should get back to my parents."

He got up. "I'd like to see you again."

She frowned. "Don't feel obligated because of my mother, Tucker."

"Your mom doesn't have anything to do with why I asked to see you. I like you. I think you're interesting."

"I like you, too. But my life is crazy. I work all the time. I'm not good dating material."

"Why don't you let me be the judge of that?"

She shook her head. "Thanks for the offer, but I'm going to have to decline."

He nodded. "Okay. I guess I'll see you around, Aubry."

Aubry watched Tucker walk away. He really did have a wonderful ass. She smiled to herself and changed her mind about searching out her parents. She decided to linger outside for a while. She could use a quiet moment. And knowing her mother, there was a chance she'd find Aubry and not so subtly ask for an update on her and Tucker.

Not that there was a "her and Tucker," and there never would be. Her life was crazy enough without adding one of the Rivers players to her agenda.

That was never, ever going to happen. She and baseball players would never mix, despite her mother's attempts to match her up with one of the guys.

It was bad enough her father owned the team, which for years meant she had been constantly surrounded by jocks. They had too much ego, too much testosterone, too much of everything.

And dating one?

That was never going to happen.

After taking some time to enjoy the peace and quiet of the night, with the gentle sound of the party in the background, Aubry decided to search out her parents. She easily found them and wandered over to where her mother stood having a rather animated conversation with her father.

Her dad was frowning. Never a good sign. When he saw her, though, he smiled.

"Aubry. Where have you been?" he asked.

"Around."

"And where is Tucker?" her mother asked.

"He left to join his friends."

"Oh. No connection between the two of you?"

Her mother looked disappointed. "We're not going to date, Mom. I don't date baseball players. Never have and never will."

"She shouldn't be dating anyone, Helen," her father said. "Her entire life right now should be focused on medicine."

She didn't necessarily agree with her father in that respect, but for tonight, she'd allow him to push that thought.

"That's a ridiculous notion, Clyde," her mother said. "Aubry is a young, vibrant, incredibly attractive woman who just happens to be at prime dating age. This is the time she should be out finding eligible men."

"No. This is the time she should be concentrating on her career. Residency is tough, and once she's through that, she has exams and a fellowship."

Aubry loved how she was being discussed as if she wasn't present, or as if her opinion on her own life didn't matter. But she also knew her parents were both arguing for her best interests, so again . . . she'd allow it. Not that it mattered anyway. She was an adult and living on her own, and she'd do what she damn well pleased. It wasn't like either her mother or her father dictated her life. Though her father checked up on her more than she liked.

"No dating for you, young lady," her father said, pulling her against him for a gentle squeeze. "You don't need the distraction."

She'd found over the years that it was much less of a hassle to placate him than argue with him. "You got it, Dad."

Her mother just shook her head and moved off to greet other guests.

Aubry moved away, too, so she could refill her glass of wine.

It didn't matter what either of them said. She was busy with work, and wasn't interested in Tucker Cassidy, or any man for that matter.

She liked her life just fine the way it was.

Why change what worked?

FOUR

IT WAS THE TOP OF THE SIXTH INNING AND TUCKER had this game in hand. The Rivers were ahead of Cincinnati by three runs. His pitch count was manageable, his curveball was working, and he was in the groove.

He felt the pitches, knew when he was in the zone and when he wasn't.

Tonight, he was in the zone. He rolled the ball around in his fingers while he took the signal from Jack Sanchez, the Rivers catcher.

Sanchez called for a fastball. That would work. The batter was down in the count, one ball to two strikes. He'd be expecting the curve, which was what Tucker had been giving him.

Ninety feet away was the third out.

Easy.

He wound up, threw the ball and the batter got a piece of it, hitting it between first and second base.

Shit.

Gavin Riley, the Rivers first baseman, fielded the ball. Tucker had already made a run off the mound, knowing he was going to have to tag the runner at first base.

It was a footrace, and they were dead even.

He made it to the first base bag a fraction of a second before the batter.

Who subsequently ran into him, then slid across his calf with his spikes.

Sonofabitch, that hurt.

They tumbled over each other, but all he heard was the umpire saying the batter was out.

He'd held on to the ball and hit the base with it in his hands before the runner. Good enough.

He got up, hobbling a little on his calf. He was fine, though, as he limped his way back to the mound.

Until the pitching coach came out, along with Sanchez.

"You're bleeding, Cassidy," the coach said.

Tucker looked down at his leg. "I am?"

"Yeah. Your uniform's torn and there's blood running down your leg."

"I'm fine."

"You're not fine."

The umpire came over to take a peek. "That looks bad." He signaled for the coach and the medical personnel.

Goddammit! He was pitching a good game.

"I'm really okay."

Coach Manny Magee stepped up to the mound along with the team doc.

"Cassidy has an injury to his left calf, Coach," the umpire said.

By now, all the infielders had crowded around, plus the umpire and the pitching coach.

"I feel fine."

Phil, the team doctor, looked at his leg then at Manny. "This is going to need stitches. Cut is pretty deep."

"Your leg looks like shit, Tucker. You pitched a good game." Manny signaled to the bullpen.

Once he did that, there was no sense in arguing.

Tucker handed the ball to the coach and walked off the field. The crowd stood and cheered for him. He tipped his hat, but the bottom line was, he could have finished the game. He'd been in a comfortable pitching groove, his pitches had landed in the strike zone, and if not for that collision with the batter, who'd gouged him in the leg, the game could have ended great.

He made his way down to the locker room, where he met up with the team doc.

"Get your pants off and let's see what's going on with that leg, Tucker," Phil said.

"It's hardly even a scratch." He took off his cleats and socks, then dragged his pants off and lay on the table.

Phil cleaned out the wound, which made him wince a little.

"It's a pretty deep wound. Needs stitches just like I thought."

"Great."

"You and Green had a hell of a run-in there at first base. How do you feel?"

"I feel fine."

"You guys always say that."

They did. No one wanted to miss any games.

"I'm going to send you over to the ER for them to do a thorough exam."

Tucker sat upright. "I don't need to go to the ER."

But Phil had already written on the chart. "I'll give them a heads-up and let them know you're on your way over. I'll put a bandage on your leg. The docs there can stitch you up. I'm a little worried about your knee."

Tucker frowned. "My knee? My knee is fine."

"Again. All you guys say that. And I saw the way you landed, then limped."

"Of course, I limped. My leg got stomped on. Come on, Phil, the game's still on."

Phil tore the form off his clipboard and handed it to him. "Off to the ER, Tucker. Your ride will be waiting for you outside."

He took the sheet from Phil and climbed back into his pants, grumbling under his breath.

He should still be out on the mound, not headed to the ER.

He was fine. Fucking fine.

And that game had been his to finish.

FIVE

ONE WOULD THINK ON A WEDNESDAY NIGHT THAT THE ER would be slow.

But not tonight. So far Aubry had covered an eight-year-old's asthma attack, a suspected myocardial infarction, an automobile accident with a non-trauma injury and a drunk who'd started his happy hour very early in the day, then had spent the past three hours vomiting. Nonstop.

Typically a lot of these cases were saved for weekends.

Maybe it was a full moon or something. Either way, she'd been busy.

She liked busy. Her shift went fast when she stayed moving. The only problem was she ended up working late updating her charts.

"Dr. Ross? There's a new patient in room seven," the intake clerk told her as she stood at the counter trying to stay ahead of said charts.

Aubry reviewed the labs on the cardiac patient, ordered new

drugs, then signed off and had a short conversation with the shift nurse about the patient's care before turning to the intake clerk. "What's the deal with the new patient?"

"Baseball player from the Rivers. He was injured during the game."

She nodded. "Heading there right now."

She grabbed the patient's chart and flipped through it on her way down the hall. When she scanned the name, she stalled for a second, then shook her head and resumed her walk to the examination room.

Unbelievable.

She opened the door to find Tucker Cassidy, still in uniform, sitting on the exam room table.

He was frowning, looking down at the floor. When he looked up, he smiled.

"Oh. Hey, Doc. I didn't expect to see you here tonight."

She laid the chart down on the table and grabbed exam gloves. "I don't suppose the injury is to your groin."

He laughed. "Not this time. I took a cleat to the calf at first base."

"I hate to be repetitious each time we see each other, but you're going to need to drop your pants."

He slid off the table and unbuttoned his pants. "This is getting to be a regular thing with us, Doc. I'm thinking you just want to get to the goods."

She rolled her eyes. "I'm afraid I won't be touching your penis or your testicles tonight."

"Too bad." He laid his torn, bloody pants on the table, then climbed on the table and lay on his stomach.

She removed the bandage the team doctor had applied. "Nice."

"Thanks. I try not to half-ass anything I do."

"Apparently. This will need several stitches."

"That's what Phil said. I don't know why he couldn't just stitch me up in the locker room."

"According to the notes he e-mailed over, he wanted to make sure your leg is sound and there are no other injuries, especially to your knee. Or to your head, since it appears you collided with the other player. Once I stitch this up, I'll do a more thorough examination."

He looked over his shoulder at her. "Which probably means you'll want me naked."

She couldn't help but smile at his sense of humor. "You'd like to think that, but I don't believe your full nudity will be necessary."

"Come on, Doc. I'm already pissed about not finishing the game. At least make the ER experience a fun one."

"I don't think this is the place you come to for a fun time, Tucker." She got out the suturing kit and scooted the stool across toward the table. "You'll need to lie still now while I clean and numb the area."

At least he was a good patient. He didn't complain and didn't move, allowing her to clean and suture the wound quickly. It took twelve stitches, but he was muscular and in good shape, so the injury shouldn't cause him much discomfort.

After she finished, she examined the rest of his leg. There were no other scrapes or scratches, and other than slight swelling around the wound area, she saw no further injuries to the back of his leg.

"You can roll over now."

He did, and she examined his knee, which was the area Phil was most concerned about.

"How does your knee feel?" she asked.

"It's fine. Same thing I told Phil."

She examined his knee. He had full range of motion without pain. She saw no redness or swelling.

"Can you put weight on it?"

"I walked in here just fine."

"Do that for me."

He hopped off the table and walked the circumference of the room without favoring the leg.

She also did a neurological exam to be sure he didn't exhibit signs of a head injury.

"I agree. You seem fine. But I still think we'll get an X-ray of your leg and knee, just to be on the safe side."

"That's a waste of time."

She lifted her gaze to his. "Remind me again—which one of us is the doctor?"

He shrugged. "Whatever you want."

She wrote the orders. "Wait here and someone will be in to take you to X-ray."

She closed the file, then started for the door.

"Wait. You're not staying here with me?"

She turned to face him. "I have other patients, Tucker."

"Sure. Right. You do. See you later, Doc."

Aubry sensed something bothered him, but it wasn't physical. She was waiting on labs for one patient, discharge papers on another. She had a few minutes, and her staff knew where she was if something came up. She leaned against the door. "Is there something you wanted to talk about?"

"No." He waited a few seconds, then asked, "Did you watch the game tonight?"

"I'm working, as you can see."

"Game was on in the waiting room when I came in."

"I don't work in the waiting room. Besides, I don't watch baseball."

She tried not to laugh at his horrified expression.

"How the hell can you not watch baseball? Your dad owns the team."

"Which doesn't mean I'm required to like baseball."

"I have to say, I'm really disappointed in you, Aubry."

"I'll try to get through the rest of my life with your disappointment."

"Okay, but, can I head out to the waiting room to watch the game? I don't know what's going on."

She looked down at him, trying very hard not to appreciate his very fine thighs, or what was going on between them. "In your underwear?"

He rolled his eyes. "I'd put my pants back on first."

"How about I put a rush on the X-ray, then you can get back to the game."

He heaved a heavy sigh. "Fine."

She left the room, handed off the paperwork and ordered the X-ray, then went to check on her other patients. In the meantime, several other patients came in so it was an hour or so before she made her way back to check on Tucker. His films were ready, so she took a look, then went back into the room.

Tucker wasn't in there. She had a pretty good idea where she'd find him.

The admissions area wasn't full, but the television was on, and there was Tucker, sitting with a group of what Aubry could only assume were fans, since they had grouped around him like he was the freaking Dalai Lama or something.

He was watching television. The other people in the waiting room weren't watching television. They were ogling Tucker, especially the young, extremely attractive woman sitting behind him who looked like she was seconds away from running her fingers through his hair. Or possibly hurdling the chairs and climbing onto his lap.

No way. Not on her shift. Besides, there were kids in the waiting room.

She headed that way and stepped in front of him.

"Tucker, I have your X-ray results."

He looked up at her. "Okay, great. Gotta go, folks. Thanks for keeping me company."

"Bye, Tucker," one of the kids said. "I hope your leg isn't too bad. I hope you don't miss your next spot in the rotation."

"Not gonna happen," Tucker said, bending over to shake the boy's hand. "And I hope your tonsils are going to be okay, too."

"Mom says they gotta come out. Does it hurt?"

"For a few days. But you get ice cream. Come on—how bad is that?"

The boy grinned.

Tucker stepped beside her as she led him down the hall and back to the exam room. "We won."

"You've made my entire night with that news."

"Yeah, I can tell."

She closed the door behind her. "Take a seat."

"Okay." He scooted back up on the table.

"You were supposed to stay in here."

"I got bored. And you know, the game."

"Uh-huh. Anyway, your X-rays are clear."

"As I knew they'd be. It's just a cut on my leg. I'm fine."

"You will be. Keep the wound dry for the next several days. Your team doctor can remove the stitches after a week. Try not to do anything to pull the stitches out."

"But I can pitch, right?"

"Yes. You can pitch."

He hopped off the table. "All right then. So I can go now?"

"Yes, you can go now. Stop at the front desk where you can pick up your release paperwork."

"Great. Thanks, Doc."

"You're welcome. Try to avoid getting hurt again."

He leaned against the table and crossed his arms, giving her a smile that did strange things to all her feminine parts. "Trust me. I'm not doing it on purpose. I could have finished the game. I was pitching like a superstar, you know."

"So modest, you athletes."

"I take it you don't like baseball players."

She was making notes in the chart, so she looked up at him. "I have nothing against athletes."

"I sense a 'but' in there."

"I really have to go."

"So if I asked you out, you'd say no because you aren't attracted to me."

She'd have to be dead not to find him attractive. He was tall, with thick black hair. His eyes alone could compel any woman to drop her panties, and the dark glasses gave him that Clark Kent/ Superman vibe that definitely gave her the quivers in all the right places. She'd seen more of his body than she had a right to, considering they weren't sleeping together, and the parts she had seen?

A-number-one amazing.

The fact he was an athlete? That did nothing for her.

"My dad bought the team when I was little. I've been around guys like you my whole life. I'm over the whole 'jock-and-awe' thing."

He let out a laugh. "Okay, so points against me because I'm a player. And when I say player, I mean sports. Not the other kind."

She opened the door to the exam room, waiting for him to walk out. "I'll have to take your word on the other kind."

"If you went out with me, you could find out."

She passed the chart to the clerk at the desk, then turned to him. "Not going to happen, Tucker."

"You've discharged me as your patient, right?"

"Yes."

"So no conflict of interest."

"Thirty seconds ago you were still my patient."

"That was thirty seconds ago. Now I'm just a guy asking you out."

They stood at the round desk where the other doctors, nurses and clerical staff wandered in and out. Currently, there were several people milling about, which meant those several people heard him ask her out. And heard her turn him down.

She was going to hear about that later.

"Don't waste your time on me. I don't have time to date—anyone."

"Here's your paperwork, Mr. Cassidy."

He smiled at Marie, the desk clerk. "Thanks."

Then he turned back to Aubry, picked up her hand and gave it a little squeeze. "I don't think you're a waste of time, Aubry. And thanks for the stitches."

"Try not to come back."

"Oh, I'll be back, but it'll be to ask you out."

"Give it up, jock. It's not going to happen."

"We'll see." He grinned, gave her a quick kiss on the cheek, then walked away.

She couldn't help staring at him as he left. The man had a very fine ass.

She heard Marie sigh behind her.

"Not happening, Marie."

"He's smooth, Aubry. And hot as hell," Marie said.

"I'm not going out with him."

"Are you saving yourself for someone in particular? Because last time I checked, Channing Tatum was married."

She pulled herself away from checking out Tucker's ass, then turned to face Marie. "Ha-ha. And no. You know I'm always here."

"Not twenty-four/seven, honey. And you should always make time for hot sex with a young stud."

"He plays for my dad's team."

"So?"

"No, Marie. First, it's some kind of conflict of interest. Second, I have my hands full just managing my residency."

Marie stared at the closed door. "Then can I have him?"

Aubry gaped at her. "You're married. You have four kids."

"I'll make time for him. I'm sure Jose won't mind. Hell, he'd probably like to get rid of me for an hour or two a week. He says I'm a pain in his ass."

"Jose adores you. He brings you flowers."

Marie leaned back in her swivel chair. "On my birthday."

"Every freaking year, Marie. He also brings you cupcakes. I would die for a man who brought me cupcakes."

Aubry looked over at her friend Katie Murphy, a fellow resident and one of her best friends since medical school. Katie loved cupcakes.

Marie shook her head at Katie and Aubry. "That's because you skinny bitches burn off everything you eat. I sit on my ass all day, and that bastard brings me cupcakes."

"And you love him for it," Aubry said.

Marie sighed. "This is true. But I'll still take your boy toy Tucker for an hour, if you decide you don't want him."

Katie pivoted, her laser sharp eyes focused entirely on Aubry. "Who the hell is Tucker and why didn't I know you had a boy toy?"

Aubry pinned Marie with a glare before turning her attention back on Katie. "I do not have a boy toy. Tucker was a patient of mine who came in tonight for stitches. He also happens to be a pitcher on my dad's team."

"Do we have anything on the board at the moment, Marie?" Katie asked.

"Nope. Board's clear. No new patients at the moment. Tests and labs are ordered and discharge papers have been filed."

"Perfect." Katie grabbed Aubry's lab coat sleeve and hauled her away from the main station, dragging her into one of the break rooms. She shut the door behind her, then faced her with a scowl.

"Okay, Dr. Ross. Spill all the details about—what's his name?"

"Tucker Cassidy. And there are no details."

Katie gave her a look.

"Okay, fine. I ran into him at a team party at my mom and dad's a week and a half ago. His now ex-girlfriend gave him a knee to the balls in the wine cellar, and I found him down there in a great deal of pain, so . . . I checked him out."

Katie grinned. "And by checked him out, I assume you fondled the package?"

"In a purely clinical way, of course."

"Of course. And how was it?"

"Katherine Murphy. I'm a doctor. I was merely performing an exam on his genitalia to check for injury."

Katie went to the vending machine, slid some money in and selected an energy drink. "Uh-huh. And was he hung?"

Aubry shook her head. "I didn't notice."

"Now I know you're lying. We always notice." Katie took a seat at the round table and a long swig of her drink. "So, you like him."

Admitting defeat, Aubry bought a chocolate milk out of the machine and pulled up a chair next to Katie. "I do like him. He's very fine looking, funny and sexy as hell. But you know how it is, Katie. I don't have time for a guy."

"Make time. Sex is a great stress reducer."

"So I've been told, but it's been so long I don't remember."

"See? This is why you should hop on the hot athlete."

"No. And how about you? You're not dating anyone."

Katie took a long swallow of her drink, then pulled a granola bar out of her coat pocket. "Who says you have to date someone to have sex?"

"That seems so . . . random and unemotional."

"I know," Katie said, unwrapping the granola bar and taking a big bite out of it. "That's what makes it so great. You get off, he gets off, there are no emotional entanglements to clutter up your already busy life. Everyone's happy."

Maybe that would work for some people, but Aubry didn't think she could make it work for her. She'd had two long-term romantic relationships in her life. One in high school, and the other during medical school. Both had been okay, but not earth-shattering.

She wanted earth-shattering, goddammit. Was that too much to ask for?

The problem was, life as a resident was hectic and unpredictable and a total time suck. She didn't have the time or energy to give to an earth-shattering romance.

So maybe some great hot sex was the answer after all.

And when hot sex popped into her head, she could definitely picture Tucker Cassidy. He had great hands. She could already imagine all the delicious things he could do to her with his hands.

"See? You're already picturing it in your head, aren't you?"

She looked up to see Katie grinning at her. She couldn't help the curve of her lips.

"Maybe."

"So go get you some hot baseball player."

She shrugged. "He said he'd see me again."

Katie nudged her with her shoulder. "So when he does, for God's sake, say yes."

SIX

THERE WAS NOTHING WORSE THAN ONE OF HIS BROTH-
ers popping in for a visit.

And even worse when it was his twin brother, Barrett.

That was the bad thing about football off-season. He saw way
more of his brothers than he wanted to.

"You know I want to come to one of your games, while I'm here,"
Barrett said, dropping his bag on the floor of the living room.

"Why are you here again?"

"I've got a meeting with my agent—actually our agent—Victoria
Baldwin. We're doing some contract stuff, then some PR shit."

"Stuff and shit. Got it. You want a beer?" Tucker asked as he
led Barrett into the kitchen of his condo.

"Yeah. Oh, hey, I saw your run-in at first base last week. You
couldn't get the hell out of the way?"

"That wasn't my fault." He pulled two beers out of the

refrigerator, popped open the tops and handed one to Barrett, who'd already made himself at home by taking a chair at the island.

"That's what you always say. But you are the klutz of the family."

Shaking his head, Tucker took a couple long swallows of his beer. He and Barrett had been at odds with each other since—hell, probably since the womb. They fought all the time and were atypical as far as twins went. It wasn't an us-against-the-world type of relationship at all. Maybe because they weren't identical twins. He had no idea.

Of course if anyone gave his brother shit, he'd be the one that was right there to defend him. Because he loved his brother. He might fight with him, but God help anyone else who did.

"You were pitching great until you fucked it all up by letting Stokes stomp all over your leg, though."

Tucker laughed at Barrett's backhanded compliment. "Yeah. I could have finished that game. My arm is feeling good so far."

"The game you pitched in Cleveland was okay. That loss wasn't on you."

He grimaced just thinking about that game. His leg had been fine, and he'd pitched six strong innings. The relief team had given up three runs and they hadn't been able to make up the deficit. "Yeah, that sucked."

"Mom says to tell you hi, and that she and Dad will be up to catch a game this month."

He nodded. "I talked to her the other day. She said something about a trip up this way but she didn't have the dates nailed down yet. Something about doing paint and fabric shopping with Katrina and the kids."

Barrett nodded. "They're in remodel mode at Grant's place. Oh, and we're having dinner with Grant and Katrina and the kids tonight."

"We are? Since when?"

"Since I told them I was going to be in town. Katrina invited me to dinner and said I was supposed to bring you, too, unless you had a game."

"Which I don't. Not tonight. You know I just got back in town after a road trip, right?"

Barrett slid him a look. "Oh, right. I keep your travel schedule on my phone so I know your whereabouts at all times."

"Fuck off, Barrett."

Barrett laughed. "Love you, too, Tucker."

He'd planned to make good use of his day off by getting in touch with Aubry. That would have to be delayed since the last thing he wanted to do was drag her over to meet his brothers.

"So, dinner, huh?" Tucker asked, his stomach grumbling at the thought.

"Yeah. You should go take a shower. You look like shit."

"I was at the gym working out, asshole."

"That's not why you look like shit. You always look bad."

"Kiss my ass. And should you really be insulting your twin's appearance?"

"I wouldn't if you actually looked like me, which you don't, unfortunately for you." Barrett flexed his considerable muscles.

Rolling his eyes, Tucker finished his beer and tossed the bottle in the recycle bin. "I'm going to take a shower."

"Good. I'm going to play a video game while you're getting pretty. Try to do that in under two hours."

In less than twenty minutes, Tucker had showered and gotten dressed.

He went out into the living room and grabbed his phone from the table behind the sofa, stared at it for a few minutes and thought about giving Aubry a call at the hospital.

Barrett turned around. "You ready?"

He nodded. "Yeah."

"In less than two hours, too. Are you sure you're pretty enough?"

"Prettier than you, asshole." He slipped his phone in his pocket, figuring he'd call Aubry later.

He drove them over to Grant's house. It took about thirty minutes to get there. He'd made sure when he rented his condo that he didn't live right damn down the street from Grant. He loved his family—all of them. But independence meant a lot to him. And while he liked seeing his brothers and enjoyed getting together with all of them, he needed to be on his own. Too much togetherness? Not necessarily a good thing.

But he had to admit, when he'd signed with the Rivers last year, he'd been happy to be in the same city as Grant. They wouldn't see each other all the time, but they'd be close enough.

Barrett, on the other hand . . .

"What the hell are you doing?" he asked as he glanced over at his brother, who was rifling through the contents of his glove compartment.

"Checking to see if you have any women's underwear in here."

Tucker shook his head. "No."

"Then what the hell are you doing in your spare time?"

"I had a girlfriend. We broke up recently." He wasn't about to tell Barrett about the incident with Laura in the wine cellar. Barrett would never let him live it down.

"Yeah? What did you do wrong?"

He pulled onto the highway, easing into traffic. "Why would you assume I was the one who did anything wrong? Maybe it was her."

"Oh, it had to be you."

"Trust me. It wasn't me."

"So tell me about it."

"She wanted to move in together. And she drank a lot. When she drank, things got ugly. We argued, I broke it off. That pissed her off."

Barrett laughed. "She sounds like a real sweet girl. You sure know how to pick 'em, Bro."

"I don't see Miss America hanging off your arm, douchebag."

"Not right now you don't, but when I'm ready to settle down? The cream of the crop will flock to me."

"Yeah, I've seen the cream of the crop you hang out with in pictures on social media."

"Naw, that's just bed buddies. I'm just playing right now."

"So the women you fuck aren't the ones you'd bring home to meet Mom and Dad?"

Barrett slid him a sly smile? "Why? You jealous of the action I get?"

"You're an asshole."

Barrett laughed. "Yeah, you're jealous."

Tucker clenched his jaw and concentrated on the road.

By the time they arrived at Grant's house, Barrett had rifled through the console in Tucker's car, flipped through his phone—including his text messages—and made a general ass of himself asking intrusive questions about Tucker's sex life, none of which were answered.

He remembered what it was like having his twin brother up in his private business.

And he hadn't missed him at all.

At least when they got to Grant's house Barrett could go annoy the shit out of him.

When they arrived at Grant's there were several work trucks parked outside.

They went to the door and rang the bell.

Nobody answered.

Barrett motioned with his head toward the side of the house. "He's probably out back where all the noise is coming from. Let's go that way."

They headed through a side gate and down a pathway. Grant was back there near the porch, talking to someone who was working on renovating the back porch. Concrete was torn up, half the porch was gone and there were a handful of guys back there.

Grant spotted them and waved them over.

"Hang on a sec," Grant said. "We're almost done here."

Then he turned back to the man standing next to him. "We need to make sure we have an adequate fan system in place so when I'm grilling the smoke doesn't reach the guests who are sitting out here."

The guy nodded. "Don't worry. We've got that in the plans."

The two of them talked for a few more minutes, then the guy walked away and Grant came over and hugged them both.

That was one thing about the Cassidy family. They might all be tough athletes, but they were always affectionate with one another. They had their mother—and their father—to thank for that. There had always been loving hugs from Mom. And their dad, Easton Cassidy, was one tough sonofabitch—one of the best quarterbacks to have ever played the game. But their father was also kind and warm and he loved his sons. He'd passed down that affection to all of them, and made sure that even though they all fought like hell with each other, and might hate each other one minute, they loved each other, too.

"How's the leg?" Grant asked him.

"It healed up fine. It was no big deal to start with. Just a cut. I've taken worse in scuffles from you guys."

Grant nodded. "No doubt. I can't believe they pulled you from the game for a little blood."

"Wouldn't have happened on the football field," Barrett said. "This is what happens when you play a pussy game like baseball."

Tucker was used to this bullshit. "We can't all be smart and play baseball. Some of us only know how to use our bodies to hit, not throw masterful pitches."

Grant let out a snort. "Good one, Tucker."

Barrett glared at Grant. "You're supposed to be on my side."

"I'm not on anyone's side when the two of you get going. Come on, let's head into the house."

"You've done a lot of remodeling already," Tucker said as Grant led them through the downstairs. "The last time I was here, the media room was still open to the rest of the basement." Now it was closed off, with a bar and entertainment area in a separate, adjacent space. Grant gave them a sample of the new sound system in the media room. It was outstanding, like being in a movie theater.

"Yeah. Katrina got started right away working on the renovations. The media room and entertainment section is done, and now that spring is here, we've dug in and are working on the outside."

"Seems like you're making some progress out there. Though it's kind of a mess right now," Barrett said.

Grant reached into the fridge, dug out three beers and handed them out. "Yeah. It's going to take a while because we're expanding the whole patio area, adding square footage and a built-in kitchen."

Tucker pulled up a seat and took a long swallow of his beer. "It's going to look great when it's done."

"It will. It'll be awesome in the summer. I might even invite you over, Tucker."

"I might even show up. Providing there's food."

"Oh, there'll be food."

"Yeah, now that you have Katrina in your life. And her little sister."

Grant nodded at Barrett. "She's picking Anya up after school today, and the two of them are going to the store to buy food to cook for dinner tonight."

"Awesome. Where's Leo?" Tucker asked.

"Football practice."

Barrett grinned. "I like hearing that. How's it going?"

"It's good. He made the team without any influence from me or Dad, despite Dad's insistence on calling the coach. It was important for Leo to know he could do it on his own. He worked his ass off, running and in the weight room. He put on twenty pounds and sprung up another two inches in height, which sure as hell didn't hurt him."

"No shit," Tucker said. "Thank God for teen boys and growth spurts, huh?"

Grant laughed. "Yeah. When spring practice started, he tried out for wide receiver and made the team."

"Good for him. We should go watch."

"You wanna give the kid a complex?" Tucker asked. "The last thing he needs is all of us on the sidelines breathing down his neck."

"Hey," Barrett said. "The whole team might need some pointers. Especially the defense, which is my specialty."

"I agree with Tucker," Grant said. "I already told the coach I'd lay low. He doesn't need some pro quarterback showing up and interfering in his practices. He knows what he's doing."

Barrett shrugged. "If you say so. But between the three of us—" Barrett looked over at Tucker. "Okay, maybe the two of us and Tucker could just pretend like he knew what he was talking about."

"Hey. Fuck off. Just because I don't play football professionally doesn't mean I don't know the game, asshole."

Barrett's lips curved. "Sure you do. Anyway, we could turn that team into a state champion."

"I think we'll stay hands off for a while, so Leo can integrate into the team on his own."

Barrett raised his hands in the air. "Okay. Dad."

Grant grinned.

The intercom system buzzed. "Hey, are you all down there?"

Tucker recognized Anya's voice, Katrina's little sister.

Grant got up and pushed the button. "Yup."

"We're back with food."

"We'll be right up," Grant said.

They headed upstairs. Katrina and Anya were in the kitchen unpacking bags of groceries.

Katrina turned around and smiled, then came over to give Tucker and Barrett hugs. "It's great to see both of you. You're just in time to help."

Barrett looked at him. "This is just like being at Mom's house."

Katrina patted Barrett's arm. "I'm going to take that as a compliment. Now go put these in the pantry."

Katrina was an internationally famous model, one of the A-list types. Gorgeous and smart, too. Why she was with his doofus of a brother, he had no idea. He sure as hell didn't see any appeal to Grant. Then again, he wasn't sleeping with him.

Thank God. Sharing a room with him as a kid had been bad enough. Grant was Katrina's problem now.

And she had two cool younger siblings, too. They had all bonded with Leo and Anya during the short time they'd known them. It was like they were part of the Cassidy family already.

And getting to be a part of the Cassidys wasn't easy. But Grant loved Katrina, Leo and Anya. And his acceptance and love for them meant the rest of the Cassidys brought them into their fold.

It helped that they were exceptional people. Easy to like, friendly and fun.

It didn't hurt that Leo liked sports, and Katrina and Anya were great cooks. Bonus points and all that.

"I hope you guys like seafood," Anya said, already dragging out pans from the cabinets.

"We're guys," Barrett said. "We eat anything."

Katrina leaned against the counter. "I know guys who are very choosy about what they eat."

"You've met the Cassidys, haven't you?" Tucker asked. "We really do eat anything."

"Including things we probably shouldn't have," Grant added. "But that was when we were kids. As far as I know, none of us have eaten dirt recently."

"I wouldn't say that yet, pretty boy," Barrett said. "Our teams play each other this year, and I intend to pound your face in the turf."

"You'll never get past my offensive line."

Katrina rolled her eyes. "Here we go again."

Anya laughed. "You two should record this conversation on a video and just press play every time you see each other."

"Flynn said to tell you that when you play against San Francisco, you're going down," Barrett said. "And he's going to be the one to take you there."

Grant grinned. "See how my brothers fear me?"

Tucker laughed and slapped Grant on the back. "You're the one who wanted to be a quarterback like Dad. Now you get to reap the rewards. And the threats."

"And that's why Tucker chose baseball," Barrett said, snatching a grape from the pile Anya was rinsing in the sink before popping it into his mouth. "Because you couldn't handle the heat."

"Oh, I've got the heat. I believe you swung and missed at several of my pitches the last time you challenged me."

"And I believe I nailed you to the ground during our football skirmish."

"Guys. Guys," Katrina said. "How about a truce? At least until after dinner?"

Grant slid in behind her and wrapped his arms around her. "You think we're fighting don't you?"

"Well, yes."

Barrett laughed. "Don't worry, honey. For us, this is a normal conversation at the breakfast table."

Katrina frowned. "Didn't it drive your mother crazy?"

"She got used to us over the years," Tucker said. "As long as no blood was shed, she learned to ignore us."

Katrina sighed. "I guess it's something I'll have to get used to as well, then. But you all make me nervous. It's like you're all seconds away from coming to blows."

"Not a chance." Grant kissed her on the cheek. "And if we are, we'll be sure to give you fair warning so you and Anya can remove yourselves to a safe place."

"Good to know," Anya said. "Now all of you can get out of the kitchen while we cook."

Tucker's lips curved as they all headed into the living room. They'd been like this for years, always bickering about everything, but mainly sports. The Cassidys were nothing if not competitive, obviously a gene passed on from their father.

It had made their lives a lot of fun growing up. And sometimes a giant pain in the ass.

But he'd chosen baseball because he loved the sport, and not for any of the bullshit reasons his brothers always accused him of.

He finished his beer, so he wandered into the kitchen. "Something smells amazing in here."

Anya looked up from the stove and grinned at him. "Shrimp creole with rice. We're also doing a corn salad on the side. And Katrina's baking bread."

His stomach reacted with a violent grumble. He was starving. "Oh, God. Can we kill off all the other guys, so only the three of us get to eat this?"

Katrina laughed. "I'd kind of like to keep Grant around, if you don't mind."

He shrugged. "If you're going to insist on that."

Leo showed up a short while later. All the guys ganged up on him to ask him about football. The kid had changed a lot in the past half a year or so. He'd gained muscle and height, as well as confidence. After he took a quick shower, they sat him down in the living room.

"So how's it going?" Tucker asked.

"It's good. The practices are great, and we're hard at it already, even though football season isn't until fall."

"That gives you time to get used to the plays and integrate yourself into the team," Barrett said.

Leo nodded. "Yeah. I'm learning a lot."

"Any girlfriends yet?"

Leo blushed, peeked over toward the kitchen, then lowered his voice. "I might have my eye on someone."

Barrett nodded his head, offering up a smug smile. "A cheerleader, right?"

"Actually, no. She's in my chemistry class."

"Even better. Nerdy girls are hot."

Grant shot Barrett a look. "You think anyone with a vagina is hot."

"Hey, I'm picky about my women."

"Since when?" Tucker asked. "You racked up more girls in high school and college than you did sacks. And that hasn't changed since you went pro—and by pro, I mean a pro at going through women."

"Don't listen to him, Leo," Barrett said. "It's not my fault women find me hot, muscular and irresistible."

"Gag." Tucker shook his head. "I just lost my appetite."

"That's too bad, because dinner is ready," Katrina said. "And you all should stop talking about sex and vaginas with my brother."

"Why?" Barrett asked with a grin. "How else is he going to learn other than from the experts?"

Grant knocked into Barrett with his body. "You're an asshole."

"Not the first time I've heard that."

Tucker slung his arm around Leo's shoulders. "We'll talk about football and the other thing later."

Leo offered up a smile and nodded.

Tucker liked the kid. He got good grades in school, was still a little shy, though not as much as he had been when they'd first met on the ranch last summer. He was growing up, and God, kids did that so fast these days. He seemed to have a good head on his shoulders, though, and Tucker knew both Grant and Katrina would make sure it stayed that way.

Dinner was amazing, and Tucker ate way more than he should have.

"Anya, this is great."

She smiled so hard he thought her face might break. "Thanks. I've been playing with making some Southern foods."

"She's chosen University of Texas for college," Grant said. "She's waiting for her acceptance letter."

"Oh yeah?" Barrett grinned. "That should make Dad happy. And Grant, of course."

Grant grinned. "Yeah, it sure does."

"We haven't told Easton yet because we don't want him to be disappointed if I don't get in," Anya said.

"I can't imagine you won't get in," Tucker said. "What college wouldn't want you?"

"Thanks. I also applied to a few other backup colleges, but U of T is what I want."

Grant smiled. "It'll make Mia happy to have you there."

Tucker could already imagine his little sister chaperoning Anya at parties and mixers. He knew Katrina would feel a lot better with Anya attending a college where a Cassidy was already in residence.

"It would make me happy, too."

"What about you, Leo?" Tucker asked. "Have you given any thoughts to colleges yet?"

Leo shook his head. "My head is filled with a new school, meeting new friends and concentrating on football right now. Plus, I'm on the baseball team, and our team is in first place. I'm hoping we'll go to the state championships."

Tucker grinned. "That would be great."

Leo nodded. "I know, right? Anyway, between that and spring football, it's pretty much all I can handle."

"I think he's got plenty of time. He can start thinking about college next year," Katrina said.

"Well, when you do, you know we'll all weigh in with our opinions," Barrett said.

Leo laughed. "I'll be happy to hear your opinions. I'll probably need them, since right now I don't have any idea."

They talked about colleges for a while, then helped clear the table and do the dishes. They'd long ago learned from their mother that the kitchen wasn't just a woman's place. You ate the food, you either helped prepare it or you cleaned it up. So Barrett and Leo put the food away while Tucker and Grant did dish duty.

After, they walked out back and surveyed the construction work that was going on. Grant and Katrina showed them the plan for the outdoor kitchen and eating area, plus the expansion near the pool.

Leo picked up a football and was tossing it in the air, so Tucker took it and threw him a few.

"You sure you know which end of that is the right one?" Grant asked him.

Tucker wanted to toss out a curse, but with the kids there, he reined in the urge. "Yeah. The pointy end."

Grant came over and took the ball from him. "Here, you'd better let me take that. Maybe you can go out there with Leo and take some passes. If you know how to catch."

"Go fuck yourself, Grant," he mumbled to his brother before taking a run out to the back of the yard to meet up with Leo.

They played a light game of catch, with Anya and Katrina included, just to work off dinner. But then Barrett tackled Grant, and the women decided they were going inside to make some iced tea, which was the signal for the game to get tougher.

"You in for this?" Tucker asked Leo.

Leo grinned. "Of course."

He slapped Leo on the back. "Let's take them down."

They blindsided Barrett on a trick play. Tucker ran with the ball, then tossed it to Leo, who skirted past a diving Grant and scored.

"Sonofabitch, that kid is fast," Grant said.

When Leo laughed, Grant said, "I mean, good job, Leo."

Barrett's gaze narrowed. "He's the enemy. Quit telling him he did good."

"Come on, he's my kid. I have to tell him when he did a good job."

Tucker couldn't help but notice the wide grin on Leo's face. He'd never had a father figure—or at least one that he remembered. Having Grant in his life now meant the world to him. That made Tucker happy for Leo.

Barrett scored on a toss from Grant after Barrett shoved a shoulder into Tucker and knocked him down—the bastard. So when they had the ball next, Tucker pulled Leo aside.

"How's your passing?"

"Uh . . . kinda sucks."

"That's okay. All you have to do is throw it up in the air. I'll catch it." He discussed the play with Leo, then they broke and faced off against Barrett and Grant.

"I'm gonna bury you," Barrett said to him.

"Quit talking shit and prepare to get your ass kicked," Tucker said.

Barrett dug in. So did Tucker. Then they were off. Tucker ran like hell, and turned to catch the ball Leo had lofted into the air. He could see the ball, and in a few steps he'd have it.

He ran smack into a pile of discarded rocks. He didn't have time to stop, so he tumbled over them and banged his head—hard—on the ground.

For a few seconds, everything went black. And everything on his body fucking hurt.

He rolled over onto his back, hoping like hell he hadn't broken anything important, like his pitching arm.

"Hey, dumbass, you hurt?"

He blinked and saw Barrett standing over him. At least he thought it was Barrett.

"Don't know."

"Shit." Barrett held out his hand. "Come on, let's get you up and check the damage."

He reached out and Barrett hauled him to his feet.

"Oh, fuck." He dropped like a rock back to the ground, dizziness making him feel like he was going to barf up the contents of that amazing dinner he'd just eaten.

"Uh-oh. That's not good," Grant said, crouching down beside him. "Did you hit your head?"

"I don't know. Maybe, when I hit the ground."

By then Katrina and Anya were out there surrounding him.

"What happened?" Katrina asked.

"He can't run for shit," Barrett said. "That's why he plays baseball."

He wanted to say something sarcastic back to his brother, but his head had started to pound. And then everyone started talking at once, which only made his head hurt worse.

"He needs to go to the ER."

That got his attention. He looked up at Katrina. "No, I don't. I'm fine."

"You are not fine. You hit your head. You're dizzy."

That much was true. But the last thing he wanted to do was go to the hospital. "I'm fine."

"I think Katrina's right," Grant said. "Come on, Barrett. Let's pull him up and we'll take a drive to the ER."

He felt hands grab him under his arms, then he was lifted. And then he got the spins again. And felt like throwing up.

Not good.

"I feel a lot better when I'm sitting down."

"Which is why we're taking you to the hospital. Moron."

If he didn't feel like shit, he'd take a swing at Barrett for calling him moron. But right now he couldn't tell which one was Grant and which one was Barrett.

"Can I go with you?" Leo asked.

"I don't think so," Grant said. "You should stay here and do your homework. I'll be sure to let you know how he is."

"I'm fine." He needed to expand his vocabulary. Soon.

His brothers managed to walk him out front and shove him in the backseat of one of Grant's cars.

"Call me," Katrina said before kissing Grant. "I want to know what the doctors say."

"They'll say he can't run for shit," Barrett said with a grin before climbing into the front seat.

Tucker just wanted to lie down and take a nap. He didn't want to go to the ER.

"Which one did you go to last time you got hurt?" Grant asked.

"Mercy General. So don't take me there."

"Why not?"

"Aubry Ross works there."

"Who's Aubry Ross?"

His stomach hurt. He hoped he didn't throw up in Grant's car. "The daughter of the team owner. She's a doctor."

Grant looked at Barrett, then grinned. "So, Mercy General it is, then."

Barrett nodded. "Yup."

"I hate you both right now."

Grant started up the car and pulled down the driveway. "We know."

SEVEN

WHEN AUBRY GRABBED THE CHART AND SAW TUCK-er's name on it, she rolled her eyes.

"Really?"

Marie nodded. "Yes, really. He's in room eleven. With his two brothers. Who, I might add, are just as good-looking as he is. The Cassidys win the hot and sexy gene pool."

She shook her head and, for a second, thought about palming Tucker off on Katie. But he was next up so she might as well do her job. And, she had to admit, she was curious.

She walked down the hall and entered the room. Tucker was lying in bed, his eyes closed. The two other guys, who were in there watching TV, stood when she came in.

Marie was right. One was tall and hot and oh dear God good-looking, with dark hair and gray eyes that pinned her with a look of concern. The other was all hard muscle and angled curves, and looked a lot more like Tucker with jet-black hair. Except his eye color was different. More blue mixed with the green. And he didn't wear glasses.

"Cassidys, I presume?"

"Yes, ma'am. I'm Grant, and this is Barrett."

"I'm Dr. Aubry Ross."

Tucker opened his eyes and smiled. "Hey."

She walked around to the bed. "Hey yourself. What did you do this time?"

"Tripped over a bunch of rocks in Grant's backyard and fell."

"And hit his head," Grant added. "I think he might have gone lights out for a few seconds. Which is why we brought him in."

"So I see on his chart. Let's sit you up, Tucker." She pressed the button that pulled the bed to a full sitting position, laid the chart down and put on a pair of exam gloves to feel around on his head. "No cuts, but you have a hell of a knot on the back of your head."

"Yeah, so I felt."

"Any headache, dizziness, or nausea?"

He paused for a second, until she pinned him with a look.

"Okay, yes to all three."

"It's probably a concussion. We'll want an X-ray and probably a CT scan to rule out anything more serious."

"Sounds fun."

"I'll get those tests ordered, and then I'll be back to discuss the results with you. Might as well get comfortable. And guys, don't let him nap, okay?"

"We're very good at keeping him awake, Doc," Barrett said.

"Good. You do that."

After Aubry left the room, Tucker lay back down. His headache had lessened to a dull pounding. He'd asked the nurse for some aspirin, but she wouldn't give him any until the doctor examined him and made a diagnosis, which really sucked. All he needed was something for his damn headache.

He was fine. This was stupid.

"Your doc is hot," Barrett said. "Are you dating her?"

"No."

"Why not?"

"Because . . . I don't know. It's complicated."

Grant stood, stretched, then leaned his back against the wall. "How is it complicated? Did you ask her out?"

"Sort of."

His lips ticked up. "So, she turned you down?"

"I'm disappointed in your lack of game, Bro," Barrett said. "Maybe I should give it a try."

This was making his headache worse. "Give it your best shot. I'm going to take a nap."

"I don't think so. Doc said no naps for you," Grant said. He grabbed the TV remote. "Let's find the sports channel on this TV and see if we can find some shitty baseball game while we wait for them to grab you for your tests."

He should have stayed home today. Then he could be sitting on his sofa watching TV—without his brothers, and without a goddamn headache.

But on the up side, at least he was seeing Aubry today, though not the way he'd wanted to.

EIGHT

AFTER RETRIEVING THE PRELIMINARY RESULTS FROM
Tucker's X-rays and CT scan, she reviewed them and made her
way back to his exam room. It was quiet in the ER tonight and
nothing epic was going on. For that she was grateful.

She opened the door to find all of them watching a baseball
game on TV.

They all stared at her. She saw genuine concern in the eyes of
Tucker's brothers. It warmed her.

"You have a concussion, Tucker. Your X-rays and CT scan are
clear, though."

"Good to know. Can I have some aspirin, now?"

She nodded. "Of course. I'll make sure they give you some
before you leave. They'll also print out some post-release instructions for you. I'd really like to not see you back here again, Tucker."

He gave her a look. "I didn't do this on purpose. This was
totally Grant's fault."

"Hey. How was it my fault? You're the one who didn't pay attention and fell over the big-ass rocks that, by the way, anyone with two eyes could see. You should have been able to spot that pile even without your glasses on."

She looked at Barrett, who nodded and said, "This is true. Big-ass rocks."

She shook her head. "Either way, this is three times now that I've had to treat you."

Grant frowned. "Three times? You were here another time besides the stitches?"

Tucker scratched the side of his nose. "No. Just that one time."

Aubry realized as soon as she'd said it, then saw the pleading look in Tucker's eyes and knew he really didn't want his brothers to know about that event that occurred in the wine cellar of her father's house. She couldn't blame him for that.

"My mistake. Twice. I'll get your discharge on file and the nurse will provide you with instructions."

"Hey . . . Aubry . . ."

She stopped. "Yes?"

He gave a look to his brothers.

"Uh, I'd really like some coffee," Grant said.

"Not me. I'm good right here."

Shaking his head, Grant grabbed Barrett by his shirt. "Coffee, Barrett. Now."

"I miss all the juicy stuff."

"Thanks for everything, Doc," Grant said as they left the room.

"You're welcome."

They closed the door, leaving Aubry alone with Tucker.

"Is there something you want to discuss?"

"Yeah. First, thanks for not mentioning the first time we met."

She laid the chart on the table next to his bed. "I can understand you not wanting your brothers to know about that. Besides,

I promised you I wouldn't ever tell anyone about that. I'm sorry for the slip."

"Not a problem. It's just that . . . you don't have any brothers or sisters, do you?"

"No. But I still understand. It wasn't your finest moment. If they knew, they'd never let you live it down."

"Understatement."

She paused, waiting, wishing she could make him feel better. She knew his head was fuzzy and likely hurting—bad. "Is there anything else? You really should get some rest."

He looked up at her. "Yeah. There is something else. Can I get your phone number? I'd like to not come here again as a way to see you."

She laughed. "I think we went through this before. There are so many reasons why the two of us shouldn't see each other— either professionally or personally. One, because you have to stop getting hurt. Two, because I lead a very busy life."

"So do I. Which doesn't mean you never have any downtime. You should get out and have some fun. You are allowed to do that, aren't you?"

"On occasion. But not often."

"So on the 'occasion' that we both have, I'd like to take you out. At least to thank you for being so concerned about the well-being of my testicles."

"I don't think I've ever been asked out quite that way before."

He grinned. "I'm nothing if not unique, Doc. So is that a yes?" He pulled out his phone.

She sighed. "I have a terrible feeling if I say no that you're going to end up in my ER again."

"I'll take a pity yes for now. And then I'll convince you I'm worth it."

She gave him her number and he entered it in his phone. Then he gave her his number. "So you don't think I'm some random spammer when I call you."

"Okay. Now that we've done that, I need to explain your after-care, which I want you to take seriously."

She told him everything he needed to know about his concussion. "We'll get you a printout before you leave."

"I'm due to pitch in three days, Doc."

"You need to take that up with your team physician. I'd like him to examine you and he can assess your readiness to pitch. You might have to sit out a game."

He heaved a big sigh. "That's not what I want to hear."

"I'm sorry, but the last thing you need is to get dizzy and drop to the ground while you're on the mound. Your health is the most important thing."

He looked down at the paper she gave him. She knew he was disappointed, so she reached down and grasped his wrist.

"Plus, it looks bad on TV."

He laughed and looked up at her. "Yeah. I get it. I'll talk to Phil and make sure he knows what went down."

"Make sure that you do, because I'll be talking to him as well."

"Damn. Okay."

She started to pull away, but he grasped her hand.

"Aubry."

"Yes?"

"Thanks. I'm glad you were here tonight. It was good to see you again."

A flood of warmth enveloped her. There was something about this man that called to her, that made her feel things she had no right to feel about anyone. Not right now, not when her work was so critical. Distractions could be bad.

And a baseball player, of all things . . .

"I'm glad I was here to help you."

"I'm not talking about the medical stuff, though you do make me feel better. You make me feel . . . a lot of things."

She shuddered in a breath when he tugged on her hand, drawing her closer.

This was all kinds of wrong, but as she leaned over him, she couldn't resist the pull of attraction. And when he cupped the back of her neck, she wanted nothing more than to feel his lips on hers.

Until the door opened. She pulled back so fast she nearly lost her balance.

"So what did we miss?" Barrett asked, holding a cup of coffee in his hand as he rounded the end of the bed. "Anything good?"

Tucker glared at his brother. "No."

"Anyway, I'll be sure you get that list of discharge instructions, Tucker," she said, trying to gather her wits about her and remember the real reason she was in his room. And it wasn't to kiss him.

She turned to his brothers. "You'll need to read those instructions as well. I wouldn't recommend he be alone tonight."

"I'm staying at his place for a few days," Barrett said. "He won't be alone."

She nodded. "Good. If you'll excuse me, I need to see to other patients."

"Thanks, Doc," Tucker said, giving her a look she recognized as regret.

"You're welcome."

She hurried out of there, hoping her face didn't appear as flaming hot from the embarrassment she felt at almost being caught kissing a patient.

Could she have acted more unprofessional? What was wrong with her, anyway? She'd been laser focused on her work since the moment she'd entered college for her undergraduate degree. Other than a short, ill-fated romance in medical school that hadn't occupied a lot of her time, there'd been nothing and no one to distract her.

Until now. And in a couple short weeks, Tucker Cassidy had completely turned her world upside down.

She was determined to turn him down when he called her for a date. There was no way she'd allow him to disrupt her carefully planned life.

She went to the station and gave the nurse discharge instructions, then took a breath.

"Heard you treated Tucker Cassidy again."

It figured Katie would be hovering nearby.

"I did. He presented with concussion symptoms. X-ray and CT scan results were negative, fortunately."

"Did he get hit with a baseball?"

"No. Playing football with his brothers. He tripped over some rocks."

"I see." Katie was entering her notes into one of the laptops and didn't look up. "He probably did it on purpose so he could come and see you again."

She turned and leaned against the station. "He did not. He'll likely miss his next pitching spot, so why would he intentionally hurt himself?"

Katie looked up from her notes, shoving a thick auburn curl behind her ear. "I was kidding. And you're being sensitive about it. What's up with that?"

She looked around. Marie was on break and everyone else was on the other side of the station. "I almost kissed him. In the exam room."

"Scandalous. And juicy. So why didn't you?"

"His brothers walked in. Otherwise, I probably would have. Which is so inappropriate."

"But probably would have been incredibly hot, right?"

She was trying not to think about the hotness of the situation. Or the regret, both positive and negative. "No. Not hot. Inappropriate, Katie."

"I don't know. He's a stud. You should have sex with him."

"And you are not helping."

"Actually, I am helping. You're wound up all the time, and you haven't gotten laid in ages. You're always so all about medicine, and not about having fun. You need to have some fun, Aubry."

She pushed off the station. "I'm not talking about this."

But Katie followed. "Seriously, Bree. When was the last time you had some incredible, mind-blowing, curl-your-toes sex?"

She gave herself a few seconds to think about it, then realized she couldn't pinpoint the last time, which meant it had been too long. "I don't remember."

"Aha. Did he ask you out again?"

"Yes."

"And?"

"He's got my number. He's going to call me. I'm going to say no."

She started moving, but Katie stopped her. "Now you're just being ridiculous."

"No, I'm being smart. Work has to take precedence. My residency is important to me. Plus, he's a jock, and you know how I feel about that."

"So, fuck him and don't think about his occupation. Then you'll feel better and he probably doesn't want a girlfriend anyway. Not after what the last one did to him."

Katie had a point. After his ex-girlfriend kneed him in the testicles, the last thing Tucker probably wanted was a girlfriend. And she wasn't looking for a boyfriend.

So what was the harm in some . . . harmless sex?

"Dr. Ross. Dr. Murphy."

She turned in the hallway to face Dr. Kenneth Chen, the attending physician in charge of emergency medicine.

Their boss.

"Hello, Dr. Chen," Katie said, always unaffected by Dr. Chen, whereas for some reason he made Aubry a nervous wreck.

"We seem to have patients in this emergency room, yet the two of you are . . . doing what, exactly? Gossiping?"

"Actually, Dr. Chen, I was consulting with Dr. Ross about my diabetic patient in room six. Now that I've finished my consult, I'm about to head back."

Dr. Chen nodded. "Carry on then, Dr. Murphy."

Katie winked at her and headed off in the opposite direction.

"I noticed you treated Tucker Cassidy, Dr. Ross."

Leave it to Dr. Chen to be on top of everything going on in his ER. "Yes, sir."

"There's no game today, so I assume it wasn't a work-related injury."

"No, Dr. Chen. He was playing football with his brothers and tripped over some rocks."

"I assume you intend to follow up on his care, as well as report it to the team?"

"I do indeed. I'll make a report to the team physician in the morning."

"Make sure that you do. Our relationship with the Rivers is important to this hospital. They send all their injuries to us. We want to insure there's follow-up."

"There will be."

"Is Mr. Cassidy still here?"

"I just left him a short while ago. Amy should be giving him discharge instructions."

"I think I'll stop in and see how he's doing. You can go about your business with your other patients."

"Yes, sir."

She couldn't get away from him fast enough. Dr. Chen was

brilliant in the ER, and she'd learned a lot in the past few years working under him. But damn if he wasn't intimidating as hell. The man didn't have a warm bone in his body. She always felt under the microscope whenever he directed his scrutiny toward her, as if she somehow didn't measure up.

She knew it was just her own mind conjuring up something that wasn't there. Her evaluations had always been decent, and she'd never had a complaint about her performance. But she also put high standards on herself. And feedback was so important to her, so she'd know whether she was on the right track.

Just once, she'd like Dr. Chen to tell her she'd done a good job. That wasn't in his nature, though. If he wasn't screaming at you that you were an incompetent moron, then you were supposed to assume you were doing a good job.

She'd be glad when her residency was over and she would no longer be under his thumb.

She was a damn good doctor.

And getting distracted by Tucker Cassidy wasn't going to help her become a better one.

NINE

TUCKER SAT IN A MEETING WITH PHIL, THE TEAM DOC-
tor, and Manny Magee, his coach.

"Is this going to become a regular thing, Cassidy?"

The last thing Tucker wanted right now was to be the recipient
of one of Manny's signature glares. You didn't want Manny glar-
ing at you. Really, you didn't want Manny paying the slightest bit
of attention to you. Manny ignoring you was a good thing. You'd
rather him yell at someone else.

"No, Manny, it isn't."

"So how come you've been to the ER twice in less than two
weeks?"

Tucker slid his fingers through his hair. "Just a fluke."

"You lost a spot in the rotation. That fucks up my schedule,
which doesn't make me happy."

And you definitely didn't want to make Manny unhappy. "It
won't happen again."

"See that it doesn't." Manny turned to Phil. "He ready to pitch now?"

Phil nodded. "He's been checked out and he's cleared."

"Good. Then we won't have to sit around and have any more of these fireside chats, right?" Manny asked him.

"No."

Manny stood. "Get your ass out there and throw some pitches. Try not to fall off the mound when you do."

Tucker prided himself on doing his job. In fact, he was damn good at it. Distractions never bothered him, whether it was fans booing him during an out-of-town game, or a field full of swarming bugs in late summer. Whatever it was, he could handle it.

He had no idea what the hell had been going on with him lately, but whatever it was, it was over now. He'd make sure of it.

He took to the field for some warm-up pitches, ignoring the athletic trainers who kept a close eye on him.

Fall off the mound. Fuck that. He'd been born to stand on this mound and throw pitches.

He started slow, since Phil and the trainers hadn't allowed him to pitch in over a week. He'd been forced to sit in the bullpen and watch someone else take his spot in the rotation. He'd chewed through about six bags of sunflower seeds, his irritation spiking with every pitch he hadn't been able to throw.

Even worse, they'd lost the game he should have been pitching.

Now, though, he was getting his groove back—especially his curveball. With every pitch he threw, he felt more and more like himself again. And when he finished his warm-up set and walked off the mound, he felt like no time had passed, as if he could pitch an entire game right now and strike out twenty-seven batters in a row.

He wished he could pitch a game right now, instead of two days from now when it was his turn in the rotation again. He was itching to prove to his coaches and the medical team that there wasn't a damn thing wrong with him.

In the meantime, though, he wanted to get in touch with Aubry. He'd put it off long enough, and these injuries had gotten in the way.

He wanted to see her if she had time, and since they were playing a day game today, he had a night off. Which meant they might be able to get together tonight.

The only way he was going to find out was to ask, so he pulled out his phone and dialed her number, which, after a few rings, went to voice mail.

Okay, so she was probably working. That made sense. He decided to text her instead.

I'm off tonight. Are you free? If so, how about dinner?

He waited a few minutes and didn't get an answer, so he shoved his phone in his bag and decided to check it later.

"Later" ended up being after his game that afternoon. Garrett Scott pitched a great game, allowing only one run, and the offense helped out by scoring four. It felt good to get a win, even if he didn't get a chance to help out. The team was what mattered.

He checked his phone and found a return text from Aubry.

Not sure you and I seeing each other is a good idea.

His lips curved. At least it wasn't an outright no.

He typed a return text to her.

Are you working tonight?

This time, she replied right away. *I worked earlier. I'm off tonight.*

He pressed the call button, and she answered.

"Hi, Tucker."

"Hey. So they occasionally give you days off, huh?"

"Shockingly, yes. And you as well?"

"We just finished up a game."

"Oh, that's right. You have midday games during the week sometimes. And how did that turn out?"

"We won."

"I'm glad to hear that."

He could tell she was trying to turn their conversation toward anything but going out, so he intended to steer it back. "So . . . about dinner?"

"Oh, right. Like I mentioned in my text message, I don't think that's a good idea."

"Why not? You're good-looking, I'm good-looking, we're around the same age. I assume you like to eat."

She laughed. "I do like to eat."

"Great. Give me your address and around seven thirty we'll do that eating thing together."

He heard her sigh. "Okay. But at dinner I'll tell you why we shouldn't see each other."

"Sounds like a plan."

She said she'd text him her address when he offered to pick her up. After he hung up, he smiled.

He had a date with Aubry tonight.

TEN

AFTER TUCKER CALLED, AUBRY HAD SPENT THE REST of the afternoon taking care of business. She paid some bills, dashed to the grocery store and did some laundry. Keeping her eye on the time, she took a quick shower and stared at herself in the mirror, feeling ridiculous for agreeing to a date with Tucker.

As if her life wasn't complicated enough. She should have said no when he asked her.

So why hadn't she?

Because you want to go out with him, idiot. That's why.

Ignoring that annoying inner voice, she dried her hair, put on makeup and went to her closet, trying to figure out what to wear.

Dinner. Nights could still be cool, so she chose a pair of black skinny pants and a long top, then slid on her boots and selected a pair of silver dangly earrings.

Okay, maybe it felt good to dress up in something besides scrubs for a change, and eat something other than microwave meals or a salad. Or, God forbid, hospital cafeteria food. Tucker was damn fine to look at, so there was that as well. How bad could it be to share a meal with a hot guy she was attracted to? He was funny, smart, and if they didn't end up in the ER because he fell off the curb and broke an ankle or something, it might just be a decent night.

It was just a date, not a relationship. Simple, easy, and fun. Not life changing or anything. She could live with that.

When the doorbell rang, she felt ridiculous for the sudden uptick in her pulse rate.

Just a date, Aubry. Remember? Light and simple.

She opened the door and swallowed at the sight of him wearing dark jeans and a button-down shirt.

"Hi," she said.

His lips ticked up. "Hi yourself."

"Come on in. I'm just about ready."

He walked in and she closed the door behind him, trying not to stare at his ass. Or imagine her hands on said ass. While he was naked.

Get a grip, woman.

Instead, she focused on what he was wearing, assessing the overall look. There was something about men in button-down shirts and blue jeans that really got to her. Maybe because she'd been surrounded by men in either suits or scrubs her entire life.

Plus . . . Tucker. Thick black hair and those glasses, and the eyes behind them. Deep, green eyes he fixed on her when he turned around.

This was what happened when she didn't have sex for a really long time. Katie and Marie were right. Her libido was definitely coming out in full force right now.

She'd have to remind herself to keep her focus tonight.

It was a date. They were going out for dinner. Nothing more.

"Nice place."

She shrugged. "Just a condo. It's really nothing much. I didn't want to buy a house—not right now, anyway, since I don't spend a lot of time here."

"Because you're always at the hospital."

She nodded. "Yes. How about you?"

"The same. I'm on the road a lot, and I want to make sure a team is going to keep me before I decide to invest in a house. So I'm leasing a condo. I don't live too far from you, actually. Just a few miles down the road."

"The new complex? The one they finished up last year? The Shenandoah Heights neighborhood?"

"Yeah. That's the one."

"I love those condos. Big porches and a great park and pool. I have a friend who lives over there. The square footage is awesome."

"It's pretty nice."

"Did you get the two bedroom or three?"

"Three. I have a big family and some of them like to visit. Between Grant and me, we can put them up."

"I'm very jealous. The floor plan for the three bedroom is very generous for a condo."

He walked into her living room. "Your place has decent space. I like your kitchen. Do you cook?"

"I hardly remember what it's like to have the time to fix a decent meal. And to be honest, I don't really know how to cook many things. How about you? Do you cook?"

"On the grill outside. Steaks and burgers and things. I do make fantastic pancakes. Plus, I can microwave the hell out of anything."

She laughed. "So your awesome kitchen is going to waste."

"Pretty much. Like tonight."

He was giving her a look, when she realized they were just standing there in the living room.

She obviously didn't entertain enough, either. Her mother would be appalled. "Oh. I'm so sorry. I'll be just a minute. Please sit down."

She dashed off to the bedroom, finger combed her hair, applied lip gloss, then took one last look in the mirror.

Decent. Okay, she looked hot. Good enough to get laid, if that's what she had in mind.

Which she didn't. At all. Much.

Okay, maybe a little.

"This is ridiculous," she whispered to herself as she grabbed her purse, her sweater, and opened the bedroom door. She pasted on her best smile and decided whatever happened—happened. She was tired of the inner war she was having with herself.

Tucker stood as she came out.

"Did I mention you look gorgeous tonight? Though you look pretty damn hot in those scrubs you wear at the hospital, too."

He was not making her inner war any easier. "Thank you."

He held the door for her, then shut it behind her. He also opened her car door and waited while she slid in before closing the door and going around to his side.

Maybe that was normal. Maybe all guys did that. But she'd dated enough in college to know that wasn't true.

"So where are we going tonight?"

"I thought I'd keep it light and easy since you were a little wary about going out with me."

She looked down at her hands. "I didn't exactly say I was wary."

"Oh, I think you made it clear. But you can trust me, Aubry. I'm a pretty great guy."

She shifted her gaze to him. "And so modest, too."

His lips curved. "Yeah, that too."

He drove toward the west end of the city, and when he pulled up in front of a light brown brick building and parked, she turned to face him.

"Are we stopping at a friend's house?"

"Nope. This is part one of our date tonight."

She had no idea what that meant, but when he came around to her side of the car, she got out. It was then she noticed the sign planted on the front lawn.

Madame Sheila's Psychic Readings.

She tilted her head and gave him a look. "Seriously?"

"Yeah. I thought it might be fun."

"I'm going to tell you up front that I don't believe in this stuff."

He shrugged. "We'll give it a go. Madame Sheila might have insight into our futures."

"Uh-huh. Sure she will."

Though she had to admit, it sounded fun. Hokey as hell, but fun.

They stepped inside the house. It was an older home, with a parlor entry. Just inside, there was a desk, with a young, very attractive brunette sitting behind it.

"May I help you?"

How very official.

Tucker gave his and Aubry's first names. The woman clicked on her laptop. "Yes, Madame Sheila will see you both shortly. I have you booked with a group appointment. Is that correct?"

Tucker turned to her. "I thought it would be more fun that way, but you can go in alone if you have some deep dark secrets you'd like to keep from me."

She laughed. "No, we can go together."

Considering the woman would likely tell her she was going to meet a tall, dark stranger, she figured her secrets—since she didn't have any—were safe.

They took a seat and waited about five minutes. It gave her time to appreciate what had to be original wood floors and the gorgeous crown molding. The solid wood archway leading into the alcove just behind Madame Sheila's assistant was something to covet. It would make a lovely sitting area—or even an office. It made Aubry want a house of her own.

Someday. Once her residency was finished and she was settled in, she'd be able to house shop, and then she'd have the place of her dreams.

"We're ready for you now," the brunette said, having appeared from down the hall. "Please come this way."

She spoke in hushed tones, like they had an audience with the Pope or something. Aubry rolled her eyes at Tucker.

"Hey, this is serious business," he said, his lips curving.

"I can hardly wait."

They were taken to a room just to the right off the hall. The room was brightly lit, surprisingly. Aubry expected complete darkness, candles, and maybe a crystal ball on the table. And of course Madame Sheila wearing robes and a turban.

Instead, there were two sofas and several comfortable chairs. And an older woman with short brown hair who smiled when they entered. She was wearing slacks and an orange blouse. No turban in sight.

"Good evening. My name is Sheila. You are Tucker and Aubry?"

Tucker walked in and shook her hand. "Yes. I'm Tucker."

"And I'm Aubry." She shook Sheila's hand.

"Please, sit down. Would you care for some coffee or tea? Or some water?"

"Nothing for me, thank you," Aubry said.

"I'm good," Tucker said.

Sheila nodded. "That'll be all for now, Brenda."

The brunette shut the door behind them.

"Well, then, I'll start my speech. I'm Sheila Aveila. I'm a psychic medium, which means I can see the past, plus the future. You booked your appointment through my assistant, Brenda, who is also my daughter. Other than that, I know nothing about the two of you. Can you confirm that?"

"Yeah. I gave her my first name and Aubry's first name and my cell phone number. Nothing else," Tucker said.

"Good. Then we'll get started." Sheila closed her eyes for a few seconds and took several deep breaths. Then she opened her eyes and stared at Aubry.

"You lost someone you loved not too long ago. Someone you cared very deeply about."

Aubry was about to say something, but Sheila held up her hand to stop her.

"Your grandmother?"

Aubry didn't know how Sheila would be aware of that. "I . . . yes."

"You have her bracelet. A charm bracelet. You keep it in your jewelry box, and when you're stressed or upset, you take it out and put it on. It gives you comfort."

No one would know that. Even Aubry's mother didn't know about her ritual. "Yes."

"That makes your grandmother happy. She's with you when you do that, and she wants you to know that someday soon, your life will get easier. But in the meantime, take comfort, because she's always with you."

Aubry didn't want to believe in this. She didn't believe in these kinds of things. Still . . .

"Thank you."

Sheila looked over at Tucker. "You . . . chaos."

Tucker laughed. "Yeah, you could say that."

"You have many relatives from your past. They look out for you. But they say you're a difficult one to manage."

"I don't doubt it."

"You have to live down a legacy, but you chose to lead your own path. It troubles you at times."

She looked over at Tucker, who was frowning. He didn't say anything to Sheila.

"Your grandfather wants me to tell you that he's so proud of your choice of career, that he appreciates you keeping the old baseball glove in . . ." Sheila frowned. "You keep it somewhere safe." She drummed her fingers on the table. "A trunk . . . a trunk in your room?"

Tucker's lips ticked up. "He knows that, does he?"

Sheila nodded. "He also wants me to tell you, like the father, goes the son. The path may be a different one, but the end result is the same. You're walking the correct road."

Tucker nodded. "Okay, I get that."

Sheila looked from Tucker to Aubry, her gaze settling between them.

"Three times the two of you have circled, and now you come together. The fates bring you in line with one another."

Okay, that was downright weird. A little vague, but still, pretty on the mark. First, the wine cellar, then twice in the ER.

A lucky guess?

Pretty damn lucky if it was.

"Love is a very powerful force. It entwines with fate and defines our destiny. Don't run from what's meant to be."

Love? Who was talking about love? Aubry swallowed. "Um, this is just our first date."

Sheila smiled. "The first of many, I hope. The aura surrounding the two of you is very strong, your colors bright. You will forge. Your families are united on the other side, with positive hopes for both of you."

Whoa. That was some deep stuff for a first date. And a lot of made up mumbo jumbo that she wasn't about to buy into.

Aubry laid her now-sweaty palms on her pants. "Well, that was so interesting."

"Thanks," Tucker said, putting his arm around Aubry. "I have pretty high hopes for our first date. I think we'll start there, and see how it goes."

Sheila smiled. "I hope you gleaned something from this reading that you found useful."

Aubry stood. "It was definitely enlightening. Thank you so much." She shook Sheila's hand, and as Tucker paid, asked her about her house. Sheila told her it had been her grandmother's house. She'd had it remodeled several years ago.

Aubry's parents were into the now and the new. She loved this old house, and would love to be able to renovate an older home someday.

After thanking Sheila again, they headed out to the car.

Once they had taken off, Tucker glanced at her. "So . . . what did you think?"

"It was weird."

"Weird bad or weird good?"

"A little of both, I think. She knew some stuff that no one else would know."

"Yeah, I got that. With the grandparents. I kept my grandpa's old baseball glove. She even knew where I keep it."

"Yes. Same thing with my grandmother's charm bracelet. How would she know that?"

He shrugged. "No idea. Unless she's the real deal and was talking to our dead relatives. Pretty cool, huh?"

She looked out the window. "I'm not sure if I'd define that as cool or not. It's a little . . . unsettling."

"Really? I found it fascinating. And then the part about you and me and the three times? No one would know that but us."

She dragged her gaze from the window and settled it on him. "You didn't tell them anything."

"No. Just gave our first names and my phone number. Besides, who else would know about us?"

She'd told Katie, but Katie had no idea Tucker was bringing her here tonight.

Fate and destiny, though? She made her own destiny, and the only part of that she was concerned with was her medical career.

The rest of it she decided she didn't want to think about. So she was going to think of this as a fun interlude and nothing more.

"I had a great time at Madame Sheila's. Thank you for taking me."

"You're welcome. You'll like what's next, too."

"There's more?"

"Of course there's more."

He pulled into the parking lot of . . .

Oh, dear God.

"Bowling? We're going bowling?"

He grinned and parked, then turned off the car and faced her. "I didn't want to do a boring first date where all we do is go out to dinner at some restaurant and make small talk. You deserve a fun first date."

"I do?"

"Yeah. Because I'll bet you work all the time and when you're not working you're probably sleeping. Or doing laundry or paying bills and shit like that."

He didn't have to know that's exactly what she'd been doing earlier. "I can have fun."

"I'm sure you can. That's why we're going bowling."

He got out and came around to fetch her. She had to admit, this was the most intriguing first date she'd ever been on.

"I don't remember the last time I went bowling. Maybe my freshman year of undergrad? And I have to tell you, even then I wasn't good at it."

"You don't have to be good at it to have fun."

"I seem to recall the last time I went bowling with a group, my date at the time made fun of my lousy score."

He stopped and laced his fingers with hers. "Then you're dating the wrong guys."

She laughed. "Apparently."

She wasn't about to tell him she hadn't been dating any guys lately. Let him think what he wanted.

They got inside, and for a weeknight, the place was booming. League play, probably. She wasn't sure she was going to be okay with that, since she was rusty as hell and would probably throw quite a few gutter balls. She didn't want everyone in there to notice.

"I hope you're hungry. They serve the best greasy hamburgers in the restaurant here."

She lifted her gaze to his. "Is that right?"

"I know you being a doctor and all, you're probably against the whole greasy hamburger thing."

"I'm a doctor, not a nutritionist. I have nothing against a nice, greasy burger."

He put his arm around her. "See how we're connecting? It's like we're meant to be."

Which got her to thinking about what Sheila said.

She immediately dismissed it. She would not go there with that whole fate and destiny stuff. She was hungry, and a burger sounded like a great idea.

Burgers and bowling—her primary objectives, and all her mind could handle at the moment.

See? Fun. Fun she could deal with. Deep stuff? No, thanks.

She smiled up at Tucker. "Let's bowl."

ELEVEN

TUCKER COULDN'T HELP HIMSELF. AS AUBRY STOOD
with the bowling ball in her hand, preparing to toss it down the alley,
he wasn't paying attention to her form or the way she swung the ball
or how many pins she knocked down. He was watching her ass.

She had a great ass. Round and curvy in all the right ways, the
kind a man wanted to put his hands on.

She knocked down six pins, swung around with a smug grin on
her face. One would think she'd just hit a strike.

"Did you see that?" she asked as she took her seat and grabbed
her beer.

"I did."

"Six pins. No gutter balls that time."

"You're up to a score of fifty-five."

"Woo!"

He couldn't help but laugh. At least she had a great sense of
humor about how bad she was.

"I might be ready for that greasy cheeseburger after this game. I feel like I've really worked up an appetite. You know, now that I'm so much better at this."

"Yes, I can tell. You've only thrown four balls in the gutter so far this game."

"Right?"

He took his turn, knocking down nine in his first try, then hitting the other for a spare. Aubry cheered for him, then got up and hit eight pins. She turned to face him, her eyes wide.

He nodded. "You can do this."

She walked over toward him. "They're in the corner. I was never very good at hitting the ones in the corner."

"Take a deep breath and aim from right to left. I have a good feeling about it."

"I'll do my best. I'd really like a spare."

"Then go get one."

She grabbed her ball and studied the lane.

He could tell this meant something to her, even though she was merely having fun. So he got up and moved behind her, sliding his hands under her elbows.

"Scoot an inch or two to the right."

She did, and he followed.

"Now make your swing in one swift move, and sight the pins when you let go. Use your wrist to flick it a little toward the pins. Does that make sense to you?"

"Yes."

He liked the feel of her body against his and was reluctant to let her go. She smelled like something sultry and a little decadent. He wanted to bury his face in her neck and kiss her, then turn her around and kiss her some more.

But now wasn't the time. He reserved that thought for later.

"You've got this, Aubry." He gave her arms a slight squeeze

before letting her go. He went back to his seat and watched as she walked up, swung, and let the ball go.

It rolled down the alley with authority, a perfect roll as it blasted the two pins down.

She raised her arms high and let out a battle cry of celebration. He stood and waited for her while she ran up and threw herself against him. He wrapped his arms around her, really liking the feel of her soft curves pressed against his body.

She pulled back, her smile wide, her eyes shining with victory. "I did it."

"You did. I knew you could."

"I got a spare. I don't suck at this after all."

"Of course you don't."

She stared at him, those intense blue eyes of hers studying him. He saw curiosity and question in her eyes. And also that same desire that gut punched him . . . hard.

He really wanted to kiss her. Right now.

But she palmed his chest, then took a very obvious step back.

"So . . . how about we finish this game, then celebrate with cheeseburgers?"

Message delivered. She wasn't ready, yet.

But he'd bet she would be before the night was over.

"Sure. And who knows? You might hit another spare, or even a strike before the end of this game."

She laughed. "Right. Like that's going to happen. Come on, stud. Game first, cheeseburgers next."

And then the really fun stuff after that.

TWELVE

AFTER A COUPLE OF BEERS AND—TUCKER HAD BEEN right—a rather fantastic greasy cheeseburger with accompanying onion rings, Aubry was more than satisfied, and a lot stuffed. Fortunately, they'd bowled another game after that to work off the meal. She'd even gotten a strike.

The night couldn't get much better.

They turned in their shoes and headed out the door.

"I had fun."

Tucker grasped her hand. "Of course you did. I told you, I'm a fun guy."

"You did tell me that. And you did the unexpected—you made me relax and have a good time."

"Good. And if that came as a surprise to you, then you're obviously working too hard."

He walked to her side of the car and opened the door. She turned to face him. "I'm supposed to work hard right now. It's my job."

He slid his hand along the side of her neck. "It can't always be about work, Aubry."

She hadn't expected this. Not now and not here, anyway. So when he bent and brushed his lips across hers, she wasn't ready. But oh, it was a nice kiss. Easy and effortless, without the awkwardness or tension she usually felt when a man kissed her for the first time. He slid his arm around her waist and tugged her close, drawing her body against his.

She reached out to grasp hold of his shirt, making contact with a solid wall of chest muscle. A dizzying array of sensations enveloped her. His scent—crisp, clean, with just a hint of musky, male sweat. A swirl of dizziness as his mouth moved over hers. She'd never swooned before, but Tucker was really good at kissing, and this wasn't even a deep, passionate kiss. He took slow kissing to a deliberate level, as if they had all the time in the world to explore each other's mouths. It made her wonder what it would be like when they were alone and he'd kiss her more thoroughly. Her toes curled at the thought.

He drew back, then rubbed his thumb over her bottom lip. "I've been wanting to kiss you for a while now."

She didn't want to admit how much his words thrilled her. "Have you?"

"Yeah. You have a great mouth, Aubry." To prove his intent, he leaned in and kissed her again, making her shudder. Making her want things she normally pushed way down on her list of things to think about.

Those "things" had instantly moved up way higher on her list.

At this moment, they were number one, especially when his hands moved over her back. When was the last time a man's hands roamed her body and did delicious things to her? Self-induced orgasms, while efficient, weren't nearly as fun as a guy taking her to the height of ecstasy.

Not that she planned on Tucker giving her an orgasm or anything.

Then again . . . why not? They were both adults. He knew what her life was like. And he traveled a lot. As long as he had no expectations of permanency, some hot awesome sex wouldn't be a bad idea at all.

Especially now that she'd gotten a tease of what it might be like.

He finally pulled away, forcing her thoughts away from sex.

He smiled down at her. "I should probably stop kissing you in the parking lot."

"Does that mean you intend to kiss me somewhere else?"

His lips curved. "I can definitely do that. Your place or mine?"

"Mine works."

"Okay."

He drove them to her house. She wasn't sure she knew what she was doing, but she knew what she felt, so she didn't want to second-guess the feelings.

It wasn't a big deal—just sex. And she'd make that clear to Tucker.

She dug out her keys and opened the front door of her condo, stepped inside, then flipped the switch. Tucker followed, shutting the door behind him.

"Would you like something to drink? I have wine and beer, plus water and soda."

"A beer sounds great, thanks."

She laid her purse down on the table next to the sofa, then went into the kitchen to grab a beer for Tucker. She opened one of the cabinets to reach for a wineglass.

"I can get that for you."

She startled, not realizing Tucker was right behind her. She melted as his hand snaked up her arm to grab the wineglass. His big body pressed up against hers, trapping her between him and the kitchen counter.

She didn't mind that at all, so she turned around.

He laid the glass down and captured her mouth in that deep, intimate kiss she'd been waiting for ever since the great first-kiss tease at the bowling alley parking lot.

It was everything she'd anticipated—and oh, so much more. Hot, demanding, his hands sliding under her shirt to roam across her bare skin. She could barely breathe, her synapses firing fast to keep up with the sensory overload of his mouth, his touch, and the feel of his body pressed against hers.

She was always fully absorbed in work, thinking that was enough to satisfy her. Now she realized she wanted so much more, like Tucker's mouth on hers, his tongue doing delicious things to hers while his hands worked their magic along the skin of her back, sliding down the top of her pants to cup the bare skin of her butt.

Her nipples tingled, her sex dampened, and she needed about ten orgasms tonight to make up for her foolish bout of celibacy over the past—however long it had been.

A sense of urgency overcame her and she lifted his shirt, suddenly needing to touch him—everywhere. When her hands slid over his abs, she groaned.

Solid wall of muscle. She needed to see this man naked. Right now.

She pulled back. "Let's go to the bedroom."

"You sure?" he asked.

She liked that he asked. "Absolutely."

He nodded, took her hand and let her lead him down the hall. She opened the door to her bedroom and walked inside toward the bed, turning to face him.

She sat on the bed and pulled off her boots, then drew her shirt off, casting it aside before standing to remove her pants, which left her in only her underwear.

"Your turn," she said.

With a smile, he took off his glasses and laid them on her bedside table, then toed off his shoes and pulled off his socks. His shirt came next.

Oh, yes. His torso was amazing. Broad shoulders, wide chest, and an amazing set of well-toned abs. She stepped over to him, needing to touch what she saw.

Now that she was close, and his glasses were off, she could really see his eyes. So gorgeous, and so intently watching her. She reached for the buckle of his belt and untethered it, pulling it apart so she could see to the button, then the zipper, drawing it down over one very impressive erection.

"Mmm. This feels familiar," she said, rubbing him through his jeans.

His eyes blazed hot. "It's fully functional again, too. Thanks to your tender care."

"Good to know. Because I intend to use the hell out of your cock tonight."

He inhaled sharply, then reached around to unhook her bra, leading the straps down her arms so he could remove it. He took a step back to admire her breasts.

"Pretty." He bent, flicked his tongue over one bud, then captured it between his lips.

She let out a moan, holding his head to her breast while he sucked and licked her nipple, his hand massaging the other breast and teasing the nipple with his thumb and forefinger. Tiny shocks of pleasure shot straight south, igniting the fire he'd started with his kisses. She squeezed his cock through his jeans, but that wasn't enough. She pushed his jeans over his hips, and he pulled away long enough to shed his pants and his briefs.

Wow. She'd examined him in the wine cellar when he was limp and in pain, and she hadn't been paying much attention then because she'd been in doctor mode.

Now? She was in woman mode, very much interested in his penis, and not at all in a clinical way. She wrapped her hand around the shaft and stroked. He thrust against her hand.

"I like you touching me," he said, sliding his hands up her arms.

She felt a skitter of goose bumps as he tangled his fingers in her hair and kissed her, wrapping his arm around her back. She sank into his embrace, letting her body align with his, skin to skin.

He put his hand on her butt, his fingers sliding into the back of her underwear to cup a handful of butt cheek. The warmth of his hand heated her, made her shove against his rock hard erection so she could rub against him.

He groaned against her lips and pushed her back toward the bed, the back of her knees hitting the mattress.

"Sit down," he said, his breathing harsh as he pulled away.

She was ever cognizant of his hard cock and all the delicious things she intended to do with it—with him—tonight.

Her long sexual drought was about to end, and she was more than ready for it, especially when he kneeled on the carpet in front of her and reached for her panties, drawing them over her hips and down her legs.

He spread her legs and smoothed his hands over her thighs.

"You are beautiful, Aubry." He pressed a kiss to her inner thigh. "And you smell amazing." He kissed his way toward her hip, then her stomach, his chest making contact with her sex.

She shivered, leaned back on the bed, resting on her elbows as Tucker teased her by not giving her what she needed the most at that moment. Instead, he used his hands and mouth to map her body. Though that definitely inspired her to wriggle against him, arch her hips, and beg for his mouth on her suddenly tingling nipples.

When he complied, she let out a satisfied moan, sliding her fingers into his hair to hold him there while he flicked his tongue against the bud. The arc of sensation shot right to her sex, making her clit tingle with the anticipation of what other delicious things he could do with his mouth. His beard scratched the tender skin of her breast in the most perfect of ways, and she could already imagine the scruff rubbing her thighs.

"Tucker."

He raised his head. "Yeah?"

"Lick me."

His lips curved. "I thought I was."

"Yes, and it feels really good. But, you know, elsewhere."

He raised himself up by planting his hands on the mattress, his arms distracting her with their corded muscle. "Care to be more specific?"

"Would you like me to draw you a map, or do you think you can figure out where I want your mouth?"

He balanced himself on one hand, using the other to map a trail from between her breasts, down her stomach, to palm her sex. "Here?"

"Yes." She was distracted by his strength, but also by the way he touched her, using his fingers to caress her in a way that definitely caught her attention. "Yes, right there."

"Does it ache, Aubry?" he asked, slipping his fingers inside her as he moved his way down her body again. "Does it ache so much you want me to lick it and suck it until you come?"

She shuddered at his words, her mind a visual of him doing just that, of what it would feel like when she burst. "Yes. Make me come, Tucker."

He draped her thighs over his shoulders, nestled her body close to his face, his warm breath a balm to her tortured senses. And when his tongue lapped along her folds, she pressed into the mattress, falling into the rapture of heat and sensation. It was a slow, languorous, billowy feeling of utter delight.

Until he put his mouth around her clit and sucked. Then, everything changed. It was like being struck by lightning in the best possible way, a sharp, sinful strike of pleasure. She let out a low moan, her hips arched off the bed, and she gave herself over to Tucker, to his devilish lips and tongue and his relentless assault on her body.

His mouth was hot, and his fingers entered her, probing her with soft, rhythmic strokes until she was certain she'd never make it out of this without a cataclysmic orgasm.

And when it hit, faster than she'd imagined, she fisted her hands in the sheets, rocked her sex against his mouth, and thoroughly fell into the release, her entire body shaking with the force of what had to be the best damn orgasm she'd had in . . .

Her mind and body were too far gone to do the math. All she could do was hold on and enjoy the quivering ride. And when she relaxed, he was there, his face looming over hers to take her mouth in a kiss that tasted of sex and hot desire.

He didn't give her a moment to catch her breath, his erection steely hard and hot against her thigh.

Which was fine with her, because she was throbbing, primed and ready for him.

And they had all night long to enjoy each other.

THIRTEEN

TUCKER'S FINGERS WERE STILL BURIED INSIDE AUBRY, the hot, pulsing contractions from her orgasm wrapping around him. His mouth was on hers, her hands roaming over his skin. Every part of him was feverishly hot and coiled with fiery need. All he wanted to do was bury his cock deep inside her until she convulsed around him.

He moved his fingers in slow, gentle movements, not wanting her to come down from that high of release. He wanted her hovering, still ready, hot and needy so he could bring her right to the brink again. Only this time, he'd be inside her.

"You ready?" he asked.

She smoothed her hand across his face, her fingertips so soft he wondered if he'd ever felt anything like that sensation before as she ran her finger over his bottom lip. And when he moved his fingers inside her, she gasped.

"I'm ready for whatever you have in mind."

For someone as reluctant as Aubry had been about being with

him, he liked that she was all-in right now, that there had been no hesitation on her part.

"Good." He bent and kissed her, then whispered against her mouth. "I have a lot in mind."

He withdrew his fingers, then licked them. "You taste good. I wonder how many times I can make you come tonight?"

Her gaze was direct. And hot. Filled with promise.

"A lot, probably. It's been kind of a sexual drought for me."

"Drought's over, babe. I have a box of condoms in my car."

Her lips lifted. "I have a box in my bathroom. I think we're good to go—for tonight, anyway."

He laughed and swept his hand over her breasts, watching them rise and fall as he brushed her nipples until they lifted into tight peaks. He bent and took a taste of each one. Soft, then hard little nubs that, when he sucked, made her moan.

She responded so damn well to him, and it made his balls quiver. He wanted to take all night long learning her body, but right now he wanted to feel what it was like to be inside of her.

"Give me just a second," she said, rolling over and getting out of bed.

He lay on his side, enjoying the view of her very fine ass as she disappeared into the connected bathroom. She returned not long after with a box of condoms in her hand. She took one out of the box and tossed it in his direction. He caught it in the air with one hand.

"Nice reflexes," she said.

"Part of my job."

"How's the leg, by the way? And the head? And your testicles?"

He laughed, pulled out a condom and rolled over to lay the box on the nightstand. "All in working order."

"Good to know." She stretched out on the bed, pulling her arms over her head. "Especially the testicles."

He tore open the wrapper on the condom, applied it, then

crawled between her legs, spreading her thighs. "Yeah, I'm going to be using my balls tonight. They're already filled with come. I'm about ready to burst from touching you and kissing you."

He spread himself over her body, leaning in close to brush his lips over hers. "And tasting you. Everything about you makes me hard."

She took in a deep breath. "Let's get you inside me, then. I'd hate to think of you suffering any longer."

He fit the tip of his cock against her, then eased inside, cupping her butt to pull her up close as he gave a first thrust.

Oh, yeah. Just as hot and tight as he imagined she'd be. And when Aubry wrapped her legs around his waist and lifted her hips, he seated himself fully inside of her. It was goddamned perfection.

She smelled like sweet cotton candy, felt like soft heaven, and as he moved within her, her body gripped his cock tight.

"You feel good," he said, reaching down to slide a hand over her hip, levering himself close so he could hit all her hot spots as well.

Her nails dug into his arms. "Oh, yes. Right there, Tucker."

She rocked back and forth against him as he pulled out, then slid in again. She was right there with him, her gaze pinned to his as they moved together in a slow, deliberate pace at first. He measured the signals she gave him. She liked it easy, and he could handle that for now. He took in the sounds she made—breathy little moans and gasps that made his balls draw up tight and made his cock harden like steel. He enjoyed watching her nipples pucker up when he rubbed his chest against her breasts.

Hell, he liked everything about being naked and inside of her. And when her moans turned to gasps and whimpers, he increased the pace, holding back the need to release. Because she was going to go first, and when her sweet little pussy tightened around him, when she dug into the mattress and raised her hips, a silent invitation for more and deeper, he gave it to her.

Sweat dripped down his back with the effort to hold back, but she was so damn good he didn't want to come. Not just yet, not when Aubry's cheeks pinkened and a dark flush spread over her breasts.

"Tucker," she said, digging her nails in harder. "So, so good. You make me want to come."

"Let go," he said, bending to kiss her, a hard driving kiss he coupled with deeper, faster thrusts. She cried out against his lips and he felt the force of her orgasm wrapping round his cock, squeezing him tight as she came.

This time, he let go, slamming hard into her with his release. He felt dizzy from it, wrapping an arm around Aubry as her body rocked underneath him.

Spent and out of breath, he nuzzled her neck, licking droplets of perspiration from her skin.

Now that had been good. Really damn good. And when he could breathe again, he told her that.

"It was pretty decent for round one," she said.

He lifted his head and looked up at her smiling face. "It's a good thing I'm in great shape. I can tell you're very demanding."

She brushed a hair away from his forehead. "I told you I'd been in a drought, didn't I?"

"Yes. I believe you mentioned that."

"So, you just happen to be the person I decided to make it rain for me."

He rolled over to his side, bringing her with him so they faced each other. "And by making it rain, I take it to mean you'd like a monsoon."

She laughed. "I believe so."

"No complaints here." He pulled her on top of him and laid his hands on her ass, kneading the soft globes. She writhed against him until he got hard again.

She grinned down at him. "I could tell from the first time I saw you that you were a rainmaker, Tucker."

FOURTEEN

AUBRY ROLLED OVER IN BED AND GLARED AT THE
clock. Five a.m.

She really hated five a.m. She yawned, then looked over at the
other side of the bed, at the dark-headed god sleeping next to her.
She couldn't help her lopsided smile.

Six times. She'd come six times last night. She was sore in places
that hadn't been sore in years. But it was a really awesome kind
of ache.

She waited for regret to set in as she got up and took a shower,
then got ready for work. By the time she dried her hair and brewed
coffee, she realized she had no regrets.

Last night had been fun, and she felt more relaxed than she'd
been in . . .

A very long time.

She sipped her coffee, leaned against the kitchen counter and
smiled.

Six orgasms would do that to a person. And God knew she needed some relaxation.

She looked up to find Tucker strolling into the kitchen wearing only his jeans—which were unzipped, showing off all that delicious skin and that vee from his lower abs to places she'd like to explore further—and his glasses.

That man was so damn sexy, glasses and all.

If only she had today off as well.

Dammit.

"I smelled coffee. You heading to work?"

She nodded. "Yes, unfortunately. Help yourself. The door locks on its own when you close it. You can take a shower or go back to bed or whatever."

He took the cup from her hand and laid it on the counter next to her, then buried his face in her neck and kissed her there. Delicious goose bumps prickled her skin. He took her mouth in a good morning kiss that made her want to tumble back into bed with him for several hours. Her entire body woke to passion and need. One would think after all those orgasms, she'd be more than satisfied.

Apparently not, because before she knew it her fingers had looped their way into his hair, and his hand was down the front of her scrubs. In a few deliberate, coaxing minutes she was primed, ready and throbbing. When he pulled her pants down to her knees and put his mouth on her, all she could do was grab the counter for support. She held on while he sucked on her clit in a very demanding way that told her he could bring her to orgasm in less than two minutes.

Or less. She cried out, not even caring as she rocked her sex against his face when she came.

"Jesus, Tucker," she said when he licked the sides of her thighs and looked up at her with a very satisfied smile. "I'm going to be late."

"You're going to be even later."

He drew a condom out of the pocket of his jeans, flipped her over onto her stomach and pushed her against the counter, shoved his jeans down over his hips, and had that condom on in record time.

She was still quivering from that mind-blasting orgasm when he entered her, pushing deep, making her gasp and moan as he thrust. He slid his hand inside her shirt to tease and pluck her nipples while he fucked her from behind.

Her mind was awash in the visuals of what she must look like bent over her kitchen counter, her hair a mess, her clothes half off, and him pumping into her. Her belly tumbled and her sex quivered listening to his harsh breaths. He gripped her hips hard, and when she pushed back against him, his encouraging words made ripples of desire flitter through her.

And when he slid his hand between her legs, she pushed him away, needing him to concentrate on pushing his big cock into her. She settled her own hand on her clit.

"Oh, yeah," he said, then pumped hard and fast into her while she made herself come—again.

And when she did, his loud groans only enhanced her orgasm. They came together with his hand on her breasts and her own between her legs.

It was wild and passionate and left her hot and sweaty, enough that when they disengaged, she turned and gave him a glare.

"Now I need another shower."

He grinned. "Uh . . . sorry?"

She shook her head, dashed into the bathroom and quickly rinsed off, combed her sex-mussed hair, then redressed and ran into the kitchen for her things.

He had a cup of coffee in his hand, but he set it on the counter and came toward her.

She held up her hand to stop him. "Don't even come near me."

His lips quirked. "Okay. Have a good day, Aubry."

Mellowing somewhat, considering she'd had two orgasms since getting out of bed this morning, she approached him, brushed her lips against his, and said, "You, too. Thanks for last night." She pulled away, then kissed him again. "And this morning."

He smiled at her. "I'll call you."

Did she want him to call her? She didn't even have time to think about it right now. "Sure. You do that."

She left in a hurry and ran to her car, trying not to break speed limits to get to the hospital in time for rounds. Dr. Chen could be horrible to his doctors who showed up late. When she got to the lounge, Katie was there.

"Oh, my God," Katie said, getting up from the table to hurry over to her. "You're always here before me. You're here before everyone. I thought you might be sick."

Aubry put her things away in her locker and tried to get her wildly beating pulse under control. "I'm fine."

"You are not fine. Your face is flushed. Are you sure you're not coming down with something?"

"No. I'm not sick." She wound her stethoscope around her neck and turned to Katie, then took a quick look at her phone. She'd made it. Barely, but she'd made it. "Shall we head out?"

"And what's on your neck?"

"Nothing." She reached out to scrub both sides of her neck. "What are you talking about?"

"Right here." Katie rubbed a spot. "It's all red. Is it a bruise?"

Aubry put her hand on the place where Katie had rubbed. "It's nothing. Probably hives because I got up late this morning. You know how Chen freaks me out."

"It's not hives. Actually, it looks kind of like a—" Katie squinted at her, then her eyes widened. "Oh, my God. You had sex."

Aubry pivoted and walked out of the lounge, Katie right on her heels.

"I'm right, aren't I? You had sex. Was it with that hot baseball player?"

She really hated that her friend knew so much about her life. "No."

"Now you're just lying to me. You had sex with him. What's his name again? Tucker, wasn't it?"

She stopped and turned to Katie. "Yes. And yes, if you must know. We had sex. Lots of it."

Katie grinned. "Awesome. No wonder you look like shit. You probably stayed up screwing all night long and you're worn out from him giving you multiple orgasms. He looks like the type of guy who'd give a woman a lot of orgasms."

Her body quivered at the mention of orgasms. She inhaled, then let it out. "Eight."

Katie's brows rose. "Eight? Really?"

"Yeah."

"Get the hell out of here. Eight? And you let him go? I'd have called in sick today and had him give me eight more."

She laughed. "Shut up. I don't call in sick to have sex. I don't call in sick, period. Even when I *am* sick."

Katie shook her head. "Then you're doing it wrong, Aubry."

"Come on." She pulled on Katie's sleeve. "We have work to do. We'll talk about sex later."

She immersed herself in her job, trying to shove thoughts of Tucker out of her head for the next several hours. Fortunately, she was busy. Not as busy as when she worked nights, but she'd had a steady stream of work. A broken arm from a job-related injury, a sick infant, and an elderly gentleman with a bowel obstruction.

Fortunately, Dr. Chen hadn't noticed she'd barely made it on time this morning, so she'd dodged a bullet there.

Late afternoon she finally found time to get a bite to eat. She got a salad in the cafeteria, grabbed her medical notes and sat in the lounge, enjoying the few minutes of peace and quiet so she could study.

Until Katie came in with her bag of food. She pulled up a chair across from Aubry at the table, laid her iced tea down, and opened her bag.

"Surely you're not going to study. Don't you ever shut off that brain of yours?"

Aubry looked up from her notes. "We have a lot to learn in a short period of time. And you never know when Chen is going to ask us about some complex brain trauma we've never heard of." She pinned Katie with a stern look. "You could stand to study more."

Katie pointed to her temple and bit into her sandwich, talking with her mouth full. "I've got it all right here, honey."

"Sure you do. What you've got is balls enough to bullshit your way through Chen's tough questions. Or you just don't care."

Katie took a sip of her drink. "Of course I care. I just don't walk on eggshells around Chen like you seem to. He wants us all to do well, and his bark is way worse than his bite. You need to relax. Didn't those eight orgasms do the trick, or are you going back for more tonight?"

"I . . ." She paused, not sure how to answer. She'd left Tucker at her place early this morning, without thought as to when, or if, she'd ever see him again.

She didn't date. She spent days and nights at the hospital, and when she was off, she studied and caught up on things she had to do at home. She'd used one of her rare nights off to go out with him last night. Surely Tucker would understand that she wasn't looking for a relationship, right?

"You what?" Katie asked, interrupting her thought process.

"I don't know. We had a fun night. Isn't that enough?"

"Of course it's not enough. You two had awesome sex, Aubry.

Wouldn't you want more of it? I mean, it isn't often we can find a man to give us one orgasm, let alone eight. Why would you let a guy like that go?"

She laid her fork down. "Because I don't have time for a guy. There's work and study and those are my priorities."

Katie sighed. "You need to reset your priorities, honey. Men can give you great orgasms—as you know so well—which reduces your stress and allows you to fully focus your efforts on work and study."

She couldn't help herself. Her lips lifted. "You have that all figured out, don't you?"

"On a spreadsheet and everything."

Aubry laughed. "Men can also be complicated."

Katie took a bite of her sandwich, swallowed, then shook her head. "No. *We're* complicated. Men are simple. Keep them well fucked and they're happy as can be."

Sliding Katie a look of disbelief, she said, "I don't believe it works that way."

"Trust me. It works that way."

"So you're saying all I have to do is fuck Tucker's brains out on a regular basis, and I won't have to worry about any emotional entanglements?"

"Absolutely. If he's an average male. And from what I've seen of him? He looks like an average male to me. Quite possibly above average."

Aubry couldn't believe she was even entertaining the idea. She had no time for this. But she had to admit the idea was tempting.

And there was no denying the side benefits would be well worth it. Tucker had seemed fun and easygoing last night. Not at all intense.

At least not until they'd gotten in bed. Then? The intensity level had been off the charts amazing, which she had no complaints about.

She hadn't been lying to him when she'd told him it had been a long dry spell for her in the sex department. Sex on a regular basis sounded so good, especially with all the pressure she was under at work.

And if she could get that without an emotional tie?

Even better.

Tucker had said he'd call. He'd pushed her about going out, so she expected her phone to buzz sometime today.

They'd make plans, and she'd see where she could fit him into her schedule.

At least sex-wise.

FIFTEEN

TUCKER PITCHED AN OKAY GAME ON THURSDAY NIGHT.
He'd given up eight hits and two runs, but his team had rallied
and won.

He could have done better. A lot better. His curve had been a
little wonky, and he hated road games, especially in Denver where
the altitude always messed with his pitches. But they'd won two of
three from Denver and he was happy to be headed home for the
next series against New York.

He'd thought a lot about Aubry while he was gone, but he
hadn't done anything about it. He figured after that intense first
night, he needed to take a step back. It wasn't in his nature to enter
a relationship, and maybe he'd had a little too much of a connection with her that night.

He liked her, but he also preferred to keep things with women
light and easy.

He'd call her when he got home. They could reconnect and have some fun again.

Once the plane landed and he got back to the private parking lot at the stadium, he grabbed his gear, said good-bye to his teammates and made the drive back to his condo. He tossed his bag down, went out and grabbed a bite to eat, then settled in on his sofa. He turned on the television and watched about an hour of sports recap on TV, then picked up his phone.

It was eleven thirty. He wondered if Aubry was still up. Or maybe she was working tonight. He probably should have asked her schedule. Or maybe texted her.

He kind of sucked about things like that. He was more of a spur-of-the-moment kind of guy.

He stared at the key pad, pondering.

If she had worked day shift, she'd likely be asleep by now. He wouldn't want to wake her. Then again, if she was dead tired, maybe she wouldn't wake up if he texted.

Shrugging, he sent the text.

Hey! You at work or sleeping?

When he didn't get a reply right away, he set his phone aside, figuring she was probably asleep.

He'd try again tomorrow.

AUBRY WAS IN THE MIDDLE OF SUTURING A PARTICU-larly difficult elbow gash when her phone buzzed in her pocket. She ignored it until she finished, gave the patient aftercare instructions, then entered discharge information into the system.

She picked up her phone and read the text message on her way down the hall.

Tucker.

It had been four days since he said he'd call. Four days without a word. And now this? She checked the time. It was after midnight.

Did he think she was available twenty four/seven for him? Maybe he thought she'd answer and he could come over for some hot, after midnight sex. Like she was some kind of escort.

Ha.

What a jackass.

Irritation shot through her.

Whatever. She slipped her phone back in her pocket and decided to ignore him.

Just like he'd ignored her for the past four days.

She didn't know what she'd expected from him. Maybe that he'd call like he said he would?

This was why she concentrated on her work and didn't do relationships.

They sucked up time and energy better devoted to her career— a career that didn't disappoint her like men often had.

SIXTEEN

THOUGH HE HADN'T PITCHED THE GAME THIS AFTER-
noon, it hadn't gone well. Tucker felt bad for Garrett Scott, because
he knew exactly what it was like when everything seemed to go
against you. Everyone's bats had been cold today, and Garrett
hadn't hit the strike zone with any of his usually stellar pitches.

They'd lost three to one, and other than Jack Sanchez's solo home
run, they'd had nothing in the way of offense. Tucker couldn't do
anything but pace and hope someone got a hit to get things moving.

It hadn't happened. They'd had guys on base in two innings,
otherwise it had been dismal. And Garrett's pitching had been way
off. He'd been lucky to only give up three runs. Tucker chalked
that up to Garrett's icy-cold control, because even with a bad game,
Garrett had managed to hold the opposing team's run production
down to three.

"Tough one today, Garrett," Tucker had said after the game.
"You'll come back for the next one."

Garrett gave a short nod, but mostly stared at his knees as he sat in front of his locker. At least they were at home, because the only thing worse than losing a home game was losing on the road.

He also knew he'd said what needed to be said. You couldn't pump up a losing pitcher. They felt bad, and nothing you could say would make them feel better, so the less said, the better. It was best to just move along.

When he stepped outside the locker room, there was an onslaught of family members and friends waiting for the players. Wives and parents and girlfriends and the like. Which was good for them.

His parents lived on the family ranch in Texas. They came up on occasion when they could, and would often drive up for his games in Dallas and Houston. But he was an adult and certainly didn't need his mom and dad to attend all his games. His brothers had pro careers of their own, though they sometimes flew in for his games as well, and now that he played for St. Louis, Grant would show up for games, which was nice.

But Grant was doing a PR thing in New York this week, so he was out of town.

Not that he expected his brother to come to all of his games. As a baseball player, he played a lot of damn games, and Grant had a life.

Still, he wondered what it might be like to have a . . . someone. Someone he knew would be there when he walked out that door after every home game.

"Tucker."

He turned around at the sound of his name, smiling when he saw his agent, Victoria Baldwin. She was with Elizabeth Riley, who was also a sports agent, along with being married to the Rivers first baseman, Gavin Riley.

He walked over to them.

"Hey, Victoria. I didn't know you were at the game today. Hi, Liz."

Victoria shook his hand, while Liz kissed him on the cheek.

"Tough loss today," Liz said. "I know Gavin will hate it. And Garrett will, too."

"Yeah, Garrett's not happy. Are you here to see him, Victoria?"

She nodded. "We have a meeting scheduled for this afternoon, though I'm sure he's not going to be in any mood to talk business."

"He'll be fine. We shake off a loss pretty fast and look forward to the next game."

Victoria laid her hand on his arm. "Of course you do, because you're all superstars. That's why I represent you."

Liz laughed. "Only the best for us, right Tori?"

"Indeed. And speaking of my clients, do you mind, Liz? I'll take a few minutes with Tucker."

"Not at all. Good seeing you."

"You too, Liz."

Liz walked away and Victoria led Tucker over to a quiet spot away from the crowd. "Just checking in. I know we talk regularly, but I want to be sure you're happy here since signing with the Rivers, that things are going well."

"It's great. I've settled in, I like the team and management. Nothing to complain about."

She smiled. "That's what I like to hear. I knew this team would be a good fit for you."

"You were right. They have great talent and everyone gets along. Management is willing to spend the money to get the right players, and the coaches know what the hell they're doing. I couldn't have asked for a better fit."

Victoria nodded. "Plus, one of your brothers lives here in town."

"Well, you can't have everything." He cracked a grin.

She laughed. "You're so bad. There's Garrett now so I have to run. If you need anything, call me, okay?"

"You got it. Thanks, Victoria."

He watched her walk away. She was smart, had been in the

business for a long time now, and she was an absolute shark in contract negotiations. He couldn't ask for a better agent.

He laid back and watched her scoop up Garrett and walk away with him, then he lingered awhile longer. Liz was there to greet Gavin, throwing her arms around him and giving him a long kiss and hug. Gavin had told him Liz used to be his agent, until the two of them got involved, and eventually married. Then they had to sever their professional relationship, but it sure looked like they had a great personal one. Gavin spotted him and waved as the two of them walked away, along with several of the other guys and their wives or girlfriends.

Nice.

He shook his head.

He had no idea why he was even thinking about all the other couples today. Not having a significant other had never bothered him before. He always worked his way past the crowds without a second thought.

So what made the idea of a . . . someone . . . pop into his head today?

He got into his car and started the engine. Was it because he'd never heard back from Aubry? Why did that bother him? He pulled out his phone. It had been two days, since he'd texted her. He punched in her number, figuring maybe this time he'd call.

She didn't answer, which meant she was probably at work.

Rather than heading home, he turned his car onto the highway in the direction of the hospital. He'd just stop in and see if she was there.

He was sure she'd be happy to see him.

IT HAD BEEN A GRUELING DAY ALREADY. SHE WAS nearing the end of her shift, and Aubry found herself watching the clock, counting down every minute.

Chen had ridden her ass about a case she'd worked this morning. A mother had brought in a child with a broken wrist. No matter what she'd done or said, the kid wouldn't stop screaming. It happened sometimes. The little girl was four, in pain, and utterly inconsolable. And the parent was nervous as hell about her little girl's broken wrist, so instead of being the rock her little girl needed, the mother had only added to the tension.

So Aubry had had a screaming child with a broken wrist, along with an extremely upset parent, and she was trying to set the arm when Chen had chosen that moment to walk in on her.

It wasn't her finest moment.

Of course, her normally gruff and not-at-all warm attending physician had somehow managed an utter personality transplant. He'd gone all smiley and sweet and calmed the highly emotional mother and got the little girl to stop crying. How he did that she had no idea, because half the time Dr. Chen made *her* want to cry. He was intimidating as hell, yet in the room he had the little girl laughing and the girl's mother in a state of absolute calm about the whole ordeal.

Aubry finally managed to set the arm and cast it without the kid screaming the entire time. And after they got the cast on the girl and the instructions relayed to the now-calm mother, Chen talked to her in the hallway.

"You didn't handle that well."

She lifted her chin. "I was handling it."

"Not from what I saw. You were tense and nervous."

"I've set broken bones before, Dr. Chen. I can assure you I knew exactly what I was doing."

"Being a doctor is about a lot more than just the medical aspect of patient care, Dr. Ross. What you had in there were two people in severe emotional distress, one of them a child. And while the procedure might seem minor to you, to them it was traumatic. Your first priority was to calm both the patient and her mother. The medical procedure could have waited, since it wasn't life threatening."

No shit, Sherlock. She didn't need him to point out the obvious to her. But he was her attending, and whatever he had to say, she needed to listen. "I understand, Dr. Chen. I'll do it better next time."

"See that you do."

He walked away, leaving her standing in the hallway feeling like a total failure.

She knew her job, and she'd always thought of herself as completely empathetic to her patients' needs, especially children. How had she so totally screwed that up today?

She headed back to the main station to update charts. It was change of shift, so she gave status reports to the incoming residents on patients who hadn't yet been discharged.

"You have a visitor."

She was charting notes and looked up at Marie. "A visitor?"

"Yes. Your hot baseball guy is in the waiting room."

She cocked a brow. "Tucker?"

"Yes. He's been here about an hour. I told him you were busy, but he said he'd wait."

Interesting. So he ignored her for several days, then just showed up here, expecting her to drop everything and see him?

She was not in the mood for this—for him. Not after the kind of day she'd had. She should make him sit out there until he got bored or tired of waiting. That would send a message to him, wouldn't it?

"So, do you want me to bring him back?" Marie asked.

"No. I'm due for a break, so I'll take care of it. Thanks, Marie."

She wandered out to the waiting room, which, fortunately, wasn't too crowded at the moment. She searched the room and found him in the corner, slouched in the chair, sound asleep. She walked over and kicked his tennis shoe.

He opened his eyes and sat up straight in the chair. "Oh, hey, Aubry."

"Tucker."

He stood, yawned. "I came by to see you."

"So I heard."

"Are you busy?"

He was kidding, right? "I'm working."

"When do you get off?"

"Not for a while."

He shoved his hand in his pocket. "Oh. I thought maybe we could grab something to eat."

"Seriously?" Since they were quickly gaining an audience of eavesdroppers, she motioned him through the doors and into a hallway. "You don't call me for days, then show up here and expect that I'll be available?"

"Hey. I texted you two days ago."

"Oh, right. A text message. At eleven-thirty at night. I'm not some chick you banged that has nothing better to do than wait for you to call, Tucker. I have a life. A career. And no, I don't have time for dinner. In fact, I don't have time for you. So you can walk through those doors and take yourself home. We're done."

She turned and walked away, assuming he'd leave.

"Hey. It works both ways, you know."

He'd caught up with her. She stopped and looked around, hoping like hell Dr. Chen had already left for the day.

"Excuse me?"

"These are modern times, Aubry. You could have called me, too. And I was in Denver for three days for a road series."

She shrugged. "Why would I call you?"

"Because you like me? Because we had fun the other night?" His lips curved.

She tipped her finger at his chest. "And you could have done

the same. Besides, you said you'd call. So I assumed you would."
No way was she going to allow him to put this on her.

"I had practice. I was busy. And I texted. But you didn't reply."

This conversation was going nowhere. "Because I was working."

"You could have replied the next day."

She rolled her eyes. "This conversation is ridiculous."

"I agree. What time do you get off work tonight?"

"I'm off in an hour and a half. Unless something big happens.
Then I might have to stay."

"Great. I'll be back in an hour and a half, and we'll go get something to eat. Then we can talk some more. Or argue more if you'd like."

"I don't—"

But he'd pulled her against him and brushed his lips against hers. "I like arguing with you, Aubry. Let's do that some more. But while we're eating. I'm hungry. See you soon."

He turned around and walked through the doors before she had a chance to tell him no.

Damn that man. He was infuriating. To think he'd assume she'd go out to dinner with him—do anything with him, was outrageous. When he came back, she'd tell him.

But he was right about one thing.

She was hungry, too. She'd barely had time to eat an energy bar today.

So maybe she'd have dinner with him. She'd let him buy, too, just for aggravating her. And then she'd tell him they weren't going to see each other anymore.

After dinner.

SEVENTEEN

TUCKER WAS BACK AT THE HOSPITAL AN HOUR AND A half later, waiting at the door for Aubry. He'd gone home, taken a shower and changed clothes so he felt a lot more awake.

Better able to do battle with Aubry.

She was in a feisty mood. And okay, maybe she had a right to be mad at him. He wasn't the best with communication. He'd obviously dropped the ball on his follow-up with her. From her point of view, she probably thought he didn't give a shit, when the opposite was true.

He'd make it up to her over dinner.

He told the main desk person he was there, and asked if she'd relay the information to Aubry. She did, and came back a few minutes later to tell him Aubry would be right out, so he took a seat in the waiting room to watch whatever was on TV. An old comedy rerun. He could live with that.

Fifteen minutes later, Aubry walked out. She'd changed out of her scrubs into a pair of jeans and a long-sleeved black button-down shirt. Her hair was soft and silky, making him itch to run his hands through it. She'd even put on makeup and lip gloss, which immediately made him think about kissing her.

She might be mad at him, but the fact that she'd taken the time to look that good meant something to him.

He stood and headed over to her. "You look amazing."

"Thanks. A patient threw up on me. I needed to take a shower."

He laughed. "You still look incredible. Sorry about the throw up."

"Why? You weren't the one who did it."

He shook his head and took her arm. "I hope it didn't ruin your appetite."

"Not at all. I'm starving."

"Me, too. Let's go. Can we just take my car? I'll drive you back here after."

She paused. "That doesn't seem to make sense from a logistical standpoint. Where are we going?"

"Not far."

She considered it for a few seconds, then nodded. "Okay."

She got into his car. He turned to face her. "First, I'm sorry. You were right. It was on me to call and I dropped the ball. And that makes me an asshole. I'm not that kind of guy. When I say I'm going to follow through, I do. I apologize for that."

He watched her expression. It had been tight as they'd walked out to the car. Now, her shoulders sagged and she exhaled. "Well. Dammit, Tucker. I was all set to argue with you. I had a good mad going on, too."

"Uh, sorry again? You're welcome to stay mad. I don't mind a good argument."

She laughed. "No, really, that's okay. Apology—both of them— accepted. Now where are we eating?"

"How do you feel about Italian?"

"I feel really good about it. Right now I'd eat fast food I'm so hungry."

He wrinkled his nose. "I eat plenty of that. And no, thanks. We're eating good food tonight."

He drove them to Il Bel Lago, a restaurant he'd heard about but hadn't eaten at yet. He turned off the engine. "I heard the food here is really good."

"Sounds great to me."

They walked inside and Tucker gave his name to the hostess, who told him it would be a few minutes.

"We'll wait in the bar," he said.

The bar was dark and modern. They took a seat at one of the tables, and a waitress came by to get their drink orders.

"I'll have Chianti," Aubry said.

"Beer for me," Tucker said, then looked over at Aubry. "How was your day?"

"Intense. Rough. Yours?"

"We had an afternoon game. We lost."

"I'm sorry. Did you pitch?"

He shook his head. "No. Garrett Scott did. But it's still tough to lose a game. Even harder when I'm not the one in control."

"You like to be in control."

His lips curved. "I'd pitch every game if they let me."

Their waitress brought their drinks.

"Thanks," Tucker said to the waitress.

"You're welcome. Sorry about the loss today."

Obviously she recognized him. "Thank you. We'll get 'em next time."

After the waitress walked away, Aubry took a sip of her wine, then said, "That must happen a lot."

"What?"

"People recognizing you. Talking to you about baseball."

He shrugged. "Not as often as you might think."

"I don't know." She leaned back in her chair, cradling her wine-glass between both hands. "St. Louis is a big baseball city. They know their players."

"And here I thought you didn't care about baseball."

"Oh, I don't. Actually, I prefer football."

He frowned. "You're joking, right?"

"I am not."

He shook his head. "Great. Just great."

"What's wrong with football?"

"Oh, nothing. Other than the fact that the Cassidys are well known for being a football dynasty."

"Is that right?" Then her eyes widened and she leaned forward. "Wait. Wait. I remember meeting Grant and Barrett when they brought you into the ER, but for some reason I didn't recognize him at the time. Grant's the Traders' quarterback, right?"

"Yes."

"Wow. I don't know why I didn't make that connection. How fascinating. And Barrett plays football, too?"

"Oh, it's worse than that. Barrett's actually my twin. He plays for the Tampa Bay Hawks. And I have another brother, Flynn, who plays for the San Francisco Sabers. My dad is Easton Cassidy, former quarterback for Green Bay and now a Hall of Famer."

She laughed. "You have got to be kidding me. You do have a big football family."

"Tell me about it."

"So why are you the only one who plays baseball?"

Not the first time he'd heard that question. "Because I like baseball."

"You never wanted to play football like the rest of your family?"

"Nope."

"So you're not playing baseball because you couldn't cut it in football or anything?"

Not the first time he'd heard that question, either. "Uh, no. I played both when I was a kid, and decided I liked baseball better. You could ask your dad—or the Rivers coach. I'm a damn good pitcher."

She laid her glass on the table and raised her hands in the air. "I believe you. And obviously you're with the Rivers now because you're good. The general manager and my dad don't put people on the team if they're not good at what they do. I just find it curious that out of this family dynasty of football players, you're the only one who chose baseball."

"You're not the first person who thinks it was because I couldn't cut it as a football player."

Their hostess came and directed them to their table. The restaurant was separate from the bar, and the décor was different as well. Well lit, yet more intimate, not as loud as the bar. They were settled into a cozy booth in the corner, providing them some privacy.

"Enjoy your meal, Mr. Cassidy," the hostess said with a bright smile.

"Thanks."

Tucker opened the menu, studied it for a minute while he made his selection, then closed it. Their waiter came by, introduced himself and told them about the specials, then asked if they wanted more to drink. Tucker looked over at Aubry.

"I'll have another Chianti."

"Another beer for me."

They ordered appetizers and their meals while their waiter was there. He walked off to get their drinks.

"Now it's my turn to apologize," Aubry said.

"For what?"

"For baiting you about football. I was just teasing you. Not about me liking football, but about why you chose baseball."

He shrugged. "I'm used to it. I've taken shit my entire life for besmirching the Cassidy name by becoming a pitcher instead of taking on football."

"You have not. Really? Hopefully not by your family."

"Nah. My brothers give me a hard time, but that's what brothers are for. My parents have always been supportive. My dad told me to do what makes me happy."

"I'm so glad to hear that. As long as the people you care about support you, they're who matter. Everyone else can go fuck themselves."

He laughed. "Thanks. That's what I've always thought."

"Look, I know exactly where you're coming from. My choice to go into medicine was a surprise to a lot of people. My mother is in finance and she helps run the Ross empire with Dad. His love of sports is legendary. It was always assumed that I, as their only child, would move into the family business and work in the front office of Ross Enterprises. But I excelled in math and science, and from a young age I knew I wanted to be a doctor."

Their waiter brought their appetizer, along with bread, and Tucker and Aubry dug in.

"Did your parents encourage you along that path?"

She nodded while pouring oil and vinegar onto a plate, then selected a slice of bread for dipping. "Absolutely. Though my uncle—not the one we were hunting for that night I met you, by the way. Uncle Davis is my mother's brother. This is my other uncle, my father's brother. Anyway, slightly off topic there. My Uncle Oliver thought it was awful of me to even consider not following in my father's footsteps. Since I'm the only heir, he said, it was my responsibility to carry on the Ross legacy. My uncle never married or had children, so he told me the continuation of our dynasty falls to me."

"Ouch. That's a pretty heavy burden to place on someone's shoulders."

"Yeah."

"It's good your parents encouraged you to do what you were meant to do, even if that means deviating from the family path."

"Yes. And I love them for it. If even once they had asked me to get my degree in business or finance so I could carry on the family name at Ross Enterprises, I'd have done it."

"Really?"

"Of course. They mean everything to me. I'd do whatever it took to make them happy, especially if carrying on the family name and business was vital to them. Fortunately, it never came to that. Dad is so proud that I'm becoming a doctor."

"That's great."

"I assume your dad is the same way."

"Yeah. He wouldn't have cared if any of us boys had gone into sports at all, as long as we did something productive with our lives, and we were happy doing it."

She speared some of the toasted ravioli and took a taste. "Mmm. This is good. Take a bite."

She put another ravioli on her fork, waving it in front of him. He grasped her wrist, then slid the fork into his mouth, chewed, and swallowed.

"You're right. It's good."

Aubry hadn't wanted to even go to dinner with Tucker, let alone find herself relaxing and having such an intense conversation about families with him. Maybe it was the two glasses of wine, but she felt calm and settled.

Or maybe it was because he'd sincerely apologized right away, and then he'd proceeded to charm her with his honesty and his candor about his life and his family. She'd been out on dates before with men who'd done nothing but scratched the surface. She already knew more about Tucker in the short period of time she'd known him than she knew about a lot of guys she'd dated for months.

"When's your next game?" she asked.

"We have five more games at home, so a decent home stretch. Then we're on the road to Chicago after that."

"How do you feel about all the travel?"

"It's part of the job." He picked up another ravioli, only this time he fed it to her. She smiled when he slipped the fork between her lips. The action was so intimate, she felt the tug in her lower belly, especially when their gazes met and held. A collision of sensation, between the delicious food, the nice buzz from the wine, and the man who confused her and definitely attracted her.

The waiter brought their dinner. She was already full, but the tempting aromas renewed her appetite. She had the champagne chicken, while Tucker had the veal. They swapped tastes of each other's food. It was delicious, a decadent delight to her senses.

"Tell me about your bad day," Tucker said as they were finishing up. "We've talked enough about me."

"It wasn't that bad, really. My attending physician was a little rough on me for not being sensitive to a patient's needs."

He leveled his gaze on hers. "What happened?"

She found herself elaborating in great detail about the child and her mother. She explained how tense the situation had been, how Chen had smoothed things over and how out of her element she'd appeared to her boss.

He nodded. "Rough situation. I'm sure you were handling it just fine, but it's hard with little kids, ya know? Even at the best of times they can be a handful. And because the kid was already upset, there was probably nothing you could have done to calm her. Your boss was just the lucky second party to come in and make things all better."

She crossed her arms and leaned back in her chair. "Really. And what makes you the expert on kids."

"Trust me, I'm no expert. But I have siblings. In addition to three brothers, I also have a little sister. When my sister, Mia, was younger, she'd scream her head off about something and one of us or Dad would try to comfort her, and nothing would help. Then Mom would come in, whisper some soft words, and that would be the end of her tirade."

"Oh, well that's the mom effect. All mothers have that calming influence."

He laughed. "You'd think that, wouldn't you, but that didn't always work on Mia. Because the very next instance it would be Mom trying to calm her down, and Dad would be the one walking in the room, saying a few 'aww, poor baby's to her, and poof. Tears gone."

"Hmm. So maybe there is some point to what you're saying."

"I'm tellin' ya, it's like magic. It's like the first person on the scene is invisible. And the second person has that special voice that does the trick. I don't know what it is, but it seems to work. It even happened with me and a couple of my brothers. Barrett and I got into fights all the time. One time he was irritating the shit out of me and I'd had enough, so I hauled off and punched him in the face. He went down, hard, and started bawling like a baby. Grant was nearby so he came in and got a towel for Barrett's bloody nose and tried to get him to stop crying."

"Let me guess," Aubry said. "He wouldn't stop, right?"

"You got it. And then Flynn, who's the oldest, comes in—and you gotta understand, Flynn is one tough sonofabitch. But here's this twelve-year-old kneeling down over Barrett being all soothing and telling him everything is going to be all right, which is basically what Grant had just said to him, but Barrett stopped crying."

Aubry shook her head. "I'm going to make it a point to be the second person in the exam room from now on whenever I have a kid as a patient. I'll send the nurse in first. She can deal with all the crying, and then I'll be the savior."

He laughed. "There's a sound plan."

"Also, you big bully. Punching your brother like that."

"Hey. Do you have any idea how many times Barrett knocked me on my ass? He had it coming."

"If you say so. Your poor mother. She was probably breaking up fights between you all the time, wasn't she?"

"She did her share, and don't do the poor mom thing. She managed us boys just fine."

"Then poor—what's your sister's name again? Mia?"

"Yes. And don't do the poor Mia thing, either. Being the youngest with four big brothers, she was a master manipulator. She had us all wrapped around her little finger."

Aubry laughed. "Okay, then. I feel better about your little sister."

They had coffee after dinner, but both of them passed on dessert.

"When do you have days off?" he asked.

"They vary. I work some weekends, and sometimes I have days off during the week."

"Me, too. Well, except for the fact that I never have weekends off. Not during the season, anyway."

"That must suck for you."

"I'm used to it. It's just part of the job." He finished his coffee, then put his cup to the side. "You should come to a game."

"I've seen plenty of games. I'm not really all that interested."

"But you haven't seen me pitch. I'm good."

"You mean you're good when someone isn't kicking you in the balls, or stomping on your leg, or when you're not falling over a pile of rocks?"

"Hey. You haven't exactly seen me at my best. On the mound, when I'm throwing the ball? That's my best."

"Humble, aren't you?"

"Athletes have to think they're the best at what they do. Otherwise, what's the point in playing?"

"I suppose." She took a sip of coffee, wondering what it was about him that intrigued her so much she was actually entertaining the idea of attending a baseball game. Her parents had dragged her to so many baseball games that now she only did it with the greatest amount of reluctance, and only when her father insisted.

"Don't you think you're a great doctor?"

"I have good days and bad days, but I haven't yet reached the God complex phase of my medical career yet."

He laughed. "I see. At what point does that occur?"

"Hopefully never. There are already plenty of those types of doctors out there—mainly the surgeons. And since I'm not a surgeon, I don't see me ever thinking of myself as godlike."

"Good to know. But just FYI? You're a really good doctor, Aubry. And I speak from experience as one of your patients."

She looked down at her cup, then up at him, not sure how to react to his praise. It wasn't something she heard often, since she mostly heard criticism, and since she saw her patients for a brief period of time, and typically only once. It wasn't like most of them were repeat customers who offered feedback on services rendered. "Thank you. I'm glad you think so."

"I think your boss, or attending physician or whatever, should tell you that more often."

"It's not his job to tell us where we're doing well. It's his job to tell us where we're falling short. To make us better."

"I guess. I don't know. Seems to me he should give you the good parts as well as the not so good."

She shook her head. "It doesn't work that way. The emergency room is a fast-paced environment, without a lot of time for 'atta girl's. If we're screwing up somewhere, there's only time to point that out, so we know what not to do in the future. If we're doing something right, we won't hear about it."

"In baseball, it's different. If I'm working with my pitching coach and a pitch is working particularly well, he'll tell me so I can work to replicate it. And of course, he'll let me know if my mechanics are off so I can correct it. But I still get to hear the good as well as the bad."

"We're in completely different fields, Tucker. You can't compare the two. You're constantly working on your craft, trying to perfect it, even the parts that are working well. Your evaluations will be completely different from mine."

He reached across the table and grasped her hand. "Aren't you doing the same thing?"

She looked down where his much larger hand covered hers. She'd never thought about all the things she'd done right during her time in medical school, through her internship and her years in residency. She'd concentrated her efforts trying to fix all the things she'd done wrong. It was a constant learning process.

But Tucker was right—she'd done good things, and she'd learned so much. She often forgot to take the time to pat herself on the back about all those good things.

"Thank you, Tucker."

"For what?"

"For reminding me that I'm good at what I do."

He smiled. "You're welcome. Try reminding yourself every day."

"I will."

He paid the bill, and they headed out toward his car. He drove her back to the hospital, stopping out front.

"Where are you parked? I'll drive you to your car."

"Here is fine. I'm parked in the physician's lot and you need an access code to get in there."

He turned in his seat to face her. "Would you like to come to my place? I really liked spending time with you tonight, Aubry. I don't want it to end yet."

Her stomach did a tumble. She'd started out the evening so

angry with him for not calling her. But at dinner, they'd had such an in-depth conversation. She'd learned a lot about him. If nothing else, she wanted to continue to learn more, to talk more with him.

"I'd like that. Wait here for me and I'll meet you."

She got out of the car and hustled her way to the elevators.

"Dr. Ross?"

She stopped and turned as one of the attendings she occasionally worked with on the night shift called her name.

"Yes, Dr. Landing."

"We've got a multiple-vehicle accident coming in. We could use all the hands we can get."

"I'm . . . off duty."

"Not now you aren't. We're shorthanded and need some help."

She sighed. As a resident, she had to do what she was told, and as a doctor, it was her duty to help the sick and injured. Thankfully she'd had that last glass of wine more than an hour ago and had enjoyed a couple of cups of coffee since then. "Of course. I'll go change and be right there."

She headed down the hallway, grabbing her phone out of her pocket. She punched in Tucker's number.

He answered right away. "Did you get lost on your way to the car?"

"Worse. There's a multi-vehicle accident on its way in. One of my attendings just stopped me and asked me to help."

"Go do your job, Aubry. I'll call you tomorrow."

She appreciated that he understood. "Okay, thanks, Tucker."

She hung up, slipped her phone in her purse and hustled her way into the locker room to change into a pair of scrubs.

EIGHTEEN

TRUE TO HIS WORD THIS TIME, AND BECAUSE HE REAL-
ized he didn't always follow through, Tucker contacted Aubry the
next afternoon. He figured after putting in some extra time at the
hospital, she might be exhausted and need some sleep, so he texted
her and said to let him know when she was awake.

She texted him just as he got to the ballpark for warm-ups.

*Got your text. Sorry. Late night that went longer than expected.
What does your evening look like?*

He smiled and sent her a return text.

*Just got to the ballpark. Have a game tonight. I'm pitching. Wanna
come?*

It took her a few minutes to reply with: *Sure.*

He laughed, because he knew she obviously didn't want to
come. She was probably tired. But he'd take what he could get. So
he texted back.

Great. Assume you'll sit in the owner's box with your dad. See you after the game.

Several minutes later, she replied.

Good luck, Tucker.

He grinned, then headed into the locker room. It was time to get into game mode and clear his mind of everything else. This was an important game. After yesterday's loss on their home turf, they needed to win this one tonight.

And it was up to him to pitch well.

AUBRY ARRIVED AT THE BALLPARK RIGHT BEFORE THE game started. She had no idea what she was doing there. She'd ended up working until ten a.m. Dr. Chen finally gave her a break and told her to take the rest of the day off, since, other than dinner with Tucker last night, she'd basically been working nonstop.

The multi-vehicle accident had been brutal. They'd lost one of the victims, unable to resuscitate him. He'd coded twice in the ambulance on the way, and the team had worked on him for forty minutes until the attending had finally, reluctantly, called it.

It was always difficult to lose a patient, but his injuries had been too severe for them to save him. Then they'd concentrated on taking care of everyone else, including the man's wife and two children who'd also been injured, though nothing life threatening. Thank goodness.

They'd recover. But a woman had lost her husband, and those kids had lost their dad. The attending physician had been the one to tell the wife that her husband hadn't made it. Some day that would be her job.

She wasn't looking forward to it. She was in the business of saving lives, not losing them.

It had been a rough night, and she'd gone home, fallen into bed and immediately passed out until she woke about five p.m., dazed and groggy. Six hours was a lot of sleep for her. She'd headed straight for her coffeemaker, eaten a bowl of oatmeal and then taken a shower, both of which had helped a lot.

Then she'd gone through her phone and seen Tucker's text. And when he'd asked if she'd come to the game, the logical part of her brain had told her to say no.

But she sensed the eagerness in his request, so here she was, in the owner's box, smiling as she greeted her dad.

He hugged her and kissed her on the cheek. "This is a surprise. You hardly ever come to the games anymore. You're always working."

"I did a double shift last night, then took a nice nap. I thought I'd pop in."

"I'm glad you're here." He put his arm around her. "It's a good series to watch."

He led her over to the bar, where she had the bartender fix her a Bloody Mary. She sat down at one of the front tables with her dad, a spot with a great view of the on-field action.

"Tell me how work is going," he said.

"Busy. Intense. Brutal at times. Had a rough night last night." She told him about her double shift.

He smoothed his hand over her hair. "What you do isn't for everyone. It takes someone with a lot of heart—and grit—to handle it. You're tough, Aubry. A lot tougher than most people. It's why at first I thought you could handle this business. But when you gravitated toward medicine, I knew you could do that as well."

"Thanks, Dad." Sometimes all she needed were her father's pep talks. He was good at being frank with her. In college, when she'd been down about how hard the workload and pressure were, he'd reminded her she was smart, and that she could handle anything. He'd also told her the Rosses weren't wusses, and she needed to rise to the challenge. He wasn't one to coddle his only daughter.

So while her mother had always given her a shoulder to lean on, her father had given her tough love.

Sometimes she'd needed both.

He sat and studied her. "You have dark circles under your eyes."

Then again, he wasn't always complimentary when she needed it the most. "Like I said—double shift yesterday. Those are the worst."

"But you love it."

As if she needed convincing. She laughed. "Yes. I love it. It's everything I imagined it would be."

He smiled and squeezed her hand. "You can handle it, Aubry. No matter what they throw at you, even when it's awful, you'll handle it."

She had always loved her father's confidence in her. "Yes, Dad. I can handle it. Where's Mom tonight?"

"It's her night with the ladies from the country club. They're going to one of the casinos."

"Uh-oh. Spending more of my inheritance, huh?" she asked with a wink.

"Yup. I guess you're just gonna have to go make your own way in life, kiddo."

She laid the back of her hand against her forehead. "Oh, woe is me."

He smiled and put his arm around her. "Come on. Let's grab a bite to eat before the game starts. You can tell me more horror stories about work."

The last thing she wanted to do was talk about work, so she engaged her father in discussions about the team, as well as Ross Enterprises. She'd been involved in the company since she was old enough to understand the rudimentary workings of what both her parents did for a living. And while she'd always found it fascinating— especially the sports angle—it had never dulled her love for medicine.

She could still appreciate her father's passion for the game, something he'd instilled in her at an early age. She'd mostly been teasing Tucker when she told him she preferred football, though that was a sport she enjoyed as well.

"The team looks solid this year," she said to her dad while they watched pregame warm-ups.

"They do. They barely missed the playoffs last year. I have high hopes for them this season."

"You've filled the team with talent, Dad. Hot bats and stellar pitching."

Her father smiled. "And here I thought you were too busy with your career to pay attention to the team."

"Oh, I pay attention. You've made some fine additions the past couple of years. I know exactly who plays for the team. I might not have time to come to every game, but I catch up on the scores and updates."

"I'm glad to hear that. Wait till you see Tucker Cassidy pitch tonight. He's a real phenom with a wicked curveball."

At the mention of Tucker's name, her stomach did a slight tumble. "Is that right?"

"Yeah. Best acquisition we've made in years."

"I can't wait to watch him." She would not tell her father how well she knew Tucker. There were some things a daughter didn't discuss with her dad.

Plus, knowing how her father felt about her dating—anyone— she didn't think he'd appreciate knowing she was seeing Tucker.

She couldn't even imagine *that* conversation. Not that she ever intended to have it with him. She'd always kept her father in the dark about her dating life. He preferred to think of her as studious and dedicated to her career.

She'd keep it that way for now. Someday, maybe when she got engaged, she'd mention there was a man in her life. Or maybe after she got married. Or possibly when she put a grandchild in her father's arms. Then there'd be no going back, and he might be distracted by a crying baby and wouldn't notice the guy standing next to her.

Her lips ticked up at the thought. Yeah, that was a long way down the road.

She focused on Tucker as he warmed up his arm, threw some pitches, slow at first, then with more speed as his velocity increased. He looked mighty fine in uniform, too. Even from up in the owner's box she could appreciate the tight fit of the pants across his thighs and butt, especially when he turned away from her.

There was something so striking about Tucker in uniform, the way he took command of the mound as if he owned it. He threw the ball with authority. He had a definite presence.

She was impressed.

Her dad was right. He looked good, at least during warm-ups. The true test would be when he faced batters.

When the game began, she leaned forward, glad she was here. Not only did she need to occupy her mind with something other than the anxiety and sadness from her job the night before; she was also interested in watching Tucker pitch.

Or maybe just watching Tucker, period. She was used to seeing him in street clothes, as just a regular guy. There, on the mound, he commanded attention, all focus on him as he studied the first batter who'd come to the plate.

Tucker held the ball, his hand behind his back as he got the signal from Sanchez, the catcher. He nodded, then turned to his side, winding up for the pitch.

His form was nearly perfect as he threw the ball, which landed in the sweet spot over the plate.

The umpire called a strike, and the crowd cheered.

She looked over at her dad. "Nice curveball."

Her father nodded. "Indeed. I've never seen anything quite like it."

He threw another pitch, very similar to the first. It hit the strike zone and the batter didn't even swing.

"He's got great hands," her father said. "Great control of his balls."

Aubry blinked and felt her face grow warm.

Of course her father was discussing Tucker's pitches. But come on. Great hands? Control of his balls? That had her mind careening off in directions that had nothing to do with Tucker's actions on the mound, and everything to do with what he could do with his hands and his balls in the bedroom.

You are not a giggling twelve-year-old girl, Aubry. Get your shit together.

Still, Tucker looked so freaking hot on that pitching mound, and she couldn't help the hot flashes. It was just embarrassing to have them around her father.

She liked Tucker's stance, and he was just so sexy, the way he studied the batters, his gaze so intense through his black glasses. She wasn't sure she'd ever seen him look so fine.

Of course, it could also be that she'd seen him naked, so she knew the perfection underneath that uniform. Not that she was fantasizing about him in any way at all. Except in every way possible.

Time to stop thinking of Tucker and sex and focus on baseball.

When he struck out the batter, she stood and clapped along with everyone else in the owner's box, effectively snapping her out of her fantasies and back into the game. Now she made herself zero in on his pitches.

The next ball was a strike—again. So impressive. It was the way he threw the ball that mesmerized her, the mechanics of it all, the way the ball seemed to arc so high, then unexpectedly drop just as it reached the plate.

Several of the batters swung and missed, or grounded out. He gave up a single in the second inning, but no runs. In the first three innings, no one on the opposing team scored.

Awesome.

Throughout the game, Tucker mixed up his pitches, of which he had several, but his curve was a beautiful thing. By the top of the eighth inning, the Rivers were up by one run. It had definitely been a pitcher's battle, which had made it fun to watch, but also nerve-wracking.

Aubry found herself leaning forward, breath held, every time Tucker threw a pitch, waiting for it to land in the right spot. And, fortunately, most of the time it did. When someone got a hit, they didn't advance beyond first base. He was good tonight, and so was the team defense. Offense needed to get on it so they could all breathe a little easier, which hadn't happened just yet.

Until Gavin Riley hit a shot into right field for a double, and then Trevor Scott doubled him home, giving them a one-run cushion going into the top of the ninth.

Tucker didn't pitch the ninth. They brought in their ace closer, who threw couldn't-hit-them fastballs. It was a fast, three-out inning, and the Rivers won the game.

Aubry stood and hugged her dad. "What a great game."

"I'm glad you came. You brought us luck."

She laughed. "Based on what I saw tonight, Dad, luck had nothing to do with it."

"Would you like to stop by the house?" her father asked.

"No, I really need to go home. But I'll come over on my next night off. Say hi to Mom for me."

"She'll be sorry she missed you."

She hugged and kissed her dad, then left. When she got to her car, she sent a text message to Tucker.

Great game. You pitched well. I enjoyed watching you. Call me later.

By the time she walked in her front door, her phone rang.

"I thought maybe you'd wait for me," Tucker said.

She laughed. "I don't think so."

"Don't want everyone on the team to know you and I are seeing each other?"

"Absolutely not."

"So, I'm your secret lover, huh?"

Her lips curved at that thought. "For now? Yes."

"I can live with that. Are you home?"

"Just got here. How about you?"

"Finished interviews, but I'm still at the ballpark."

She knew better than to do this, but she wanted the company. "You could come over, if you'd like. I know you're probably hungry. I could fix you something."

"You don't have to do that. Do you work tomorrow?"

"Yes."

"I don't want to keep you up late. I can grab something on the way over, that way you don't have to cook. Are you hungry?"

"No. The suite had plenty of food."

"Then I'll grab a quick burger, and I'll see you soon."

"Okay."

She hung up, went in the bathroom to brush her teeth and hair, then looked in the mirror. She still wore her jeans, blouse and boots and pondered changing clothes.

Changing into what, exactly? She pondered that thought for a few minutes, wondered why she was making such a big deal about it, then decided to change into a pair of comfortable lounge pants and a long-sleeved Henley.

Much better, and less restrictive. She realized she already had thoughts of Tucker's hands on her, and her body responded with a rush of heat.

Yes, she was definitely glad she'd invited him over. Maybe it was the tension from yesterday, but she needed that release that only he could provide. Sure, she could do it herself, but it would be much more fun to enjoy some fun sex with Tucker.

While she waited for him, she made a cup of tea, then picked up one of her medical books and did some research.

About twenty minutes later there was a knock on the door. She went to open it.

She looked him over. "I don't see a burger bag."

He smiled at her. "I ate it on the way over."

"You must have been hungry."

"I was."

He came in and she shut the door, watching as he made his way into her kitchen to lean against the island. He looked good in his jeans and long-sleeved cotton shirt. Of course, he always looked good.

"You obviously worked up an appetite with the way you pitched tonight."

He turned to face her. "Glad I was able to entertain you."

"I was definitely entertained. And my dad is impressed."

He slipped the tips of his fingers into the front pockets of his jeans. "Is that right?"

"Yes. He spoke very highly of you."

"That's good to know. And did you tell him about us?"

She laughed, walking over to stand in front of him. She grasped one of his belt loops and tugged on it. "Definitely not."

He pushed off the island and wrapped an arm around her, drawing her against him. "I'm okay with being your dirty little secret, Aubry."

She thought he was going to kiss her, his lips hovering just a fraction of an inch away from hers. Their gazes collided, his breath mixing with hers as her lips parted, anticipation making her pulse rate kick up.

"For now," he added, before his mouth came down on hers.

NINETEEN

WATCHING TUCKER PLAY TONIGHT SHE'D WITNESSED mechanics and precision, every move perfection. But when he kissed her, it was messy and spontaneous, one hand sifting through her hair as the other found its way to her back, lifting her shirt to roam across her skin. She moaned against his lips and used her hands to map the muscles of his forearms and shoulders.

He moved into her, his cock hard and insistent as he deepened the kiss. A delicious headiness swirled within her, her skin prickling with awareness as he moved his lips from her mouth to her neck, laving her throat with his tongue. She couldn't help her deep moans as need held her in its grasp. She was caught up in a daze of hazy passion and grasped tight to Tucker, her legs shaking as he cupped her breast, pulling the fabric of her bra down to tease and pluck her nipples.

And when he drew down her pants, she helped him, stepping

out of them, needing to be naked, wanting him to touch her, taste her, give her the orgasm she so desperately craved.

He slipped his hand down the front of her panties, and she whimpered.

He stepped in closer to her, wrapping his other arm around her to hold her steady.

"Shh," he said. "I know what you need."

His hand was warm as he cupped her sex, then slid lower, his fingers slipping inside her. The heel of his hand rubbed her clit as he moved his fingers within her.

It was so damn perfect. Tucker's touch hit those spots that sent strikes of shocking pleasure straight to her core.

His gaze met hers. "Like that?"

She arched her hips toward him. "Yes. Just like that."

He kissed her, and she melted against him, around him, unable to hold back as the sensations overtook her. All she felt was heat surrounding her, the feel of his mouth and tongue and the movements of his hand and fingers. She felt consumed and let herself fall.

Her orgasm shook her, and she grabbed Tucker's wrist, holding his hand right where she needed it as she was wracked by wave after wave of undulating tremors that left her weak and light-headed.

He took her down easy, slowing the intensity of his kiss, removing his fingers but still holding tight to her body.

She reached up to touch his face, running her fingers over the stubble of beard across his chin. She brushed her lips across his, taking a long, satisfied breath.

"That was good." She slid her hand over his chest. "I needed that."

"I could tell." He rested his forehead against hers. "But we're not finished yet. I'm just getting warmed up."

She patted his chest. "That's what I like about you, Tucker. You have stamina."

He grinned, then took her hand, pressed a kiss to the back of it, and led her into the bedroom.

She pulled off her shirt and took off her bra and underwear, then grabbed a condom from her nightstand. "I moved them closer. You know, so they're handy."

He smiled. "Good thought."

She sat on the bed to watch him undress.

"I like you like this," she said as he climbed on the bed next to her.

"Like what?"

She wrapped her fingers around his cock. "Naked and hard."

TUCKER WATCHED AS AUBRY SAT BACK ON HER HEELS and stroked his cock. Was there anything hotter than watching a woman touch your dick?

He didn't think so. His balls tightened and his breath caught as she bent forward and put her sweet mouth around the crest. All he saw was a flash of pink tongue wrapping around his cockhead, and he grabbed a handful of sheet, hoping he could hold out long enough to enjoy the hell out of this.

Her mouth was hot, wet, and as she suctioned a tight seal around him and slid his cock between her lips, his stomach tightened.

He raised up to sift his fingers through her hair. "God, that's good, babe."

It felt so goddamned good he wanted this to last forever. He also wanted to come, hard—to jettison hot spurts along her tongue until he was empty and satisfied.

And as she used one hand to stroke the base and her other to cup his balls and give them a gentle squeeze, he already knew which of his desires was going to win.

Because he'd thought about this a lot, imagined her hot and wicked mouth on his dick.

The reality was more than he had ever imagined.

He lifted his hips, feeding more of his cock into her mouth.

"I'm ready to come, Aubry. I want to shoot into your mouth."

She hummed along the side of his cock, then squeezed her lips tighter together.

That's all it took. The first spurts spilled along her tongue as he erupted, his hips arching off the bed. Aubry held tight to the base of his cock as he gave her all he had, jerking in rhythmic spasms until he was spent.

She licked him fully, then laid her head on his thigh while he came down from that incredible high. It took him a minute or two and several deep breaths before he could even find the strength to run his hand over her hair.

"That," he said, "was damn good."

"Glad you thought so." She lifted her head and looked up at him. "But we're still not done."

He finally looked down at her. "You're a tough taskmaster. I'm going to need a few minutes of recovery time."

She laughed. "I'll get us something to drink. What would you like?"

"A beer sounds good."

She slid off the bed. "I'll be right back."

He admired her fantastic ass and the soft sway of her hips as she disappeared from the bedroom. While she was gone, he mentally replayed that phenomenal blow job in his head.

And his dick started to harden.

He looked down at it and shook his head. "So much for recovery time."

"Who are you talking to?" she asked as she came back in, handing him his beer. She'd poured a glass of wine for herself.

"My cock."

She arched a brow and climbed onto the bed, crossing her legs as she faced him. "Is this something you do often?"

"Not really."

She took a sip of wine. "Can I ask the topic of conversation?"

"The blow job you gave me. I was mentally replaying it in my head, and I started to get hard. Then I chastised my cock for having a one-track mind."

She laughed. "I hardly think it's the fault of your penis that you enjoyed what I did. But, thanks for the compliment." She raised her glass toward him.

"No, really. Thank you." He tipped his beer toward her in a toast, and they both drank.

He took several long, deep swallows of beer, then set the bottle on the nightstand. He took the wineglass from her hand and put it next to his beer, then pulled her on top of him, sliding his hands along the smooth skin of her back. When he moved his hands to her lower back and pressed in, she moaned.

"Feel good?" he asked.

"You have no idea."

He realized she worked long hours, all of them on her feet. She probably needed a good back massage. He rolled her off of him, then slid off the bed and grabbed a pillow, positioning it at the edge of the bed.

"Come on."

She rolled onto her side to look at him. "Come on and what?"

"Bend over the bed."

She grinned. "I like where this is going."

He laughed. "Well, it might go there, but really, I'm going to give you a massage."

"Now I definitely like where this is going."

She slid off the bed and into his arms. Her lips met his in a tangle of tongues and lips that left him hot, hard and definitely ready to spin her around and slide inside of her.

Instead, he turned her around and bent her over the bed, positioning her hips and stomach against the pillow to be sure she was comfortable.

Of course, this position also gave him a prime view of her very sweet ass, which didn't help his raging hard-on.

His erection could wait, though he did position it up against her butt as he leaned over and laid his hands on her lower back. He pressed in, feeling the tight tension in her muscles.

She moaned, and his cock twitched.

"That feels good," she murmured, her eyes closed.

"Relax and let me work my magic."

Her lips curved. "Mmm-hmm. Magic hands."

He liked that she enjoyed what he was doing, that he could get her to unwind. He felt the muscles give under his hands as he worked deeper.

That's when he saw the mirror across the room, positioned on the wall. He could see himself, and Aubry. Which meant if he fucked her this way, they could both watch.

His dick was hard as steel now. He could imagine pumping into her, twisting her a little to the side so he could watch his cock sliding in and out of her.

He sucked in a deep breath and let it out, his hands drifting down.

"Tucker." Her voice went lower, and she raised her butt up, her sex teasing his cock, her thighs clamping around him.

He smoothed his hands over the twin globes of her ass, then drew his hands up over her lower back again, mixing the therapeutic with the sexual. He wanted her relaxed, but turned on, too.

And when he smoothed his hands over her butt this time, he let his hand slide lower, this time between her legs.

She was wet, ready, her body quivering with the same anticipation he felt.

He opened the nightstand drawer where she kept her condoms, grabbed one and put it on, then positioned himself between her thighs.

"Aubry. Look at the mirror."

She lifted her head and their gazes collided in the mirror.

"Now watch."

He entered her and watched as her face changed to one of deep passion as he seated himself fully inside of her. To feel her and to look at her made his balls tighten.

He leaned back to see his cock going in and out of her pussy. Oh, yeah, now that was a beautiful sight. And something he wanted Aubry to see.

He shifted to his side, repositioning her just so.

"Now look," he said.

She made a low sound in her throat, then pushed back against him before pulling forward again. "I see. I feel you. Oh, it feels so good."

She worked in tandem with him, pushing back as he thrust into her. He grasped her hips and drove in deep, then eased out, prolonging the pleasure for both of them. And when she reached between her legs to touch herself, it was all he could do to keep from losing it, from coming right then. Between feeling the way her body gripped him and watching her in the mirror, he was ready to go off.

But Aubry would come first.

"Come on, baby," he said, giving her fast thrusts as she touched herself. "I want to feel you tighten around me. Make yourself come and make me come, too."

Her breathing quickened, and the sounds she made as she brought herself to climax nearly shredded him. And as she pushed against him, tilted her head back and came, he let go, shoving deep inside of her, watching both of them in the mirror as he grabbed her hips and shuddered against her.

He'd never watched anything hotter, especially since Aubry's gaze was riveted to the mirror, watching them.

Out of breath, he held on to her and came down from that incredible high. He smoothed his hand over her back, then leaned over to press a kiss to her shoulder.

She smiled at him in the mirror. "Great back rub."

He grinned. "Glad you liked it."

"Oh, I more than liked it. But now my legs are shaking."

He laughed and disengaged, then turned her around and kissed her.

"I also need a shower now," she said. "You made me sweat."

He cupped her butt and drew her against him. "You probably need another back rub, too."

"Mmm." She tipped her fingers across his jaw. "I might. Though I might pass out on you if you massage my back again."

She was probably exhausted from work the night before, spending time at his game and having sex with him instead of getting caught up on sleep.

They took a shower, then crawled into bed.

"Roll over on your side."

She frowned. "Why?"

"Because I'm going to rub your back."

"Tucker, I wasn't serious—"

"Roll over, Aubry."

She did, and this time he kept his intentions to only the back rub. He dug in and found all those sore muscles, this time in her upper back. He liked hearing her groans of approval and tried not to let his dick get involved.

Within ten minutes, she was asleep. He listened to the sounds of her rhythmic breathing and smoothed his hand back and forth over her hip.

Yeah, this was pretty damn good.

Content, he curled his body around hers, pulled the covers over them both, and closed his eyes.

TWENTY

IT WASN'T OFTEN THAT AUBRY HAD A CHANCE TO GO out and eat with her friends, but after a particularly intense day at work on Friday night, Katie had decided they needed drinks and food, and Aubry wasn't going to be allowed to say no. So she found herself seated at a table at a trendy bar-slash-restaurant, not far from the hospital, with Katie and several other residents, after they'd finished their reports and were sprung for the night.

"Brutal," David said, downing his third shot of tequila. "I had a fifty-six-year-old with epigastric spasms and Chen looking over my shoulder the entire time. I nearly broke out in a sweat. I had the diagnosis and treatment plan right. I mean, I'm a third-year resident, not a goddamn intern. I don't need him to hold my hand."

David was a brilliant resident who knew what he was doing. He was the golden god of the emergency room—graduated at the top of his class and would no doubt go on to do great things. Hearing him bitch about Chen gave Aubry some comfort. At least she knew Chen wasn't singling her out.

Katie scooped up spinach dip with her chip, slid it into her mouth and swallowed, then nodded. "He did the same thing to me. I had a myocardial infarction with COPD complications and Chen stood in the room staring me down as I called for the treatment plan like it was my first day. I'm telling you, the man is downright unnerving."

"He does it on purpose, you know," Rick said.

Rick was another one of the residents. Aubry looked over at him. "Do you think so?"

"Sure. He figures if he can't rattle you during a crisis, then you can handle your shit. If he flusters you, then you need work."

Katie waved a chip at Rick. "You might be right about that. So we should just start ignoring him."

Aubry laughed and took a sip of her cocktail. "Ignore him. Right. Good luck with that."

"Does he quiz you when you're working with a patient?" David asked them.

"Oh, my God," Katie said. "All the time." She settled into her best impression of Dr. Chen, because Katie did him best. She sat up straight in her chair and put on a sour face. "'Dr. Murphy, what is the proper treatment plan for a patient presenting with acute diverticulitis?' Keep in mind, all the while I've got the patient screaming in pain in the bed and I'm supposed to answer questions?"

Katie rolled her eyes. "Like I didn't learn that during medical school? I mean come on. Ask me some hard questions."

"He just wants us to be the best, you know."

Katie pinned Aubry with a look. "Oh, come on. He's a pain in the ass and I don't think he's busy enough. We were swamped in the ER tonight. Two car accidents with multiple injuries, two heart attacks, three fractures, multiple sutures and several gastric cases."

"And a partridge in a pear tree," David added.

"Exactly," Katie said. "One would have thought he might have directed his attention to patient care instead of poking first-year questions at us like his residents were a bunch of imbeciles."

Rick took a sip of his beer and nodded. "I'm with Katie on this. We could have used a hand, not a pop quiz."

Aubry sighed. "Maybe you're all right about that." She rolled her head, trying to ease the tension in her neck. "Either way, we got through another night."

"I'll drink to that," Katie said, and signaled their waitress for another round. As she did, she looked up at the bar and turned to Aubry. "Hey, Aubry, your hot baseball guy is on TV tonight."

Aubry twisted in her chair to check out the television. "He's not pitching. The camera just panned to him watching the game. Walter Segundo is up tonight."

"What hot guy is that?" David asked.

"Aubry's dating one of the players on the Rivers," Katie said.

Aubry pinned Katie with a look before redirecting. "I'm not exactly dating him."

"Fine. Whatever." Katie scooped up the last of the spinach dip. "Aubry's having sex with one of the Rivers' players."

"That clarifies things so nicely. Thank you so much, Katie." Aubry shot her friend a scathing look.

Katie just grinned. "You're welcome."

"Which player?" Rick asked.

She hadn't wanted anyone to know. But now they did, so she supposed there was no point in trying to hide anything. "Tucker Cassidy."

Rick nodded. "Good pitcher. He was a great acquisition for the Rivers."

She knew all about his acquisition, but she never told people about her father, and very few people made the connection. Katie knew, but that was about it. "Was he?"

"Yeah." Rick went into a deep explanation of Tucker's earned run average and his curveball while they watched the game.

"So," David said. "Tucker Cassidy, huh? Never figured you were the type to date a baseball player."

Aubry leaned back in her chair, so not happy to be the topic of conversation. "I never figured you were the type to date a stripper."

David flashed a glare at Rick.

Rick raised his hand. "Don't look at me, man. I didn't tell her."

David shrugged. "She's a nice girl. Working her way through college by dancing. And I burn off steam sometimes by going to strip clubs."

"So is it serious?" Aubry asked.

David shook his head. "Nah. She's busy with school and I'm busy with work. We're just having some fun together."

"Honey, we never judge," Katie said. "I would totally date a stripper. Of the male variety, just to be clear. And I won't keep it a secret should that ever happen. Not that anyone can keep a secret around the hospital. It's like gossip central, especially at the main station."

Aubry took a look swallow of her drink. "Speaking of gossip—Rick—word's out about you and Felicia."

Rick gave them all a blank stare. "What about me and Felicia?"

"You're dating Felicia?" David asked. "How come I didn't know that?"

"Probably because you spend all your time practicing medicine instead of listening to the gossip at the main station," Aubry said.

David nodded. "That must be." He turned to Rick. "Felicia, huh?"

Rick shrugged. "Maybe. I don't know. It's kind of touchy since she's one of the nurses on shift. We'll see how it goes."

Aubry laid her hand on his arm. "She's amazing. Sharp, funny, gorgeous."

Rick's lips curved as he took a drink of his beer. "Yeah, I know."

"Our friend might be falling in love," Katie said with a shake of her head.

"Hey now," Rick said. "No one said anything about love. We're just dating."

Katie offered up a smug smile. "And now we have confirmation."

Aubry laughed, glad the topic of conversation had turned to someone other than her. It gave her time to glance up at the television, hoping for another glimpse of Tucker.

The Rivers were still at home and were ahead by two runs. As Aubry took another glance at the TV, they panned over to the dugout again, and this time she caught sight of Tucker leaning against the rail, eating sunflower seeds while talking to his teammates, and looking sexier than any man had a right to.

Her sex clenched as she recalled all the different ways he'd touched her last night, and all the times she'd come. Tucker was very . . . thorough.

She picked up her phone and looked at the time. "I . . . have to go."

"Got a hot date with the hot pitcher?" Katie asked.

She didn't even bother to deny it. "Maybe."

"Can you get me game tickets?" Rick asked.

She stood and grabbed her bag, then looked down at him. "Why? Are you thinking of taking Felicia to a game?"

He smiled up at her. "Maybe."

"Then I'll see what I can do."

She left the bar and headed down to the ballpark, purposely avoiding the owner's suite. She didn't want to have to explain to her father what she was doing there twice in one week. It was already the top of the eighth inning anyway, so it wasn't like she'd be staying long. With an all-access pass, she could pretty much sit anywhere there was an available seat.

She chose one along the third baseline above the visitor's dugout. It was a cool night since it had rained earlier in the day. Glad she had brought her pullover jacket, she snuggled into it to watch the last two innings. And she also had a great view of the Rivers' dugout from here, so she could see all the players.

And Tucker.

Not that she'd come just to ogle one hot man. She'd come because the game had looked really good, and since she could get into the ballpark for free, why not, right?

That was her rationalization and she was sticking with it.

Cincinnati was still down by two runs, but the meaty part of their order was up to bat in this inning. Segundo was still pitching and continued to look strong. He struck out the first batter, the second lined out to the shortstop, and he had the third in the hole with one ball and two strikes.

Until the batter hit a fastball between second and third for a base hit.

Well, crap. She bought a soda and settled in to see if Segundo would be able to pitch himself out. He walked the next batter, probably intentionally, though he didn't make it look that way, but she knew enough about pitching to know an intentional walk, even if he did try to make it look unintentional. The next batter up hit several foul balls and Segundo finally worked him to two balls, two strikes when Segundo took a long breather, shook off several of Sanchez's signals and wound up. He threw the ball and the batter swung.

And missed.

The crowd stood and cheered. Aubry did, too. The pitcher had dodged a bullet, but he'd looked remarkably calm doing it.

The Rivers were up to bat in the bottom half of the inning. Sanchez was up first.

Sanchez singled just past first base, Fielding hit it right to the third baseman, so he was out. They pulled up a pinch hitter to hit for the pitcher, so it looked like Segundo's night was over. The pinch hitter, Lopez, took a ball and a strike to start things off. Then Lopez knocked out a single into left field, which moved Sanchez to third base and Lopez to first.

Now it was getting interesting. Aubry leaned onto the edge of her seat, her heart pumping.

With one out, the top of the batting order came up. Gavin Riley was up and hit a long fly sacrifice to deep center field, which scored Sanchez but left them with two outs and Lopez still at first base. They ended up stranding him when the next batter grounded out, but they'd scored another run going into the top of the ninth.

Their ace closer came in and walked one batter, struck out two and the final batter hit a pop fly that was easily caught by Trevor Shay to end the game.

Aubry stood and smiled. Even though she'd only been there for two innings, they'd been an exciting two innings. With medical school and her internship and residency, she hadn't taken a lot of time for baseball in the past few years. Plus, her parents had always dragged her to games, and she'd had to admit she'd grown to resent it—and the game.

Now, though? She remembered why she enjoyed baseball.

She sent a text message to Tucker. *I'm at the stadium. Would you like to meet up?*

It didn't take him long to reply. *Yeah. Invited to a party. Wanna come with me?*

Did she? She had planned on just having him over to her place for some alone time. A party was something entirely different. It was like . . . dating. And they were most assuredly not dating.

She thought about it a minute, then shrugged and sent him a return text.

Sure. Should I meet you somewhere?

He texted her back. *I'll pick you up in about an hour.*

Since she figured she'd have plenty of time because of media interviews and postgame meetings, she dashed home to take a shower and change clothes. She'd headed to the bar right after her shift at the hospital ended and she needed to freshen up. After drying her hair and putting on makeup, she chose a pair of black jeans, heels and a silk top, layering a few of her favorite silver chains over the top. She laid out her leather jacket near her purse, then perused herself in the mirror.

She shook her head. Typically, at the end of a particularly grueling work shift, she'd be home in yoga pants and a tank top, a bowl of popcorn on the side table in the living room and a book in her lap.

The woman looking back at her in the mirror? So not her.

What was she doing, anyway? What was she doing with Tucker? This was so unlike her. Her career was everything to her, and for the past several years it had been the only thing.

Sure, sex with Tucker was great and all, but sex had never been a priority for her. When it came around, great. If it was lacking, she could survive without it. And she'd never been the type of woman who saw herself as incomplete without a man in her life, so it wasn't like being with Tucker—being with any man—was something she desperately needed.

So what was the allure? Was it loneliness, a piece of her life she hadn't consciously realized she'd been missing? Or was it Tucker?

Her doorbell rang, so her soul-searching questions remained unanswered for now.

Tucker was there, wearing a black button-down shirt and dark jeans, and looked just damned edible, as always.

"You look hot," he said, stepping inside and pulling her toward him to brush his lips against hers.

"Thanks. So do you." She grabbed her jacket and her purse, then turned to face him. "I'm ready to go."

"Great." He led her out the door and to his car, opening her side and waiting for her to get in before heading over to his side.

Once they were on the way, she looked over at him. "So tell me about this party."

"It's for Liz Riley's birthday. She's married to Gavin Riley."

"I know Liz very well since she works a lot with the team as a sports agent."

"Right. Sure you do. Anyway, we're all meeting at Gavin and Liz's house. Not a big thing, just a few people from the team. Wives, girlfriends, some friends."

If she'd known about this, she might not have come. Anyone connected to her father—like Liz—like the team—could tell her father about her seeing Tucker. She wasn't sure she was ready for her dad to know she was dating one of the players.

Which she most certainly wasn't.

Or she supposed she was, since going to a party with him could definitely be considered a date.

"You're chewing your lip."

She looked over at Tucker. "Excuse me?"

He pointed to her face as he drove. "You're chewing your bottom lip. Like you're worried or thinking or something."

She licked her lip. "I'm fine."

"Did you have a bad day at work?"

She shrugged. "My day was fine. Normal for me."

He pulled onto the highway, merged over into the fast lane. After a mile or so, he asked, "Then what's bothering you?"

"Nothing's bothering me."

"Something is, because I've seen you do that thing with your lip before."

She looked at him. "Really. And you know me so well that you think it's because something's bothering me."

"Yes."

He was so confident. Then again, he was also right, which kind of irritated her. She decided not to answer him and looked out the window. Trees were in bloom, color had started to burst into her city. Spring had definitely sprung in St. Louis, which brightened her mood immensely despite all the rain they'd had lately.

Besides, rain was a good thing. It renewed everything.

"So are you gonna tell me or not?"

She shifted her attention back to Tucker. "Tell you what?"

"What's bugging you?"

She finally sighed. "The party."

He took a quick glance her way. "Liz's party?"

"Yes."

"You don't want to go."

"I didn't say that, it's just—people there know me."

"Okay. And that's a problem."

"Maybe."

His fingers flexed on the steering wheel, and she could tell that she'd upset him, which hadn't been her intent.

"It's because you don't want anyone you know to know that we're seeing each other, especially anyone in baseball or connected to baseball who knows your dad."

When he said the words out loud, it sounded petty and ridiculous. What difference did it make if she was dating one of the players? There was nothing in their contracts that prohibited it, and certainly nothing about it that would get her father riled up. He'd likely not care at all. He'd probably never know. It wasn't like anyone other than Liz routinely spoke to her dad. She was worrying for nothing.

She was just going to go and mingle with people she knew and have fun and quit worrying about it.

"Actually, everything's fine. I'm not concerned at all."

He looked like he didn't quite believe her. "Are you sure?"

She gave him her most sincere smile. "Absolutely."

He exited the highway and pulled onto a street with enormous trees. It was dark and a little foreboding, and the house was huge.

When they pulled to the end of the long, dark driveway she noticed a lot of cars. Like, a lot of cars.

"Okay, then," he said, putting his car into park before turning to her and laying his hand on her thigh. "Let's go party our asses off, Aubry."

TWENTY-ONE

LIZ ANSWERED THE DOOR LOOKING LIKE A KNOCKOUT, as always. In her mid-thirties, was Aubry's guess, and she looked late twenties at most. Her stunning red hair was cut in a short bob, the silken ends sweeping along her chin. And, despite a busy career as a sports agent, being married to Gavin Riley, the team's first baseman, and dealing with the couple's two-year-old daughter, Genevieve, she'd never known a woman more put together, on top of . . .

Everything.

"I'm so glad you're here, Tucker," Liz said, her eyes widening as she turned from him to Aubry.

"Aubry." Liz enveloped her in a tight hug. "I didn't expect to see you. And you're with Tucker?"

"Yes."

"You have to come with me. We have some catching up to do. Tucker, go grab a beer with the guys. They're downstairs."

"Yes, ma'am." He looked over at Aubry. "You okay?"

"Fine. I'll catch up with you later."

"Don't worry about him," Liz said, her arm firmly linked in Aubry's. "All the guys are downstairs shooting pool or playing video games or whatever it is they all do when they're not watching sports."

Liz led her into the kitchen. "First, we get a drink. Mixed or beer or wine?"

"A glass of white would be great. And I'm not picky."

"All right, then. I'm trying out a new chardonnay tonight, so we'll both have a glass."

Liz poured them each a glass of the chardonnay, handed a glass to Aubry, then leaned against the counter. "Before we head into the family room to join everyone else, I have to ask—how long have you been dating Tucker?"

She took a sip of the wine before answering. "Oh, Liz. This is very good."

"It is, isn't it? I tried it at one of our favorite restaurants the other night and knew right away I'd have to have some."

"It's crisp, not sweet, but not too dry, either. It's perfect."

"And you're avoiding my question." Liz's eyes sparkled with amusement.

"Sorry. Not long. We're hardly dating, really."

Liz's brows rose. "Which means what, exactly? That you're just friends or you're just in it for the sex?"

Aubry laughed. "I don't know. It's too early to make a call. I like him. The sex is good. But as far as a relationship, I don't know. My work keeps me busy and I haven't really had any kind of relationship since my undergrad years. Who has time?"

Liz waved her hand back and forth. "You have to make time for the things that are important, Aubry."

"I am making time right now. For the sex part."

"Hmm." Liz studied her. "But you're not having sex with him right now. You're here. At my party."

"Happy birthday, by the way."

She laughed. "Thank you. It's just an excuse to have people over and have a good time. I'm ignoring birthdays for the most part these days."

"Why? You're gorgeous and you look about my age."

"You win best compliment of the night since you're what? Twenty-two?"

Now it was Aubry's turn to laugh. "Now *I* feel complimented."

"How is doctoring going these days?"

"Intense but rewarding. You know I switched over to emergency medicine, right?"

"Yes. Do you like it?"

"I love it. But it does occupy a lot of my time."

Liz nodded. "Hence the lack of a hot man in your life."

"Right."

"Honey, you've got one now, don't you?"

"For the moment."

Liz pushed off the counter and grabbed the bottle. "Come on, let's join the other ladies. But before we do, a word of advice."

"Sure."

"Tucker's a great guy, Aubry. He's smart, damn fine looking, and he's got a good career ahead of him. You could do a lot worse, you know?"

"I do."

"So maybe take a few deep breaths, step away from being all-work-all-the-time-Aubry, and have some damn fun. No one says you have to marry the guy."

"My friend Katie tells me that all the time."

Liz nudged her with her hip. "Your friend Katie is very smart. You should listen to her."

They joined a group of the wives and girlfriends of players, along with sports agent Victoria Baldwin, who was good friends with Liz. Liz also introduced her to a few of her neighbors. All in all, a great group of women.

"Where's Genevieve?" she asked Liz.

"Spending the night with Gavin's parents. Since my birthday is actually tomorrow, it's an early gift to me so Gavin and I could enjoy an adults only party. No kids, no little one getting up in the middle of it all, and we get to sleep in tomorrow."

"Anyone who's a parent knows what an amazing gift that is," Shawnelle Coleman, one of the players' wives said. "And since I have two kids who are spending the night with their grandparents tonight, believe me, I appreciate it just as much."

Shawnelle lifted her glass of wine in a toast. Aubry couldn't relate since she didn't have kids yet, but she was definitely enjoying her chardonnay, so she was glad to toast with the other women.

She was happy to see Alicia Riley, who was engaged to Garrett Scott. "How's the wedding planning going?"

"Actually, pretty smooth so far. Now that baseball season is in full swing again, it might be a little harder to manage everything."

Liz waved her hand. "Don't be ridiculous. You're a Riley, and you have all your sisters-in-law and your cousin Jenna to help you out. Whatever you can't deal with, we can pitch in to assist."

Alicia grinned. "This is true."

"I imagine it's tough for you being on the road with the Rivers all the time," Aubry said, "plus trying to plan a wedding."

Alicia shrugged. "That's my life as a physical therapist for the team, so I'm pretty used to it. Plus, it keeps me close to Garrett, so I don't mind. And like Liz said, between my mother and my Aunt Kathleen, plus Liz and Jenna and Savannah and everyone else, I have a lot of help. I don't think there's any detail that'll get missed as far as the wedding."

"Not if we have anything to say about it," Liz said with a confident smile.

"It sounds like you have things well in hand. Or at least a lot of hands to help."

Alicia nodded. "Hopefully so. And still able to juggle the job along with the wedding planning. Oh, and speaking of the job, I was wondering how yours was going in emergency medicine."

"It's going well, thanks."

"You were originally going to specialize in obstetrics, right?" Alicia asked her.

Aubry nodded. "Yes. But then during my internship I did a rotation in the emergency room, and I fell in love."

Victoria smirked. "With blood and guts."

Aubry laughed. "Something like that. More like the fast pace of the ER department. I had several conversations with some of the doctors there during my rotation, and every day I spent in the ER lit a fire in my blood. I couldn't sleep at night because I kept thinking about it. I knew it was where I was supposed to be and it was then I decided emergency medicine was my calling."

"It's intense, isn't it?" Liz asked.

"It can be. But the care we give is immediate, and often lifesaving. That's what I enjoy about it."

"I'm sure it's very exciting. But so much work," Shawnelle said.

"Spoken by the lawyer," Liz said. "Now there's someone with an amazing career."

"Spoken by the sports agent," Shawnelle shot back. "I think we all do our share of intense work, honey."

Liz nodded. "That's true. As long as we love what we do, it doesn't matter how intense it is, does it?"

"You have a point," Aubry said. "There are days I'm so busy and so involved in what I'm doing, the hours just fly by. And I'm never bored."

"I can't imagine you would be," Alicia said. "What you're doing is so rewarding."

Aubry smiled at her. "Thank you. You're a caregiver yourself. Often an athlete's future is in your hands. Your job in rehab is so important."

"Thanks. I love what I do."

They all talked work for a while, until Liz went to answer a knock at the door. Even though it was late, having started the party after the baseball game, it was Friday night and a lot of people had come, which was nice for Liz.

Aubry eventually followed the women downstairs.

There were quite a few men there as well. As Liz had said earlier, several were playing pool. There was also a dartboard, some pinball games and a video game system. All in all, it was one hell of a setup. There was a very nice bar against one of the walls, so a bunch of the guys sat there drinking. She spotted Tucker talking with Gavin Riley and Dedrick Coleman, Shawnelle's husband.

Aubry, Liz and Shawnelle wandered over to listen to them talk about another team.

"I don't know," Gavin said. "They've got a power hitter in Green, with Soong in the cleanup position, but the bottom of their order is weak. Tucker, I think you could go strong against them, especially if they can't hit your curve."

"But their pitching is solid, and you might find yourselves up against Peters, who has one hell of an ERA so far this season," Tucker said. "Still, your bats are hot right now. I'd say we take at least two from them."

"You're talking about Cleveland?" Liz asked.

Gavin nodded, and put his arm around Liz as she came up beside him. "We have a three game series with them next week."

Shawnelle slid in next to her husband, Dedrick, and Aubry didn't quite know what to do. Until Tucker motioned for her to join him, so she did, scooting up next to his side.

He slipped his arm around her. "Having fun?"

"Yes. Definitely." Which was the truth. Despite her trepidation about coming here, she was having a great time surrounded by very smart, fun women. And she was tired of second-guessing her decision to be with Tucker. She decided Liz was right. It wasn't like she was thinking down the road or toward the future. It was best to just stay in the "right now" with him.

And right now, his fingers drew circles along her back and his touch made her tingle.

What was it about Tucker's hands on her that could send skitters of sensual awareness down her spine?

She supposed it was too early to ask him if he was ready to leave, but for some reason, she wanted to be alone with him. Like now. She slid her hand along his arm and did the same thing to him, letting her palm rest against his chest, her nails digging in just enough to get his attention.

He looked at her with a questioning glance, then smiled as her hand snaked lower, toward his belt buckle. She kept her movements unobtrusive and easygoing so no one would notice. Nothing overt, just enough so only Tucker was aware of what she was doing.

"Something you want?" he asked.

"Definitely."

He smiled, his movements picking up with a little more intent across her back. When his hand rested on her hip, his fingers tapping on her butt, she inhaled—deeply.

"Tucker."

The wicked look he gave her was filled with intent and promise. "Yes, Aubry."

She shifted her gaze to everyone around her, realizing they were engaged in conversation and not paying attention to them, which was a good thing since at the moment she was very much hot and bothered. When her gaze met Tucker's again, she realized he was still focused on her.

"We'll continue this conversation later," she said.

"Yeah. We will."

Funny how very little had been said between them, but so much had been implied.

But it was good to know they were both on the same page.

AUBRY MADE HIM HARD. JUST HER TOUCHING HIM made him hard, not to mention her hands roaming over his body. Oh, sure, she made it look all innocent, but the looks she gave him, and just the goddamned way she breathed, turned him on.

And now she rested her hand on his thigh while she sipped her wine and talked to her friends like she didn't know exactly what she was doing.

He finally had to think about something else until his erection subsided, then he slid off the bar stool to get away from Aubry and cool down.

He headed over to watch some of the guys play darts, figuring that would pull his attention from the hot woman who made him want to grab her by the hand, drag her out to the car and bury himself inside of her until the ache making his balls throb went away.

And thinking in those terms wasn't helping, because now he had a visual of fucking her in the backseat of his car.

Darts. He needed to concentrate on the dart game.

"You should put your tongue back in your mouth, man. People are starting to notice."

He shot a glare to Trevor Shay. "Fuck off."

Trevor laughed. "It's kind of obvious that you have it bad for Aubry."

Tucker shrugged. "We just started seeing each other. No big deal."

"It's the beginning, when things are really hot and heavy. It is a big deal, when you can't get enough of each other."

"Is that how it was with you and Haven?"

Trevor's gaze drifted over to where Haven stood in the middle of the crowd of women. As if she knew he was staring at her, she looked up and smiled. Trevor smiled back. "It's still like that."

Tucker shook his head. "She's so got you hooked."

"Yup."

"And you don't have a problem with that."

"Not at all. Why would I? She's gorgeous, smart, and we've known each other a long time—long enough to clear all the bullshit out of the way. She knows the worst parts of me, and for some reason she loves me anyway. So yeah—I'm man enough to admit I love her."

"You make it sound so simple."

Trevor pushed off the wall and looked at him. "Once you find someone you want to spend the rest of your life with, it really is that simple. Ask any of the guys who are married or with one woman long term. They'll all tell you the same thing."

"What thing?" Gavin asked as he and Garrett came over.

"We're talking about our women," Trevor said.

"What about them?" Garrett asked.

"How you know when the right one comes along."

"Oh." Gavin grabbed his beer from the table next to him and took a long swallow. "Yeah. You might fight it, kicking and screaming for a while. A lot of us don't realize she's staring us straight in the face because giving up our freedom is a hard thing to reckon with. But once we think about what it might be like to live without her, it doesn't take long for common sense to kick in."

"What if you're not ready to settle down yet?" Tucker asked.

"That's easy," Gavin said, putting his beer down and grabbing his darts. "Then she's not the right woman for you."

Gavin walked away.

"So Aubry's not the one?" Garrett asked.

"I have no idea. I like her, but it's still early. I mean we just got together, you know?"

Garrett smiled. "Sometimes it hits you like a strike of lightning and it doesn't take any time at all to realize she's the one. And sometimes it doesn't matter how much time you spend with a woman, because she's never going to be the one for you, man."

"Yeah. I see what you mean."

Garrett patted him on the back. "Trust me, it's all about instinct. You'll figure it out."

Garrett and Trevor went over to take their spots by the dartboard, leaving Tucker to think as he leaned against the wall and sipped his beer.

Was it really that simple? He hadn't thought much about finding the right woman—or any woman—to settle down with. He liked his lifestyle the way it was, figuring he had plenty of time yet to find the woman of his dreams.

But he'd never really thought about how that might happen. Or when that might happen. Or how he'd know when the right woman came along, that she really was the right one.

Ah, hell. Why was he even thinking about it, anyway? He and Aubry were just going out, having sex and a good time.

He wandered over and played a few games of pool with the guys, drank a few beers, ate some amazing food, then ended up sitting upstairs and talking with the gang. It was a good group. He liked the guys, had meshed well with the team, and felt at home here—more at home than he'd ever felt before. His style of pitching worked well for this organization, and the sense of camaraderie he felt with this group of players was more like a brotherhood than he'd ever gotten with any other team.

Plus it was a winning team, and he liked playing for winners. They all had the same mind-set, too. Play hard, and win.

The party started to wind down, so he made his way over to Aubry. She was in the kitchen, a glass of wine in one hand, the other waving in the air as she talked in an animated fashion to several of the women. He leaned against the doorway to watch her. She'd say something, then stop and listen intently as someone else took over the conversation.

She'd been accepted, too. He was aware a lot of the women already knew her since she was Clyde Ross's daughter, but she seemed comfortable with all of them. And when she tilted her head back and laughed at something Liz said—oh, man, that sound shot straight to his balls.

There was nothing like a woman who knew how to laugh, who could have fun and be so completely unguarded like that.

He stepped into the room. "Okay, what are you all talking about?"

Liz turned around. "Women and multiple orgasms. And the men who can give them to us. We haven't gotten around to questioning Aubry about that yet, Tucker."

He grabbed Aubry's hand. "She'll let you know tomorrow."

Everyone laughed. They said their good-byes and thanked Liz and Gavin for inviting them to the party, then headed out.

Aubry leaned against him as they made their way to the car. He stopped in the street, pulling her toward him for a kiss.

She came into his arms and met his lips. The kiss was hot and passionate, making him wish they were already home so he could undress her and be inside of her, something he'd been thinking about for a few hours now.

He pulled away and she licked her lips, still holding on to him. Her nails dug into his forearms.

"Don't drive too fast, but let's get somewhere where we can get naked, okay?"

"You got it."

They ended up at his place, since it was like a mile closer than hers, and he was out of patience, especially since Aubry kept running her hand up and down his thigh on the drive home.

He pulled into the driveway, got out and came over to her side. She was already out and closed the door, so he took her hand and led her to the front door.

He wasn't the type of guy to get anxious about sex. This wasn't his first time, and she wasn't his first woman. Over the years, he'd learned to be patient and he could wait for it. But Aubry had him pent up all night long, thinking about getting her alone, so by the time he closed the front door, he was ready.

Hell, more than ready.

So was she, apparently, because he hadn't even found the light switch before she pushed him against the wall and shoved her body against his. He wrapped his arms around her and bent to take her mouth in a kiss that fired his passion fast and hot.

He fused his tongue to hers, his cock went instantly hard, and he shoved his hands into her hair, holding her head in place so he could explore her mouth, take the kiss deeper. He rocked his cock against her body. In response, she let out a soft, throaty moan that shot straight to his balls. Her hands roamed over him, her nails dug into him, and if he didn't get her naked right goddamned now he might just explode.

The problem was, it felt really damn good to feel her against him, all her soft parts against his hard parts. He didn't want to move his cock away from her since he was nestled between her legs, rocking against her.

"You keep doing that and you'll make me come."

He lifted his head and looked down at her. "Through all that denim?"

"Okay, it might take me a while, but it sure feels good."

"It'll feel even better without clothes."

She pushed her hips against him. "Then what are we doing in the hall? Let's get naked."

He grinned, then reached around to cup her butt, drawing her closer. "I was getting there, it's just that you feel really good, Aubry."

Her breath escaped, a slight gasp with it. "Naked, Tucker. Now."

"Yes, ma'am."

He took her by the hand and led her to his bedroom. He didn't even bother flipping on the lights, because he knew where all the furniture was in his room. She didn't, though, which was fine with him, because it forced Aubry to stay close to him. He had her tucked against his side, loving the feel of her soft curves as he directed her to his bed and sat her down on the edge. He bent and pulled off her heels, the ones that made her legs look long and made him think about her wrapping those long legs around him while he pumped into her.

His dick twitched.

Yeah, slow down, buddy.

He raised up and undid the button on her jeans, then the zipper, his fingers colliding with satiny skin as he drew the jeans over her hips and down her legs.

He wasn't a patient man. Not when sex was involved. And damn if these jeans weren't glued to her legs. He wanted to tear them off but the moonlight streaming in through the windows reflected off her face, and she was watching him undress her. He crooked a half smile at her.

"I think women wear these jeans on purpose."

She cocked a brow. "Really. For what reason."

He sat on his heels. "Multiple purposes, actually. One, they make your ass and legs look amazing."

She smiled at him. "Thanks."

"And two, they take fucking forever to get off of you, so you force us to be patient."

"I don't recall asking you to be patient. Right now I don't care if you cut them off. You remember I was the one who suggested we get naked."

That was the right answer. He hurriedly jerked them down her legs and tossed them onto the nearby chair, then smoothed his hands up her legs, unable to resist touching every inch of exposed skin.

"Now who's the one forcing patience?" Aubry glared down at him.

He grinned. "But there are so many awesome places on you to put my hands. And my mouth."

He kissed her thighs, then spread her legs, laying his lips on that sweet spot right where her inner thigh touched the tantalizing lace of her panties. She took in a sharp breath, and that was the sound he wanted to hear, especially when it was followed by a moan when he put his mouth on her sex. Even through her underwear, he tasted her—that sweet, salty, unique flavor that belonged only to Aubry.

He wanted more, so he drew her panties aside and licked her. She moaned, louder and longer this time.

"Oh, God yes. Do that again," she said. "Just like that. For a really long time. Until I come."

He could work with that direction. He slipped his tongue inside of her, then licked the length of her, slow and easy. He listened to the sounds she made, using those keys as a road map and enjoying every step of the journey. She tasted like tart honey and he could stay here and lick her up for hours. But eventually she tensed, writhed against him and he could tell she was almost there, so he gave her a little more pressure with his tongue and quickened his pace.

And when she arched against his face and shuddered, crying out his name, he knew she was coming. He tasted her sweet release, lapped it up, his hands on her hips holding her while she shuddered. He kept his mouth on her, giving her that contact she needed until her hips relaxed to the bed.

God, that was good. Feeling Aubry writhe all over his bed, listening to her moans, tasting her—it was all he could do not to interrupt her pleasure by shoving his cock in her until he came. Until they both came. But she tasted so damn sweet, and he wanted her to come first. Now that she had, he wanted to hear those cries again. This time, while he was inside of her.

He crawled up her body, planting kisses along her hip and rib cage, lifting her shirt as he did. He drew it over her head, then unhooked her bra and removed that, too. He made quick work of getting rid of his own clothes, then dropped down on top of her, rubbing his chest against her nipples.

"Mmm," Aubry said.

"Good?"

"Yeah. Let's do more of . . . all of that. But with your cock inside of me this time. I could use another orgasm."

He liked Aubry's open and aggressive approach to sex. He'd been with women who weren't vocal, who didn't tell him what they liked. Not that he minded shy. He could coax a response. But he much preferred a confident woman who knew what she wanted and wasn't afraid to ask for it.

And he definitely wanted to give it to her. He grabbed a condom from his nightstand, then reached for her legs, pulling her to the edge of his bed.

"Oh, I like where this is going."

He grasped his dick, stroked it. "This is going in your pussy."

She laughed. "Hurry up."

"You're taking all the romance out of it, Aubry."

"Aww. And does that hurt your tender little feelings?"

Now it was his turn to laugh. "I'll give you some feelings."

He tore open the condom and put it on, then put his hand over her sex. Her breath sharpened—deep, harsh, her expression changing from playful to very serious as he swept his fingers over her clit.

He wanted her ready for him, and when she lifted against his hand, her eyes closing as he moved his thumb back and forth over the hardening nub, he knew she was primed.

That's when he cupped her butt, raised her up and slid inside of her.

Her eyes opened and she met his gaze, grabbing his arms to draw him deeper.

She lifted her hips, giving him access to her.

"Damn, you're pretty here," he said, looking at her—at them, where they were joined. "I can see my cock going in and out of you. Your pussy lips grab me, sucking onto me as I slide out of you. You're so tight and hot and wet, Aubry. All I want to do is stay buried inside of you, to feel you squeeze my cock like this."

The grip she held on him and the way she looked at him when he fucked her was torture of the best kind. Her gaze was direct and passion filled, and he could feel her wrapping herself around him, inside and out. It was a heady feeling, putting him in a fog of pleasure like he'd never felt before.

He could get so lost in her, in the sensations she wove around him. Her scent, the way she looked at him, the way it felt to be inside of her.

He gripped her hip and raised her leg, nestling against her to take her mouth in a kiss that made him lose himself even further. He tangled his fingers in her hair, breathing in her scent as he drove his cock in deeper. And when she sucked on his tongue, it took everything in him to hold off, to wait, when all he wanted to do was spill inside of her.

Just a few seconds longer. He'd go when she went.

And when she came, it was goddamned perfect. She whimpered against his mouth, squeezed his cock with contractions and raked her nails along his arm. He was pretty sure blinding white lightning hit parts of his brain when he let go. He rocked hard and deep into her as he gave her everything he had.

Spent and sweating, he wrapped his arm around her and just . . . stilled, absorbing the thrumming beats of both their hearts as they settled.

Aubry ran her fingers through his hair with one hand while rubbing his back with the other.

"I might need a shower," she said. "You're sweating on me."

He raised his head to look down at her. "You complaining?"

Her lips curled. "Not a bit."

He finally got up and pulled her to a standing position. "Let's go."

They took a quick shower and he washed her back, kissing all the red spots he'd put on her body with his day's growth of beard.

Her skin was tender, and he'd scratched it. But she didn't seem to mind, which was a good thing, because he sure as hell liked touching her—especially with his mouth.

They got out of the shower and dried off. She went into his closet and came out wearing one of his T-shirts.

He didn't mind that, either. He grabbed a pair of sweats and climbed into those.

"I don't know about you, but I'm hungry," he said.

"You are, huh?"

"Yeah. Sex always revs up my appetite."

She shook her head. "Don't look at me, Tucker. I'm no great cook."

"Surely between the two of us we can come up with something simple."

"Do you have eggs and bacon? I can manage those."

He led her down the hall and into the kitchen. "Surprisingly enough, that's one of my specialties, too. That and tuna. I can open a can of tuna like you've never seen anyone do before."

She reached into his fridge and grabbed the carton of eggs. "I'm pretty good with tuna, too. And bowls of cereal. I also make some incredible toast."

He took out two pans and started laying the bacon in one.

"I hope you don't like fancy eggs," she said. "I can only make scrambled."

He laughed. "Scrambled works for me."

"You should find a girlfriend who's a good cook. That should be tops on your list."

He shifted toward her and put his arm around her, tugging her close. When she looked up at him, he kissed her. "Cooking skills is not high on my list of criteria when picking out women I like."

She gave him a look. "Really. And what kinds of talents are important to you?"

He let go of her and concentrated on the sizzling bacon. "Oh, you know, the typical things—earning potential and blow job skills."

She laughed. "Of course."

He liked that she wasn't easily insulted, and that she didn't take him too seriously.

They finished the eggs and bacon and added toast, then sat down to eat.

While she ate, Aubry kept studying him.

"Do I have food on my face?"

"No, I was just wondering about your glasses. Did you ever think about having surgery to fix your vision?"

"I've thought about it, but I see really well with my glasses and I didn't want corrective surgery to change the way I zero in on the plate when I pitch."

She laid her fork down. "So you think if they corrected your vision it would change your pitching."

"Yeah. The team suggested it. I turned them down. I see just fine with my glasses, and my pitching shows it. No reason to change what works, ya know?"

He scooped a forkful of eggs into his mouth, and she smiled at him.

"Definitely not."

After he took a drink of juice, he said, "Besides, you have to admit these glasses make me look dead sexy."

Aubry laughed. "I can't deny that. I was just curious. I wore glasses from the time I was six years old until midway through college. I couldn't wear contact lenses because they bothered my eyes. Then I had the corrective vision surgery. That's why I was wondering if you'd explored the option."

He pushed his empty plate to the side, then leaned across the table to look at her. "You have beautiful eyes, Aubry. But they'd be just as beautiful if you still wore your glasses. In fact, I'd wager you looked hot in your glasses."

"Thank you. And you are very sexy in your glasses."

"I know."

She rolled her eyes. "And so humble, too."

"Right?"

She shook her head, then took her plate to the sink and rinsed it. She started to grab the pans but Tucker was right there.

"Leave those. The maid will take care of them."

She turned around. "You have a maid?"

"No. But you don't need to do the dishes. Let's go to bed."

"I can't go to bed now. I just ate." She finished washing the pans and handed them off to him to dry.

He laid the dishes in the drying rack, then leaned against the kitchen counter. "So . . . what do you want to do? Watch some TV?"

"That'll do for now."

They curled up on the sofa and Tucker used the remote to scroll.

"That one," she said as a horror movie came up.

"Are you sure this won't give you nightmares?"

She leveled a look at him. "I work in the ER. I don't get nightmares. Besides, this is fake. I deal with some real horrors."

"Duly noted."

After the movie ended, he clicked off the remote and stood, then reached for her hand. "Come on. Bed. You yawned your way through the last half hour."

Stifling another yawn, she let him haul her to her feet. "But it was riveting stuff. Honest."

"Uh-huh."

"I'm still going to want hot, passionate sex when we get to bed."

"I'm happy to oblige."

He had some spare toothbrushes in the bathroom, so she opened one of the packages and brushed her teeth, then fell onto the bed. When Tucker climbed in next to her, she snuggled her butt against his crotch, closed her eyes and was out cold in less than a minute.

So much for hot riveting sex. He smiled and closed his eyes.

TWENTY-TWO

AUBRY WOKE TO THE SMELL OF COFFEE. SHE TURNED over onto her back and stretched, then realized as soon as she opened her eyes that she was most definitely not in her own bed.

Right. Tucker's bed. Where she'd demanded hot sex and then promptly passed out.

Oh, well. She got up, went into the bathroom and brushed her teeth. She thought about getting dressed, then decided it was too much effort at the moment, choosing instead to follow the coffee smell.

She paused at the end of the hall as she spied Tucker. He wore only his sweats, slung low on his hips as he sipped a cup of coffee. He leaned against the kitchen counter and looked out the window.

He had the most chiseled abs of any man she'd ever been with. And those hip bones . . . God, those hip bones. Did men know what those things did to women? Maybe they did and they wore their pants low like that so women would leach out brain cells, think only of sex and want to drop their panties on command.

If he asked, she'd drop hers. It was a horrifying realization considering she wasn't some hormonal teenager. She was a smart professional. A freaking doctor, for God's sake. She'd seen naked men before—plenty of them. Many of them had damn fine bodies, too.

But not like Tucker. She was melting all over herself and there was nothing to do but appreciate the hell out of his anatomy.

In a purely nonclinical way.

She should be ashamed of herself. But she wasn't. Nope, not a bit.

Gathering her wits around her, she walked into the kitchen trying to get hold of herself.

Tucker spotted her and smiled. "Hey, you're awake."

"I smelled coffee."

"Like an aphrodisiac, isn't it?"

He turned around and grabbed a cup out of the cabinet while she continued to admire his hip bones.

The aphrodisiac? That was him, not the coffee, and she was becoming more and more aroused every second. Pretty soon she'd be wide awake and she wouldn't even need coffee.

But he brewed her a cup, so she accepted it from him with a murmured thanks, fixed it the way she liked it and took a few sips, letting the caffeine infuse her senses. Along with the eye candy.

"Sleep well?" he asked.

"Like the dead. Sorry for crashing on you."

His lips curved. "Not a problem. I was pretty tired, too, so I'm not sure I could have performed for you anyway."

"Oh, I don't know. I have a feeling you're up for it no matter how tired you are."

"You must think pretty highly of me. I'm gonna take that as a compliment."

"You do that."

As the coffee worked its magic, so did the sight of Tucker, his hair sleep mussed, his body calling to her in ways she wasn't about to try to fathom.

Purely and simply, she'd woken up on the side of arousal this morning. She laid her cup down and went over to him, sliding her fingertips along the waistband of his pants.

He looked down at her and she caught the flare of instant desire in his eyes, happy to know he was on the same page.

She moved into him, pressing her body against his. She raised up on her toes, slid her hand in his tousled hair and kissed him, tasting the lingering flavor of coffee on his lips. He kissed her back, wrapping his arm around her to pull her closer.

Yes. Oh yes. Some hot, heady passion was exactly what she needed this morning.

She reached between them, sliding her hand into his sweats. He wasn't wearing underwear, so she wrapped her hand around his hard cock. He groaned, thrusting his tongue into her mouth, the action of his mouth and her hand on his shaft inciting her to a feverish arousal.

It was all consuming, this desire she had for him. The best part was, she felt it in return, in the way he thrust his cock into her hand, the sounds he made and how he tunneled his fingers into her hair as he kissed her.

She pulled away from the kiss, pressed her hands on his chest for some distance, and took in the look of raw passion in his gaze. He was breathing heavily as he stared her down—like some fire-breathing dragon. And wasn't that just the sexiest thing? She'd established he was the hottest man she'd ever laid eyes on, the reason for her state this morning.

She couldn't get enough of him, her mind and body already fixated on him. On sex.

She drew down his pants, releasing his cock, then dropped to her knees.

"Oh, yeah," Tucker said, tipping her chin up so she met his gaze. "Suck my cock, Aubry. Put your sweet, hot lips around me and suck it."

Hearing his words and seeing his gaze fixated on her unraveled her. She lifted his cock, winding her hands around the shaft, stroking him, wanting to give him pleasure because he always made her feel so good.

Now it was her turn to make him feel good.

TUCKER DREW IN A BREATH, THEN HELD IT AS AUBRY wrapped her lips around his cock, drawing his shaft into her warm, wet mouth.

He shuddered as he watched his cock disappear between her lips. It was like a large piece of heaven wrapped around his dick. Or maybe the sweet fires of hell. He couldn't be sure, but right now he didn't care. All he knew was it felt really damn good to have her mouth around him—to see her swirling her tongue over the crest, then engulfing his cock to the hilt. His balls throbbed as he fought to keep from thrusting as hard as he could into the soft cavern of her throat.

Instead, he eased in and out, watching her cheeks hollow as she took him deep.

She made him shudder as she pulled away, then wrapped her tongue around the head of his cock. She gripped him at the base, stroking him as she bathed his shaft in sweet, hot licks that made his balls quiver.

And when she tilted her head back, met his gaze and put her mouth around his cock again, each inch of his shaft disappearing slowly between her lips, he nearly lost it right then.

He let out a low groan.

"You're killing me," he said. "And you're gonna make me come."

Her only response was a satisfied hum against his cock, which only made it worse. Or better, he supposed, because it felt really damn good.

He slid his hand around the back of her neck, holding her in place as he thrust deep, then withdrew. She gave him hard suction, clamping her lips tight together, squeezing the head of his dick against the roof of her mouth until he was ready to explode into her hot, wet mouth.

"I'm gonna come, Aubry. Right now."

She didn't back away, instead leaned in and took his cock fully into her mouth. When his cockhead hit her throat and she swallowed, squeezing him, he knew he couldn't hold back any longer.

His entire body shuddered as he climaxed, a jettison of hot come spurting along her soft tongue. Aubry's throat worked to take it in, and he watched her swallow while he convulsed with pleasure until he was shaking with it.

Spent, he reached down to pull her up from the floor, then took her mouth in a kiss that tasted of him. She wound her tongue around his, her soft moans making him twitch despite the blistering orgasm she'd just given him.

Now it was time to give her a little taste of what she'd done for him. He bent and pulled her underwear down, then put his mouth on her.

She hummed in satisfaction as he rolled his tongue over her sex.

"Oh, yes, Tucker. Right there. I woke up so hot this morning. I'm so ready to come."

He loved hearing her say that, loved knowing she'd woken up aroused and ready for sex. He found the spot that made her moan and kept his tongue there, pressing in, giving her what she needed. He added his fingers, sliding them inside of her, pumping her, fucking her, listening to her cries of pleasure as she came apart for him.

There was nothing sweeter than having her come for him, to taste her as she trembled against him. He got up and kissed her, held her while she shuddered through the aftershocks until she settled.

She laid her head on his shoulder. "Now I'm hungry."

He laughed. "Let's go take a shower, then we'll get some breakfast."

They cleaned up and headed out to a restaurant to eat.

"When's your next game?" she asked as she dove into some oatmeal and fruit.

"Tonight."

Her eyes widened. "Am I keeping you from getting to the ballpark?"

"No. I don't head over until this afternoon."

"Okay."

"How about you? When do you work?"

"I have a shift tonight."

"Now it's my turn to ask if I'm keeping you from work."

She laughed. "Trust me. Nothing keeps me from work or I get in trouble. I report at three."

"Okay. Thanks for spending the night with me."

"I enjoyed it. But, you know, we can't make a habit of it."

Interesting thing for her to say. "Yeah? Why's that?"

She shrugged and finished her glass of juice. "You're busy. I'm busy. It's that whole career thing."

He leaned back in the booth. "We've managed just fine so far, haven't we? You haven't missed work yet, have you?"

"No."

"And I haven't missed a game. So we're doing okay, aren't we?"

"I guess so."

He studied her. "Unless that's your polite way of saying you'd like to dump me."

Her lips curved and she reached across the table to grab his hand. "Trust me, Tucker. I like what you've got."

"Good. Then quit trying to end it. We're good. We're having fun together. So stop trying to complicate something that, so far, isn't complicated."

Now she studied him, before finally nodding.

"Okay. Uncomplicated it is."

He wondered if she'd brought it up because of the work schedule thing, or if it was something else. Because, really, what they were doing was as uncomplicated as it could get. Sure, they both had busy schedules, but so far they'd been able to work around them. And he liked Aubry—a lot. He wanted to keep seeing her. But if she had reservations about it—about him . . .

He decided to shrug it off and just go with the way things were for now. Aubry was pretty upfront and outspoken. If she had issues, she'd tell him.

He definitely had no issues. He liked being with her, liked seeing her, touching her and having sex with her. He knew she didn't want to complicate her life, and after that debacle with Laura, the last thing he wanted was a difficult relationship.

So far, the two of them were working well.

He intended to keep it that way.

TWENTY-THREE

AUBRY HAD HER HANDS FULL WITH A PATIENT WITH abdominal pain, another with a broken ankle, one with a bloody nose that wouldn't clot properly and one with an upper-respiratory infection. She'd been running nonstop since she got to work this morning, which made for a good day as far as the passage of time, but it sure as hell had been hectic.

"Room twelve is vomiting blood," Olivia, the nurse said as she passed her in the hall.

"Tell him to quit sniffling. He's drawing all that blood down his throat. And is the clotting agent working yet?"

Olivia nodded. "It seems to be slowing down the bleeding. I'm heading back in there now to check."

"I'll be there shortly. I need to check the X-rays for the abdominal patient."

She reviewed the X-rays, which didn't tell her what she needed to know, so she found the intern in charge of her abdominal patient.

"What do you see on this X-ray?"

The intern, Max, studied it. "Not much, really. Nothing to account for the amount of pain the patient is in. We've ruled out appendix and gall bladder."

She nodded. "What would you do next?"

Max looked at her. "I'd order a CT scan of the upper and lower abdominal region."

"Good call. Get that done and go monitor the patient. Let me know when we have the results."

Max nodded and went to order the tests.

That taken care of, she went in to check on her nosebleed patient. True to what Olivia had told her, the clotting agent was working and his bleeding had stopped. She packed his nose and decided to keep him there to make sure the bleeding didn't start up again. Hopefully within an hour he'd be on his way, with instructions to see a specialist about his inability to appropriately clot.

They'd gotten X-rays back on the upper-respiratory patient, which fortunately revealed no pneumonia, just a bad case of bronchitis. She sent the older woman on her way with antibiotics and an inhaler, and a note to follow up with her personal physician.

Since she actually had a minute to breathe, she went to grab an energy drink. She had downed that when her phone buzzed.

It was Tucker. *In the waiting area. You busy?*

She rolled her eyes. She hadn't seen him in a couple days. Conflicting schedules and all. But he had kept in touch and they'd talked.

But now, to just show up here? For some reason he must think she worked in an office, and he could drop by anytime. She was going to have to set him straight about that.

Like now, when she had those few minutes to breathe. She headed out to the waiting area where he stood at the desk talking to Charlene, the intake coordinator.

He looked up when he saw her and smiled.

So typical. He wore loose jeans, a long-sleeved cotton shirt pushed up to the elbows, and he looked gorgeous.

She, on the other hand, had her hair pushed behind her ears and her scrubs were covered in . . . God only knew what. She felt disgusting.

"Hey," he said, heading over to her. "I was in the area so I thought I'd drop by."

"I'm really busy. You should call or text and make an appointment."

He laughed. "I haven't fallen or torn anything up, Doc. I don't need an ER appointment."

"That's not what I meant."

"Oh. You meant like an appointment for a date. Well, aren't you all important."

She shook her head. "That's not what I meant, either."

Her hair had fallen in her face and he tucked the strand behind her ear. "Having a rough day?"

His voice was soft and comforting and she was being a bitch.

Her shitty day was not his fault. "It's been busy."

"I can go. Why don't you call me when you get off work?"

He turned to walk away but she grabbed his wrist. "No. It's okay. I'd like you to stay. I have a patient I have to deal with first, but . . . stay."

His gaze melted her, made her wish they were anywhere but here right now.

"Okay. I'll just hang out here."

"No. Come back with me. There's a lounge you can wait in."

He smiled. "Sure."

She walked him back to the doctors' lounge. No one was in there—of course—because it was just that kind of day.

"There's a vending machine. It has soda and water and snacks. And a TV with a sports channel."

"I'm good for now."

She looked up at him. "I'll just check on that patient and be right back. If I'm not—"

He put his hands on her arms. "Aubry. I'm a big boy. I can take care of myself. If you get busy, don't worry about me, okay?"

"Okay."

He brushed his lips against hers. "I'll either see you soon or I'll talk to you later."

She nodded, then hurried off. She ran into Max on her way to the patient's room.

"CT scan is ordered. I was just going to arrange to have the patient taken in."

"All right. Let me know when we have the results."

After Max walked off, she finished charting her patients' records, then went back to check on incoming.

Those were all handled, so she headed back to the lounge.

Tucker was in there playing a game on his phone.

"You're still here."

He stood and slid his phone in his pocket. "You weren't gone long."

"I'm waiting on test results for a patient."

"How long will that take?"

"Maybe an hour."

He looked around. "Got a broom closet we can fool around in?"

She laughed. "That stuff only happens on those television shows."

"What? You've never gotten it on in the hospital?"

"Uh, no."

He took her hand and led her out of the lounge. "You're doing it all wrong, then, Dr. Ross."

"What are you doing?"

"Finding us a closet or one of those—what do you call them— on-call rooms?"

She tugged at his hand, horrified that he'd even consider the notion. "Tucker. We cannot do this."

He didn't stop, until they ran into Katie.

"Hey, where are you two headed? And I'm Katie, by the way," she said to Tucker.

"Tucker. Nice to meet you, Katie."

"Back to the lounge," Aubry said.

"Actually, we're looking for some privacy," Tucker said.

Katie's eyes widened, then she grinned. "How fun for the two of you. I'd suggest room thirty-four at the end of hallway two. Unless we're slammed, they never place patients that far away. It's very private, and no one will come looking for you there."

"And how do you know that?" Aubry asked.

Katie just gave her a crooked smile, then retrieved a granola bar from her pocket. "You two have fun."

"Thanks," Tucker said. "Now where's this hallway and room thirty-four?"

Aubry shook her head. "No way."

"Fine. I'll just ask for directions, but then it won't be so private."

"Are you serious about this?"

He let go of her wrist. "Clock's ticking, Doc. And we can just kiss a little if you're afraid about being caught. Nothing has to happen that you don't want to happen."

She could definitely use a few minutes of kissing. Tucker always managed to relax her, and her day had been frenetic at best. "Fine."

She took his hand and led him around several corners and down a long hallway until they got to the last room on the right, room thirty-four.

"Jesus. This is far away. Do you really have this many patients?"

"Sometimes. Especially in the winter, during flu season. We get jammed then. But right now? No."

"Good." He closed the door, then pushed her against it and laid

his mouth on hers in a deep, passionate kiss that made her forget
all about her lousy day. All she thought about was Tucker's hands
on her hips, his fingertips squeezing into her flesh as his kiss made
her feel boneless. She sagged against him and he drew her scrubs
up, placing those awesome hands of his over her skin. And when
he dipped his hand inside her pants, sliding his fingers into her
underwear to cup her sex, she had a fleeting thought to object.

That thought vanished in an instant, arousal taking over when
he whispered against her ear.

"Let me make you come, Aubry."

"Yes." It's what she wanted, what she needed more than anything
right now. And maybe a small part of her recognized the danger in
the situation, which only served to heighten her sense of arousal.

He stroked her sex, his fingers dipping inside of her while he
used the heel of his hand to rub against her clit. It wasn't going to
take her long. She was ready, so ready to come. And his words only
made it easier.

"You're so hot, so wet, Aubry. I want to feel you come apart for me,
to feel your pussy squeezing my fingers. After you go off, I'm going to
push you up against the door, drag your pants down and shove my
cock in you. I'm going to fuck you hard and fast until I come."

His words shot right through her, making her quiver. She shuddered, lifting her hips against his fingers until a shock of pure
pleasure burst inside of her. She gripped his hand and rocked
against it as she came. He grabbed her chin and turned her, kissing
her, absorbing her orgasmic cries.

She was still shaking when he flipped her around, pushed her
against the door and jerked her pants down. She heard the sounds
of his zipper and the tear of the condom wrapper. Suddenly she felt
his warm body pressed against hers, and then he was positioning
himself against her, inside her, making her want to scream with
delight as he thrust.

Instead, she bit down on her bottom lip, forcing herself to remain silent as he drove into her. But when he snaked his hands around her front and into her top, pulled her bra down to grab hold of her breast, she couldn't help the moan that escaped.

"I love fucking you like this," he said, pumping hard and fast into her. "Just the two of us, knowing exactly what we both want and taking it, no matter who's around."

She'd never been more aroused, more in need than she was at this moment. She reached down to touch herself.

"That's it," Tucker said. "Make yourself come again, Aubry. Let me feel it, and then I'll come inside of you."

She knew they needed to hurry, that someone could hear them, could walk in here at any moment. That realization only increased her need, her desire to get off with Tucker inside of her.

"I feel your pussy gripping me tight," Tucker said, his voice all hard edges and soft seduction. "Now make me come."

She was panting, nearly breathless as she neared the edge. Tucker teased her lips with his thumb. She licked it, but then when he slipped his thumb inside her mouth, she sucked, rewarded with his harsh groan. He shoved his cock in deeper and she climaxed, waves of orgasm washing over her. She didn't care where she was then, because all she needed at that moment was him, his cock pumping hard into her as he came and giving her the best orgasm she'd ever had, consuming her in its intensity.

She flattened her palms on the door as she fought to catch her breath. Tucker laid against her back, kissing her neck, his breathing as raspy as hers.

"Wow," was all she could manage, her throat had gone utterly dry.

"Yeah," he said. "Wow for sure."

When they disengaged, they tucked into the bathroom and cleaned up. She straightened her scrubs, fixed her hair and checked herself in the mirror. Other than rosy cheeks, she looked . . . normal.

Good.

"I need to get back to work," she said.

"Okay." He drew her into his arms and planted a long, hot kiss on her that, under normal circumstances, would have led them back to bed. But since they hadn't actually started in bed, and they weren't at home, she reluctantly pulled away.

"Tucker . . ."

"Yeah, I know." He gave her a lopsided smile. "Oh, I actually stopped by to find out when your next day off is."

She thought about it for a second. "Tuesday."

He grinned. "Hey, that works out. So's mine. How about a date?"

She laid her hand on his chest. "Sounds perfect."

"I have an out-of-town series coming up, but I'll call you."

"Okay. Can you find your way out the way we came? I think it would be best if—"

He brushed his lips against hers. "Yeah. I can. Bye, Aubry."

"See you later, Tucker."

He slipped out the door and disappeared. She waited a minute, then headed back to the station to retrieve the chart on her patient. Since she hadn't been beeped, she knew there had been no new incoming patients while she'd been . . . otherwise occupied.

The CT results were in on her abdominal patient, so she found Max and they went over treatment options. After she finished there, she went to update the chart.

"You were absent for a while," Katie said, eyeing her with a mix of curiosity and amusement.

"Oh. Uh. Tucker and I grabbed a bite to eat."

Katie let out a snort. "You two might have grabbed a bite, but it was more likely of each other, not food."

Aubry concentrated on the laptop in front of her, ignoring her friend. "I have no idea what you mean."

"What I mean is there are red marks on your neck, and you're wearing a post-sex glow on your face, not an I-had-an-awesome-chicken-sandwich glow."

She turned to Katie. "You are way too observant."

Katie shrugged. "I am when other people are having sex. And here in the hospital? You naughty girl."

An hour ago Aubry would have laughed off the suggestion that she'd have sex in the hospital. Now? "I'm not even going to blush."

"I wouldn't, either. Someone needs to have some fun around here." Katie studied her. "So . . . was it?"

"Was it what?"

"Fun."

She laughed. "It was amazing. Tucker definitely brings out my bad side."

Katie linked her arm in Aubry's. "There's nothing wrong with that. You've been good for way too long. Time to tap into your inner bad girl. Now that you've had fake food, let's go get some of the real stuff before it gets busy in here again."

She followed Katie toward the cafeteria, thinking about what her friend had said.

Is that what she'd done? She'd always followed the straight and narrow. College, then medical school and now her residency, never once deviating from her carefully chosen path. Her father had always told her that her career was vital, and she should never allow anything—or anyone—to distract her.

She never had before. Not that she'd been a saint. But she wasn't a bad girl, never had been. She'd had her share of fun, just never the kind that would get her in trouble.

Tucker, though? He'd tapped into her wild side, the part of her that had fantasized about doing crazy things.

Like having sex in the hospital.

He could be trouble, in so many ways.

TWENTY-FOUR

THEY'D WON ONE GAME AND LOST TWO IN PITTS-burgh. Tucker had pitched one of the losses, and he felt pretty shitty about that.

He knew they weren't going to win every time he pitched, but still, he hadn't been on his game. He'd given up two earned runs. Something had been off and he'd thought about it ever since that game. He still couldn't put his finger on what was wrong, even now as he and the other pitchers ran through warm-ups.

"You're still bugged about that loss the other night."

He looked over at Garrett Scott, who was throwing balls next to him. "Yeah."

"Let it go. It was just one game. You're going to lose a lot of games, Tucker."

"I know that. But my curveball was off that night. My curve is never off."

"Did you talk to Bobby about it?"

That's what he should do. As pitching coach for the Rivers, Bobby Sloan could spot a problem with a pitcher's mechanics better than anyone. "Not yet."

"Do it. Trust me, Bobby will know if there's something off about your curve."

"I will. Thanks."

"And Tucker?"

"Yeah."

"Let go of that game. It's one down, and a lot more coming up. You let that one get in your head, it'll fuck you up for the rest of the season."

He nodded. "You're right about that. Consider it gone."

Garrett laughed. "If only everyone took my advice so easily."

"What a crock, Garrett. Who listens to you?" Tommy Mahoney asked.

"All of my peers should, Mahoney. Like you. Because I'm full of wisdom."

"What you're full of is shit," Tommy said with a laugh.

Garrett shook his head. "And that's why you're a relief pitcher, and not a starter."

"No. I'm a relief pitcher because someone has to come in and save the game after you've fucked it up."

Now it was Tucker's turn to chime in. "Come on, Mahoney. You know that's not how it works. You come in and take over when we have to take a piss."

"And you can suck my dick, Cassidy."

Several of the other pitchers came over, both starters and relievers, and they all spent several minutes giving each other shit. It was a good stress reliever, and something they did a lot to ease tension. No one ever took offense since they all respected each other's work. Tucker relied on middle inning relievers and closers.

Without them to save games, he'd be toast and he knew it. So did Garrett and the other starting pitchers.

"All right, assholes." Bobby Sloan, the pitching coach, came over and broke up their jawing session. "Now that you're all done insulting each other, how about you shut up and start putting up?"

They all dispersed and walked away to throw, but Tucker hesitated, then headed over to where Bobby and the assistants stood to watch. "Bobby. Have you got a minute?"

"Yeah. What's up?"

"I think there might be something off with my curve. I felt it the other night during the game."

"Okay. Let's set you up with a catcher and I'll watch you throw. Mix in some of your other pitches, too."

Bobby pulled one of the catchers over to the mound, as well as one of his teammates to stand in as batter, which made it easier for Tucker to visualize the strike zone. Tucker was already warmed up, so he took the catcher's signals and threw as if in a game situation, trying to throw strikes.

He threw several pitches, several of which the batter hit. He missed quite a few as well, but Tucker didn't pay attention to that. He wanted to concentrate more on the style of his curveball, the mechanics of getting the ball where he wanted it to go.

"Okay, that's enough. Thanks, guys," Bobby said to the batter and catcher.

Bobby walked over to him. "The pitches looked good to me, Cassidy. I don't see anything off with your mechanics. The curve looked like it was supposed to. Your body was in the right position and the ball sailed normally, no matter what pitch you threw."

That was good to hear. "Okay, thanks."

"Hey, you had an off night. Sometimes it's the weather or the crowd. Sometimes, especially with the curveball, it just ain't gonna work that night, no matter how you throw it, ya know?"

Tucker scratched the side of his nose. "Well, that's the problem. I don't know about that. My curve always works. Except that night."

Bobby laughed and slapped him on the back. "You're young. You've had a lot of success and very little failure. Welcome to the big leagues, kid. And get used to some of that failure. It's going to happen. But it's good that you evaluate it. Keep doing that, you'll do great things."

"Thanks, Coach." He walked away to join the rest of the pitchers for practice.

Maybe Bobby was right and he was overthinking the other night. He'd suffered losses before and had never thought anything of it. Sometimes the other team just had hot bats, and other times he'd gotten behind in the count too many times. He'd never let a loss bother him like this one did, but he'd always been confident in his curve. It was his trademark pitch and it worked for him.

He needed to shake it off, because tomorrow night he was pitching again.

And he needed to be able to count on his curveball.

TWENTY-FIVE

AUBRY GOT UP EARLY ON HER DAY OFF, KNOWING SHE
had to catch up on studying, laundry and paperwork. She also had
to get her car licensed, so she took care of that detail before she
forgot—again. She worked quickly and managed to finish everything on her to-do list before heading over to her parents' house to
have lunch with them.

She walked in the door and found her parents outside on the
terrace.

"Hi, sweetheart." Her mother got up and came over to give her
a hug and a kiss on the cheek. "It's such a beautiful day, we thought
we'd have lunch outside."

"It is nice out here."

Her dad came over and kissed her cheek. "You look pretty today."

"Thanks, Dad." She'd worn capris and a short-sleeved top along
with comfortable sandals, because she wanted to go shopping after
lunch.

Shopping for her date with Tucker tonight, though he hadn't told her where they were going.

She considered telling her parents about Tucker, then thought better of it.

Not yet. She wasn't even sure where they were headed, and her mother was so fixated on her having a relationship, while her father was the exact opposite.

Definitely not yet.

"How is everything at work?" her dad asked.

"Fine. Busy as usual."

"Any interesting cases?"

She smiled. "Nothing we want to get into over lunch."

Her mother grimaced. "Yes, please, Clyde. My stomach can't handle all that blood and gore while we're trying to eat."

Her father looked at Aubry. "This is why I always took you to see the horror movies and left your mother at home."

Aubry laughed.

They ate lunch and caught up on family gossip and news. One of her cousins had gotten engaged, which surprised Aubry, but she was so thrilled for her.

"I'm so happy for Jade. I didn't know she and Mark were serious."

"Neither did I," her mother said. "But Farrah tells me he was so romantic about the proposal. He took her to the park and proposed in the rose garden."

Aubry melted. "Oh, how sweet."

"Seems a little soon to me," her father said. "And Jade is still working on her master's degree. I hope they don't rush things to where it screws up her plans for her future."

Her mother waved her hand back and forth. "Oh, Clyde. Where's your sense of romance? I'm sure the two of them will figure that all out."

"She has to think of her future financial well-being, and that means her career. She needs to finish school and get her career established, just like Aubry."

Her mother leaned back in her chair. "What if Aubry fell in love with someone tomorrow?"

Her father shook his head. "Aubry's head needs to stay focused on finishing her residency, applying for a fellowship. Plenty of time later for love, marriage and babies. It's too soon."

Nothing like being talked about as if she wasn't in the room. She loved her father with all her heart, but his thoughts on career versus home and family were awfully rigid. She understood he wanted her to be independent and have a career, but there had to be room for her to have a personal life as well.

"I'm sure I could handle both, Dad."

He shot her a look of disbelief. "When would you even have time? You work all the time, and when you aren't doing that, you're studying and keeping up with managing your caseload. There's so much to learn being a doctor, Aubry. No. There's no time for romance in your life. Not now, anyway. You'll have time for that later."

It was as if he'd dismissed the notion she could have a relationship with someone. Like he'd banned the thought. He was treating her like a child all over again, telling her what she could and couldn't have.

Well, screw that.

She wanted to blurt out that she'd found plenty of time for romance in the past month with Tucker, but that would be a stupid thing to do and would set her up for failure. If she wanted to introduce Tucker as someone she was . . .

What exactly was she doing with Tucker, anyway? She hadn't—they hadn't defined it. And did it matter? Did it matter to her? It hadn't until now. The only reason she was even thinking of it was because her father's objections to mixing career and dating were really pissing her off, making her want to fling her relationship with Tucker in his face and show him that she could manage her career and a private life just fine, thank you very much.

But not today.

Still . . .

"You know, Dad, it's the twenty-first century, and women juggle career and relationship quite well these days. In fact, many very smart women manage to have successful careers, a healthy marriage and children. Shockingly, all at the same time."

"Well, of course. And someday I'm sure you'll be able to do that."

She pinned him with a look. "But for some reason I couldn't handle that now?"

He calmly took a sip of his iced tea, seemingly unaware that Aubry was about to spring from her seat and strangle her father in anger. Instead, he shook his head.

"Residency is a full-time job, a night and day endeavor. You're on call, you have cases to research, and your exams to prepare for. I can't see how you could successfully handle a relationship, let alone marriage and family."

He had no faith in her ability to manage her time. Like she could only deal with one thing. "Several of the residents are married. One has a child."

"And I'm sure it's quite a juggling act for them and very difficult."

And now he was making judgments about her friends' lives. Did she even know this man at all? She started to argue, but her mother shook her head, making her swallow the argument.

After lunch, her father kissed her good-bye and told her he had some calls to make, which left her alone with her mother. They carried the plates into the kitchen and laid them in the sink, where Aubry helped her mother with the dishes.

"Don't take your father's words to heart, Aubry. He can be so single-minded on some topics, especially where you're concerned. But you know he only has your best interests at heart."

"He made me angry, Mom. It's like he doesn't trust me to know what's best for my career. For my own life. I'm not a child anymore. I can make my own decisions. And how dare he presume to know how difficult someone else's life is? People he doesn't even know."

Her mother swept her hand up and down Aubry's arm. "Well, it's not the first time he's done that, and not just with you. He can be . . . difficult at times."

Aubry choked out a laugh. "Difficult? That's an understatement. I don't know how you can keep from throwing plates at him."

Her mother smiled. "He can also be sweet and kind and very open-minded."

Aubry huffed out a sigh of disgust. "I haven't seen much of that where I'm concerned."

"I know you're perfectly capable of handling your own life, sweetheart. You're an adult now. You have been for a while. Your dad, though, still sees you as his baby girl. He only wants the best things for you. He wants you to succeed."

She leaned against the kitchen counter. "And he thinks I can't do that without his guidance. Or maybe I should say his bullying tactics."

"Oh, honey. He's not a bully."

She shot her mother a look. "Isn't he? What would happen if I brought a guy over to meet the two of you? Could you imagine how that would go over?"

Her mother tilted her head, giving Aubry a questioning look. "Is there a guy?"

She trusted her mother above anyone else. "There might be. I don't know yet."

"If you have a young man you want us to meet, you let me know and I'll prepare your father for it. I'll make sure he's on his best behavior."

Aubry raised a brow. "And how will you do that? Are you going to drug him?"

Her mother laughed. "No. But trust me, I do wield some influence where your father is concerned. You have nothing to worry about. He might come across as brusque and bullish at times, but, Aubry, he loves you."

She sighed. "I know he does."

"So bring your young man over for dinner, and let's get your father used to the idea that you're a grown woman who's handling her own life just fine."

She'd think about it. In the meantime, she'd push thoughts of her father's opinions aside and concentrate on her date with Tucker tonight.

TWENTY-SIX

AFTER SPENDING THE AFTERNOON WITH HER MOTHER, who decided to go shopping with her, Aubry dashed home just in time to get ready for her date. Tucker had told her he'd pick her up at six and she could dress casual.

She'd bought a new blouse for tonight, so she put on her tight jeans, wedge sandals and the button-down silky red top, with a black tank underneath. She did her makeup, brushed out her hair, and finished off the look with her favorite lip gloss just as the doorbell rang.

She opened the door and couldn't help the sigh of pleasure as Tucker stood there wearing dark jeans and a navy blue button-down shirt. His hair was getting a little long, which made it curl at the ends, making her want to sift her fingers through its thick softness. Unable to resist, she stepped up to him, slid her hand in his hair and kissed him.

He wrapped an arm around her, tugged her close and deepened the kiss. She moaned against his mouth.

When they broke apart, she read the heated passion in his eyes.

"Keep that up and I'll never be able to give you your surprise tonight."

She invited him in and closed the door. "Ooh. There's a surprise?"

"There is."

"Now I'm excited."

His lips curved. "I hope you like it. I thought it might be fun."

"Are we going bowling again?"

He laughed. "Not bowling."

"Now I'm curious and excited."

"Good. Let's go."

He drove them into Clayton, to a shopping center where he parked and they got out.

When she saw where they were headed, she turned to him. "Really?"

"Yeah."

She grinned as they stepped inside, having figured out what was happening. It was a kitchen setup, but definitely industrial, with a long stainless steel island, a stove and lots of tools. Tools she was definitely unfamiliar with.

There was no one else here yet.

"We'll just sit in the middle," Tucker said, leading her to a spot in the center of the stainless steel island.

They were going to take a cooking class. She sat on the stool, then pivoted to face him. "What made you come up with this idea?"

"I figured since neither of us knew how to cook, maybe we could get some tips here. And, you know, stay in more often."

When he waggled his brows, she laughed. "I like where your mind goes, Tucker Cassidy."

"I figured you might. Plus, you know, we'd also go hungry less often."

She shook her head. "Always thinking with your stomach."

He leaned into her. "Either my stomach or my cock. Mostly my cock."

She laughed.

The instructor came out, a tall, energetic and super friendly woman named Patricia, who informed them that tonight they'd learn how to make an appetizer, main course and dessert.

Aubry looked around. "Where are the rest of the people?"

"I booked us a private couple's class. More fun that way."

She smiled at him. "Let's hope you still think it's fun when we get to the end of the class."

He pulled her against him. "Oh, it'll definitely be fun. I can feel it."

She liked his confidence.

The first thing they were going to learn was how to make pasta.

"Whoa," she said. "This sounds daunting."

Tucker put his arm around her. "You're a doctor. You do amazing things to help people every day, Aubry. Surely you're not going to be intimidated by a little pasta, are you?"

She inhaled a deep breath. "I guess not."

They put on aprons, Aubry rolled up her sleeves and they got to work on the eggs and flour, cutting the eggs into the flour and making the dough for the pasta. Aubry was intrigued by the pasta machine, and she watched with delight as Tucker had fun rolling the dough through the machine. They seemed to ace this part, and she set the pasta on the rack to dry.

She looked at him. "That seemed to actually work."

"It did, didn't it?" he said with a grin.

For the appetizer, they sliced the caps off mushrooms and dug out the insides to make stuffed mushrooms, mixing in cheese, garlic and bread crumbs before putting them in the oven to bake.

For dessert they were making almond biscotti, which made

Aubry's mouth water and her stomach grumble. She decided to start that, while Tucker worked on the spaghetti sauce and meatballs. It was truly a team effort, and the smells were divine.

Fortunately, the cooking school also provided wine, an awesome bonus. She sipped wine and made her log roll for the biscotti, tucked it into the oven and turned to see if she could help Tucker, who seemed to be mastering his sauce. She grabbed a spoon and slid it into the pan for a taste.

"This is delicious," she said.

He looked at her. "Of course it is."

She laughed, but she admired his confidence. She also believed that confidence would be what it would take to become a decent cook. You had to believe you could do it. It was a lot like medicine. Not for sissies. You had to believe in yourself.

She could do this. *They* could do this.

She helped him with the meatballs, and after those were ready, they added them to the simmering sauce while she went back to finish up the biscotti.

Their instructor was fantastic, not hovering, but giving direction and staying nearby to give them pointers, advising them how to manage the cook times and which items to prep at what times. Since it was just the two of them, it gave Aubry peace of mind to know Patricia wasn't going to let them screw this up.

When their stuffed mushrooms were finished, they actually had time to sit and savor their wine and appetizer together. She fed one to Tucker, feeling nervous as he chewed, then swallowed.

"This is really good. Here, try one."

She tasted it, as surprised as he was that they had cooked something that had turned out so well.

"It is good."

"You two are funny," Patricia said, tasting one of their mushrooms.

"Why?"

"You seem surprised that you can cook."

Aubry laughed. "We can make eggs and bacon. That's about it."

"Don't forget we can also do toast," Tucker added.

"Right," Aubry said. "Toast."

"Buy some cookbooks and start experimenting," Patricia said. "You might surprise yourselves with all the dishes you can make."

Since her biscotti was done, and it smelled amazing, Aubry set a pot filled with water on to boil, then filled it with the spaghetti noodles. It wasn't long before the main course was ready, homemade noodles and meatballs covered with sauce.

"I'm going to be honest with you here," she said to Tucker.

"Honest about what?"

"I've never been so nervous about anything in my entire life."

He gave her a quick kiss, then raised his fork to hers. "Here's to testing our culinary prowess."

They both tasted at the same time.

"This doesn't suck," he said.

The noodles were cooked well, and the meatballs were flavorful. The sauce was great, too. They might not be experts and this dish certainly wasn't restaurant quality, but for a first effort, Tucker was right. It didn't suck.

"We might actually be able to handle this cooking thing," she said.

"Yeah."

"Or maybe it's just the wine talking."

Patricia came by and filled a small plate with their main course and took a taste.

"It's not the wine talking. You both did good."

Aubry felt like she'd just aced her MCATs all over again. "Yes!" She high-fived Tucker.

"Now enjoy your dinner," Patricia said. "And the wine."

"Thanks," Tucker said. "We will."

Aubry wasn't a foodie. She enjoyed eating, but most of the time she was at work and food was just whatever she could grab to keep from starving. Tonight, though, she savored every bite, wishing she could box it up, take it home and keep it forever.

She'd never been a cook. She'd spent all her time at the hospital, studying, or, before that, in school, so cooking had never been something she'd mastered. Now, though, she felt like it was a challenge she could devote more time to.

"I'm going to order some cookbooks and start fixing meals for us to eat," she said.

"That'll require gadgets," Tucker said, sliding another piece of meatball into his mouth.

"You mean like pots and pans? I have some of those."

"This homemade pasta is good. I'd like to work on that again. And this sauce is pretty damn good, too."

She took a sip of her wine and nodded. "The sauce is incredible. The fresh herbs really made a difference. I wish I had a house with a big yard so I could have an herb garden."

He laid his fork down and picked up his glass of wine to take a sip. "What's stopping you from buying a house?"

She shrugged. "I don't know. It's not something I've ever thought about doing. It's just me, and I don't really need the space. The condo has always been adequate for my needs."

"Except you can't grow a garden in those tiny backyards that come with a condo."

"So true. What about you?"

"Same thing. Just me, and I lease the condo in case I get traded. In my business, unless you know you're going to be with one team for the long haul, you don't set down roots."

"Good point." And just the thought of Tucker being traded caused an ache in her stomach. She was enjoying her time with him.

Maybe too much?

That was something she didn't intend to think about tonight. Not when she was having so much fun.

She took another swallow of wine and decided to ponder the thought of a house instead. She'd always intended to buy a house after she got settled . . . somewhere. After residency, when she figured out where she'd end up practicing medicine.

What prevented her from buying now, though? She could always sell if she decided to move for work. Just the thought of being able to plant a garden, grow some tomatoes and herbs, excited her.

It was a sudden epiphany. She could sell her condo and buy a house.

"What are you thinking about over there? You went quiet all of a sudden."

"Oh, sorry. I was thinking about how I've put things on hold until after my residency. Things like buying a house. And then wondering why I couldn't just do that now."

He finished off his glass of wine, then set it on the table. "No reason you couldn't buy now, is there? Unless you're going to be moving."

"I could apply for a fellowship to a hospital in another state. But I like the hospital I'm working in. And St. Louis is my home."

"So your ultimate goal is to stay here."

She'd never thought in those terms before, had always kept herself in the here and now, refusing to think that far down the road. "I don't know. Maybe that is what I'm saying."

"So buy yourself a house, Aubry. Do whatever the hell it is you want to do. You've worked your ass off these past few years in medical school and residency. Isn't it time you reap the rewards of that?"

She stared at him.

He smiled back at her. "What?"

"No one has ever told me to just go for it before, to do whatever I want to do."

He leaned forward and grasped her hands. "I find that hard to believe."

"It's the truth."

"Then let me say it again. You should do what you want to do. Whatever it is you want to do. Because you deserve to have whatever makes you happy."

Something inside her heart clenched. She didn't know what it was, and sitting here with a cooking instructor monitoring them wasn't the place to dissect it.

Or maybe she did know what it was, and this either wasn't the time or place, or she wasn't ready to face it yet. So she tucked it back into her heart and brushed her lips across Tucker's.

"Thank you."

"You're welcome. Now how about that biscotti?"

TWENTY-SEVEN

TUCKER NEVER THOUGHT HE'D HAVE HIS TRUCK PILED
up with fancy pots and pans and gadgets to make food. But as he
carted all the boxes into the house, he had to admit, he was pretty
excited.

Now he just had to actually use it all. Which he would, right
away, since his brothers Barrett and Flynn were coming over. He
and Aubry had decided they should cook together, and when he
told her his brothers were flying in for a visit, she suggested they
cook for them.

His brothers definitely liked to eat, just like he did. They'd
make good guinea pigs for him and Aubry.

Since their cooking class two weeks ago, he and Aubry had bought
a few cookbooks and tried out some recipes. Nothing too fancy, but
they'd made some dishes. Successful ones, too. But his supply of cook-
ware and accessories was limited, and they always seemed to end up at
his place, so he had decided to do a little shopping and stock up.

He might actually have a knack for this cooking thing. If nothing else, he'd eat a lot less take-out food. And that wasn't a bad thing.

He had everything washed, dried and put away when the doorbell rang. It was Aubry, holding two bags of groceries.

"There's more in the car," she said. "If you'd like to go get those, I'll start putting these away."

"Okay." He went out and grabbed the rest of the bags, shut the trunk of her car and came back inside.

"I'm making guesses as to where you want this stuff," she said as he laid the bags on the island.

"Wherever you want to put things is fine."

They unloaded all the bags, then Aubry leaned against the island.

"Okay. I got amazing salmon steaks. I'm already hungry just thinking about it."

"Me, too."

"When do your brothers get in?"

He grabbed his phone and checked the time. "They should be here soon."

"I also bought beer. Like, lots of beer. You said the guys like beer."

He laughed. "Yeah, I noticed the beer. I already had some, but they drink like fish. I think we'll have plenty."

"I got wine, too, which is chilling in the fridge. I should probably start the marinade for the salmon."

She started toward the fridge, but he grabbed her hand. "There's no hurry on that, Aubry. You should open the wine, pour yourself a glass and relax."

She looked at him like he'd just sprouted two heads. "Relax? We're cooking for your brothers tonight. How am I supposed to relax? I'm still a novice at this cooking thing, Tucker."

"And my brothers eat hot dogs from the microwave. They're hardly culinary connoisseurs. So . . . chill, okay?"

She took a deep breath, then let it out. "Clearly, I'm slightly nervous about this. You and I playing in the kitchen together is one thing. Cooking for someone else is different."

He pulled her toward him, brushing his fingers against her hand. "They're not someone else. They're my brothers. You could fix them a bowl of cereal and they'd be happy. Just relax."

"Fine. I'm opening the wine."

He smiled, shook his head and grabbed a beer as she went for the wine. Just then, the doorbell rang.

"Get your wine. I'll get the door."

He opened the door to his brothers Barrett and Flynn.

"Hey, asshole," Barrett said, but then hugged him as he stepped inside.

"Hey yourself, dickhead."

"I don't smell anything, other than you," Flynn said, hugging him. "Is dinner ready yet?"

He hugged Flynn. "We haven't started yet. Waiting for you to pitch in."

They laid their bags inside the front door.

"I can cook a masterpiece of a meal for you with hot dogs and a cucumber," Flynn said. "Let me at your kitchen."

Barrett snorted. "I'd rather go for fast food than eat something you've cooked, Flynn."

"You've obviously never eaten my cooking," Flynn said, he and Barrett following Tucker into the kitchen. "I'm good at this shit."

Aubry was leaning against the counter, glass of wine in her hand. "Aubry, you met Barrett before. This is my brother Flynn."

She pushed off the counter and shook Flynn's hand. "Nice to meet you, Flynn."

"You too, Aubry. I hear you and my brother have become master chefs."

She laughed. "Hardly. I hope Tucker didn't set your expectations too high for this meal. We're very new at cooking." She turned to Tucker. "Maybe I should have bought hot dogs as a backup, just in case."

"Don't worry, honey," Barrett said. "We're here to help pitch in."

"Yeah, if we were nuking hot dogs," Tucker said. "Which we aren't."

Barrett glared at Tucker. "Screw you. I can cook."

"No, you can make hot dogs, Barrett. I can cook," Flynn said.

"Neither of you can cook." Tucker went to the fridge and grabbed three beers, handing two over to his brothers and keeping one for himself. "Aubry and I are in charge of this meal tonight."

"So Barrett and I will just hang out and look pretty," Flynn said.

"That's what you two are good at," Tucker said. "The hanging out part. Not the pretty part."

Aubry hid her smirk as she followed the three brothers into the living room. If nothing else, this evening should be entertaining. When she'd met Grant and Barrett a while back, she'd been in work mode, treating Tucker for an injury, so she hadn't had much time or focus to truly capture the camaraderie among the brothers. Now, though, and despite a little trepidation about the upcoming dinner she and Tucker were cooking, she intended to relax and enjoy this.

She slid into a spot on the sofa next to Tucker. "Tucker tells me you're in town for one of the kid's school events? Grant's girlfriend's brother, if I recall?"

"Yeah," Flynn said. "Leo plays football, but right now he's playing baseball. His team is in the championships, so we decided since we were both traveling, we'd head over here and catch the championship games."

"How exciting for him."

"No doubt they'll win," Tucker said. "He's developing into a hell of a stud for a kid who didn't play much sports not that long ago."

"Grant's influence," Barrett said to Aubry. "And ours. You can't mix with this family and escape without the sports bug."

"Except for Mia—" Tucker turned to Aubry. "Our little sister. She's in college, and happy to be away from the nonstop sports talk and roughhousing that goes on whenever we're together."

"Does this mean you all play football or baseball whenever you're together?"

"Baseball?" Flynn laughed. "Who'd want to play that pussy game?"

Tucker pinned Flynn with a look. "I will lay you flat and shove a baseball down your throat."

"You could try, but between Barrett and me, you'd be the one eating it."

"Barrett's my twin. He'll take my side."

"Think again," Barrett said to Tucker. "When it comes to football or baseball, you already know what I'll choose."

Aubry laughed. "Poor Tucker." She rubbed his back. "That's okay. I might not be able to go up against these two, but there are sharp knives in the kitchen, and I have performed surgery before. I can wield them like weapons."

"Oh, I like you," Flynn said. "You talk a tough game. But can you take a beating in a game situation?"

Being an only child, Aubry never had to deal with sibling teasing. However, she'd borne the brunt of harsh competition from peers and harassment from instructors. She knew better than to back down when a challenge was issued. "Bring it."

"I like her, too," Barrett said. "But what's she doing with you, Tucker?"

"Kiss my ass, Barrett."

With a smile, Aubry pushed off the sofa and stood. "You three can sit here and spar. I'm going to go fix the sauce for the salmon."

Tucker moved to stand. "I'll help you."

She shook her head. "You hang out here. This is a one-person job."

TUCKER SAT BACK AND DRANK HIS BEER, HAPPY TO have his brothers—and Aubry—here.

"I need to stretch," Flynn said, standing. "Let's go out back so I can walk around."

"This is what happens when you get old and take too many hits," Barrett said, standing to follow him.

"Fuck you. And I can still put you down."

"You can try."

Tucker shook his head, grinned and stopped in the kitchen to grab three more beers. He pulled Aubry into his arms and kissed her, lingering for a long, satisfying kiss, but not too long. The last thing he wanted was for his dick to get hard. His brothers would never let him live that down.

When he pulled away, she smiled up at him.

"I like your brothers," she said, laying her palms flat on his chest.

"If you do, you're the only one. Besides my parents."

She laughed and patted his chest. "Go outside with them."

"Are you sure? I don't mind hanging in here to help you."

"You can help when it's time to cook the salmon and make the sides. I've got this covered right now."

"Okay."

He kissed her again, unable to stop himself from deepening the kiss, pulling her tighter against him.

"Hey, you two. Knock that off," Barrett said. "We need beer out here. You can make out later."

Aubry pulled away. "Go."

Tucker smiled at her. "Yes, ma'am."

He grabbed the beers and headed out back to the deck, where Barrett and Tucker had already grabbed chairs.

"Can't keep your hands off of her, can you?" Barrett asked. "Not that I blame you. She's pretty."

"She's more than pretty," Flynn said, accepting the beer Tucker handed him. "A doctor, too, huh? Barrett told me about your trip to the ER. She's the one who treated you?"

Tucker sat in one of the chairs and popped the top on his can of beer. "Yeah. She's a hell of a lot smarter than I am."

"Yeah, well, who isn't?" Flynn winked at him, then took a long swallow of beer.

More than accustomed to nonstop insults from his brothers, Tucker ignored that one from Flynn.

"Are you gonna be able to make Leo's game tomorrow?" Barrett asked him.

Tucker nodded. "It's a day game, and early enough before I have to report to the stadium that I should be able to see most, if not all, of it."

"We'll hold a seat for you," Flynn said. "Unless some hot mom shows up. Then you're on your own."

Tucker laughed. "Always thinking of family, aren't you, Flynn?"

"You know it."

"Where are you two headed after this stop?"

"Flying out to San Francisco to look at some property for Flynn," Barrett said.

Tucker raised a brow. "Are you looking to buy a house, Flynn?"

"Eventually. Things are pretty settled with the Sabers now, so I might consider that. We'll look at houses. But this is commercial property."

"Really. Are you thinking of investing?"

"He's thinking of opening a restaurant," Barrett said.

Tucker turned in his chair to face Flynn. "No shit."

"Thinking about it."

"I had no idea you were even interested in doing something like that. And why?"

Flynn shrugged. "I like food."

Tucker laughed. "Come on. No bullshit."

Flynn leaned forward in his chair, rolling the can of beer around in his hands. "It's something I've been toying with for a while now. San Francisco extended my contract and considers me a franchise player. I'm staying put there, and I want to put my signature on the place. Plus, I seriously like food. And I *can* cook, assholes."

"But you wouldn't be the chef there or anything," Barrett said.

"Of course not, dipshit. You hire an experienced chef to run your restaurant. But it's a way for me to stay connected to the city."

Tucker was impressed, though he shouldn't be. As the oldest Cassidy, Flynn had always had the smarts, the leadership ability and the ambition to do anything he wanted in life. That he also loved football had been an added bonus for the family.

"Do you need investors?" Tucker asked. "If you do, hit me up. I might be interested."

"Thanks. I'll let you know."

Tucker stood. "I don't know about you guys, but I'm getting hungry. I'm going to head inside to help Aubry with dinner."

Flynn got up. "Let's all go help."

"You can all cook," Barrett said. "I'll put myself in charge of drinks."

"Taking on the hard tasks again?" Tucker asked as they walked inside.

"You know me. Always willing to fall on the grenade."

Tucker shook his head and followed his brothers inside.

TWENTY-EIGHT

DINNER WAS A ROUSING SUCCESS, THOUGH AUBRY
knew she and Tucker couldn't take all the credit. Flynn had pitched
in, and despite Tucker giving his brother a hard time, she had to
admit Flynn knew his way around a kitchen. He'd decided to put
himself in charge of the grilled vegetables. She'd handed them
over to him, and he'd sliced them, seasoned them and prepared
them with meticulousness, then baked them until they were a golden,
crisp perfection.

She leaned against the counter, watching in awe.

"How did you learn to do that?"

He shrugged. "Our mom is a great cook, so you sit around
talking with her enough, you pick up a few things. Plus, I'm a big
fan of food and I hate takeout. So I've practiced at home."

"I'd say you know what you're doing."

He looked out the window where Tucker was busy with the

grill, Barrett talking to him. "Don't tell my brothers. I have a reputation as a badass."

She laughed. "Your secret is safe with me."

She'd prepared the seasoned potatoes, and those were ready just as Tucker came in with the grilled salmon. She'd also tried her hand at the topping sauce for the salmon, a honey mustard glaze that she hoped was as good as it sounded.

It had been a very unusual experience to say the least. She'd fully expected Tucker and his brothers to sit in the living room, drink beer and talk or watch sports, or possibly hang out outside. Despite Tucker's intention to assist her with this meal, she'd figured he'd want to catch up with his brothers, and she wouldn't have minded cooking by herself.

What she hadn't expected was for all of them to roll up their sleeves and help her. Tucker handled grilling the salmon, and Barrett had washed all the prep dishes.

It was definitely a team effort.

She opened another bottle of wine and set it on the dining room table to let it breathe while they laid the food out and set the table.

Barrett was the one who held her chair out for her. She turned to him and smiled. "Thanks."

"It's the least I can do for the beautiful woman who made this amazing meal for me."

"Quit hitting on my girlfriend, Barrett," Tucker said, nudging his brother aside to sit next to Aubry.

Tucker had called her his girlfriend. In front of his brothers. That was fairly monumental, especially for a guy. Aubry was touched by his display.

"Thank you all so much for the help," she said. "I hope you enjoy the meal."

"It looks great, and smells even better," Flynn said. "I know it's going to be good."

"Enough talking," Barrett said, lifting his fork. "Let's eat."

They poured wine, and ate. Aubry took a bite of the salmon, which melted on her tongue.

"This turned out perfectly, Tucker," she said. "Just the right amount of grill time."

"It is pretty good," Flynn said. "I like the sauce, too. Is that honey in there?"

Aubry nodded. "It's a pretty simple glaze, with white wine, balsamic vinegar, honey, Dijon mustard and garlic."

Flynn nodded. "It's great. For a little different flavor, you might try marinating your salmon in soy sauce, brown sugar, bourbon and ginger. Add a little lime juice and some garlic, and just a touch of black pepper. It's tangy and really damn good."

Aubry's eyes widened. "That sounds delicious."

Tucker pinned Flynn with a look. "I can't believe you have a recipe in your head."

Flynn shrugged. "I told you. I cook."

"Flynn's thinking of opening a restaurant in San Francisco," Barrett said to Aubry.

"Really?" Aubry asked. "That would be amazing."

Flynn glared at Barrett. "Do you have to tell everyone we know?"

Barrett grinned. "Pretty much, yeah."

"Uh-oh," Aubry said. "Was I not supposed to know? I'm sorry if it's a secret."

"It's not a secret," Flynn said. "I just haven't decided yet if I'm going to do it. After our visit here in St. Louis, we're going to fly out to San Francisco and look at commercial property. I'm still thinking about it, though."

"Opening a restaurant is serious business," Tucker said. "I know a lot of athletes who've done it, but I've heard it's very difficult. Do you have a chef in mind?"

Flynn shook his head. "Right now I'm just considering the

project. First I'll look into location and property. Then we'll take it from there and see what happens."

"I told you, if you need investors, let me know," Tucker said. "I believe anything you put your head and body into, you can make work."

Flynn looked at Tucker, then nodded. "Thanks, Bro. That means a lot."

Aubry loved the look that passed between the brothers. That was a tight bond.

"You're not getting any money from me," Barrett said. "I'm just going to go with you and tell you over and over that it's a dumb idea."

Flynn laughed. "Yeah, I knew I could count on you, Barrett."

"I think it's very exciting," Aubry said to Flynn. "I do wish you luck. You seem passionate about food. I think you could make it work."

"Thanks."

Dinner was a success, and the more time she spent around Tucker's brothers, the more she liked them. Barrett was funny, Flynn was more serious, but still had a good sense of humor. And it was quite obvious that despite all the teasing, they all loved each other very much.

It was also clear that Tucker enjoyed having his brothers around. With them spread out playing sports in different areas of the country, he probably didn't get a chance to see them all that often. So she didn't mind at all that they stayed up very late.

She stifled a yawn and finally stood and said, "I hate to be a terrible partier, but I have an early call tomorrow, so I'm going to bed."

"We should head to bed, too," Flynn said, standing.

She put up a hand. "Don't be ridiculous. Stay up as long as you like. I can guarantee that as a doctor, I fall asleep in seconds and will sleep like the dead. Lessons learned from my internship."

Tucker put his arm around her. "You sure?"

She nodded. "Absolutely. Have fun catching up with your brothers." She kissed him good night, hugged Flynn and Barrett, then took herself to Tucker's bedroom.

She could have gone home to her own condo, but it was late and she'd brought a bag with her scrubs for tomorrow.

Besides, Tucker had asked her to stay, and she wanted to. Something about sleeping next to his body at night had become so natural, so seemingly perfect.

And tonight she was too damn tired to dissect all the reasons why, so she undressed, washed her face and brushed her teeth and crawled into Tucker's bed, pulling up the covers without thinking about their relationship.

Instead, she smiled and turned off the beside lamp, closed her eyes and was instantly asleep.

TWENTY-NINE

"LEO'S GOT A GOOD ARM," TUCKER SAID. "LEFT FIELD is a good position for him. Plus he's fast, so he can run down base hits."

Tucker's brother Grant nodded. "His on-base percentage is decent, too. He's enjoying playing baseball."

Tucker turned to his brother and grinned. "You sound surprised."

"Grant thinks it should be all about football," Leo's older sister Anya said. "Kind of like your other brothers."

"Hey, kid. I didn't say a word."

"It was implied, Barrett." Anya winked at him.

"Actually, he's enjoying both sports," Katrina said. "I'm just happy he's found something that fulfills him. My little brother is a different kid this year."

"Yeah," Anya said. "A lot less surly. And, unfortunately, a lot more outgoing. You can hardly shut him up now. I miss the quiet, hides-in-his-room-all-the-time Leo."

Katrina nudged her sister. "You do not."

Anya gave her sister a quirky smile.

Tucker enjoyed Grant's fiancée Katrina and her siblings. And Grant loved them all, which meant they were family now.

With the pitcher on Leo's team throwing a strikeout to end the inning, they were now up to bat and Tucker waited for Leo to get his turn. He hadn't yet seen him bat, but hoped for something good from Leo and his team. He wasn't disappointed—the first and second batters singled, then the third batter drove in two runs with a double, putting Leo's team up two runs in the bottom of the first inning. The fourth batter grounded out, and Leo was fifth in the order, so he was up next.

"I am so nervous," Katrina said.

Grant took her hand. "He's going to do great, so relax."

Leo took the first pitch, a called strike.

"Oh, God. He's going to suck," Anya said.

"He isn't going to suck," Tucker said. "He's waiting to see what the pitcher's got."

He took the second pitch, a ball up and high. The pitcher for the other team was good, but hadn't settled into his groove yet. He was all over the place in terms of pitch placement, so Leo was being smart in waiting for the right pitch.

Soon it was a full count, and Leo had fouled off about four pitches.

"He's going to strike out, isn't he?" Anya asked.

"No, he's going to line one out to left field."

She looked over at Tucker. "How do you know that?"

"Trust me. I just know."

Two pitches later, Leo launched a double into left field. Everyone stood and yelled his name, clapping loudly.

When Tucker sat, Katrina looked over at him. "You were right. How did you know?"

"Easy. I know what their pitcher was throwing, and based on the way Leo was swinging the bat and hitting those balls foul, it was only a matter of time until he connected."

"I'm impressed," Katrina said.

"Me, too," Anya said.

Grant leaned over his shoulder. "Fucking smartass."

Tucker grinned.

Leo's team ended up winning the game by four runs, a good start to the championship. They met up with him at the entrance to the locker room after the game. Tucker hung back while Leo got hugs from Grant, Katrina and Anya, and a huge pat on the back from Barrett and Flynn. Then he stepped in and shook Leo's hand.

"You did good, kid."

Leo smiled. "Thanks."

"You should probably rethink the whole football thing. Based on your talent, football's a waste of time."

"Hey," Grant said, frowning.

Tucker winked at Leo, who laughed. "Yeah, we should talk about that over pizza."

Tucker and Leo walked away, but not before he heard Grant mumble something about kicking Tucker's ass.

Unfortunately, he couldn't join them for pizza since he had a game of his own to play. So he shook Leo's hand, wished him luck on the rest of his games and said he'd try to get to another, but they'd for sure connect at Grant's house as soon as possible to talk baseball. He said good-bye to his brothers, kissed Katrina on the cheek and hugged Anya, then drove to the ballpark.

He got into uniform and headed out to the mound for warm-ups. He'd been working on all his pitches, but mainly his curve-ball, hoping he'd see improvement on whatever quirk it was that screwed him up on his last game.

He wasn't anxious—he was determined.

Tonight, he was going to win this one.

AUBRY FINISHED WORK AT SEVEN THIRTY, SO SHE cleaned up at the hospital, changed clothes and drove over to the ballpark, then made her way to the owner's box. Her parents were both there tonight.

Her mom gave her a hug.

"I'm surprised to see you here," her mom said. "Dad's over talking to one of the sponsors he invited to join us tonight."

"That's okay." She grabbed some water and took a seat next to her mom. "I'll chat with him when he's free."

She checked the score. The Rivers were up by one run, and it was the bottom of the third. The Rivers had one man on base and no outs.

"Did you just get off work?"

Aubry nodded. "I didn't have anything going on, so I thought I'd catch the rest of the game."

"It's a good game so far. Tucker Cassidy is pitching."

That's why she was here. "Looks like he's held them off so far."

"Philadelphia has a good team, but yes, no runs on their side yet."

Just then, Trevor Shay hit a triple, scoring the runner on first base. The owner's box erupted with cheers. Aubry stood and yelled, too.

Tucker had a nice three-run lead when he took the mound at the bottom of the third.

"So, Mom," she said while there was a lull in the action and her dad was busy with clients. "What if I asked to bring a guy over to dinner?"

Her mother gave her a sideways look. "I assume this isn't sim-ply a 'what if' situation. You have a certain someone in mind."

"I do."

"You know you're always welcome to bring someone over to meet your father and me, Aubry. Who is he?"

She debated telling her mother. She'd been debating this for a while now. But it was time. She looked around to check her father's whereabouts. He was seated at the far end of the owner's box, talking up the sponsor, so he was out of earshot. "Tucker Cassidy."

Her mother beamed a smile. "Good choice. Nice young man."

Aubry relaxed her shoulders. "Thanks. I think so."

"How long has this been going on?"

"A little while now. I like him, Mom."

"Obviously you do, since I don't recall the last time you brought someone over for dinner."

"Dad's not going to like it."

Her mother dismissed that statement with a wave of her hand. "Your dad wants you to remain single—and his baby girl—forever. He'll get over it."

"He's always talking about how I should focus on medicine, to the exclusion of a social life."

"He worries about you, and your father is a career man. That's always been his priority. But he likes Tucker. I don't see this as a problem."

They talked dates that would work, and she felt a lot more at ease about asking Tucker to officially have dinner with her parents.

"Hey, sweetheart." Her dad finally came over, leaning down to kiss her cheek. "I'm sorry I was tied up earlier."

She smiled up at him. "It's not a problem. I knew you were busy."

"Shouldn't you be getting some rest, or studying?"

She patted her father's arm. "I'm good, Dad. I wanted to catch the game."

"Well, I'm glad to see you. Just don't stay up too late."

When he walked away, she looked at her mother and rolled her eyes. "It's like I'm eight years old. He'll never see me as a grown-up."

Her mother laughed. "He's always worried about you. And it's his prerogative as your father. Indulge him."

"Fine."

She settled in to watch Tucker pitch. He looked good tonight, in more ways than one. In typical fashion, he looked hot as hell in his Rivers uniform, commanding the mound with his body. He'd given up several hits, but overall his pitches were hitting their mark.

Aubry had always watched games with a detached, slightly disinterested concentration. Now, with Tucker pitching, she took more of a vested interest, her stomach tied up in knots each time Tucker took the mound. She leaned forward, observing his movements, the release of the ball and the batter's reaction to it.

It was nerve-wracking. She didn't know how Tucker did this.

By the middle of the seventh, the score was six to two in favor of the Rivers. It was a comfortable lead for Tucker, but Aubry was still nervous. She got up to stretch and grab something to drink.

Her father came over to stand next to her as she looked out the windows.

"How was work today? Anything interesting?"

"We had an appendicitis attack, a few broken bones, a chronic migraine, someone who had fallen off their stepladder at home and strained their back and a woman pregnant with triplets who came in with premature labor. A pretty routine day."

He put his arm around her. "You're doing so well, Aubry. But I'm worried about you."

She tilted her head back to look at her father's face. "Why would you be worried about me?"

"You work so hard and such long hours. And here you are at the game tonight when you should be at home sleeping."

She smiled and leaned her head against his chest. "I'm fine. If I'd been exhausted, that's where I would have gone."

"Still, it's unusual for you to come to so many games."

She laughed, then stepped away. "Maybe I've taken a sudden interest in baseball. And maybe I just need to spend a little less time working and sleeping, and get out more. See my family. Is that okay?"

He studied her as if he could read her mind. He'd always had that uncanny ability. "It's more than okay. You know your mother and I love to spend time with you."

"I'm glad to hear that. The Rivers are looking good."

"That they are. I think we have a team that'll be in contention this year."

Glad that she'd managed to get her father off the topic of her and on to his team, she listened while he talked team statistics for a while, then made her way back to her seat to watch the rest of the game.

Tucker ended up pitching through the eighth inning, and the closer came in to finish off the ninth. The Rivers had won without giving up more runs. Tucker had looked sharp, his pitches hitting where they needed to.

He should be happy.

She sent him a text message letting him know she was at the ballpark. She knew he'd be busy giving interviews for a bit, so she visited with her parents awhile until her phone rang.

"Are you still in the park?" Tucker asked.

"Yes."

"Meet me downstairs by the locker room in ten."

"Okay."

She hung up, said good night to her parents, then made her way down to the locker room hallway.

Tucker was already there, waiting for her.

He came over and kissed her. She had to admit, watching him tonight made her hungry for more than just a good baseball game.

She slid her hands up his arms, feeling the muscle that had thrown those amazing pitches.

"You did well tonight. Congratulations on your win."

"Thanks. I could have done better."

"Are you serious? You won the game."

He shrugged. "My curve has been a little off."

"Really? Not that I noticed. You looked really sharp out there tonight."

"It's not a big deal. I'll work it out. Thanks for coming to the game." He swept his hand over her hair. "Aren't you tired?"

She laughed. "Now you sound like my father, who told me I should be home and in bed."

He brushed his lips across hers. "You should be home and in bed."

She lingered at his lips. "Then take me there."

"Let's go." He held her hand and led her out the door and to his car. "I'll drive you to your car."

He dropped her at her car, then followed her to her condo. She got out and waited for him to park, enjoying the way he walked as he made his way to her front door. He pushed her against the door, his body crowding hers in the best possible way as he pressed the length of his body to hers and kissed her.

She felt wrapped up in him. All of him, from his mouth to his thighs to all the delicious parts of him in between. She breathed him in as he wound his tongue around hers, sucking her tongue in his mouth, making her moan with desperate desire.

She pressed her keys to his chest, a silent signal to get them into the house right now.

He broke the kiss only long enough to open her front door and pull her inside. He shut the door, locked it, then pushed her against it—this time inside, where it was private, where they were alone.

Then his mouth was on hers again and he was touching her, making her acutely aware of all of her senses.

She wondered if she'd ever grow tired of this—of sex with Tucker. It seemed like every time they were together, all she wanted was for him to kiss her, to touch her, her thoughts straying to the two of them shedding clothes and getting naked together.

Grow tired of him? Not anytime soon.

He cupped her butt, lifting her against his erection. She dropped her purse to the floor, kicked her shoes off, wishing she could will herself naked so he could touch all of her skin. She reached for his shirt and slid her hands under it to feel the warmth of his body, rewarded with his insistent groan.

When she palmed his shaft through the denim of his jeans, rubbing where it was oh so hard, he deepened the kiss, making her feverish with need. She was suddenly too hot with all these clothes on. She pushed him back and pulled her shirt off, then undid the clasp on her bra and removed that, too.

Tucker's gaze consumed her, all that raw heat and desire devouring her. He took a step forward and captured one of her aching nipples between his lips, flicking it with his tongue before drawing it into his mouth to suck.

All she could do was hold on to him as pure, delicious sensation rocked her straight to her core, making her tremble as he licked and sucked her nipples, teasing her until she thought she might die from the decadent pleasure.

When he pulled away, she thought he'd lead her to the bedroom. Instead, he undid the buckle of his jeans, then the zipper, pulling his cock out for her. She licked her lips and dropped to her knees, engulfing him.

"Christ, Aubry. That's good. Suck it hard."

She gave him what he needed—what she needed. She was so far

gone, so in rapture of what they gave each other, that she would have taken him right over the edge if he had let her. But he pulled her up and kissed her again, tugging at her hair in a way that let her know this ravaging passion she felt wasn't one-sided.

And when he dropped to the floor and pulled her there with him, she knew they'd never make it to the bedroom.

"Condom's in my pocket," he said, reaching there while she wriggled out of her jeans and underwear.

Tucker had put on the condom, so she straddled him, balancing her thighs on either side of his hips. She leaned forward, splaying her hands across his chest as she slid onto his cock.

She quivered as she seated herself fully on top of him, her body achingly filled with his cock. She dug her nails into his chest.

"That's good," she said. "That's oh so good."

He gripped her hips and lifted into her. "Yeah, it is. Now ride me and make us both come."

She rocked against him, her body clenching as she rolled back and forth. And when he reached up and grasped her breasts to tease her nipples, sparks of sensation shot like an out-of-control fire right to her sex, making her gasp and writhe against him.

Rubbing her clit against him was exquisite, a brutally sweet sensation that drove her close to orgasm. She could feel her pussy tighten around his cock, could feel the way he swelled impossibly larger inside of her each time he thrust, dragging her closer to the edge.

"That's it, babe," he said, his fingers digging into her hips. "Make us come."

She was panting, her body on the ragged edge where reality was no longer possible. She was all nerve endings, every part of her tuned in to their connection, to the intense way Tucker made eye contact with her as he drove into her. She wasn't just one person any longer—she was part of him, just as he was part of her.

And when she came apart, when her orgasm tore through her, she cried out as wave after wave of undulating pleasure rippled within her.

"That's it," Tucker said, thrusting rapidly, then groaning as he came with her.

She collapsed on top of him, still feeling the quaking aftereffects of one very sublime orgasm.

After a few minutes, she came to the realization that they were on the hardwood floor in the hallway.

She lifted up. "This has to be uncomfortable on your back."

He grinned up at her. "My back wasn't what I was thinking about when I was inside you."

Warmth spread through her and she leaned down to brush her lips across his.

She climbed off and they headed down the hall, cleaned up in the bathroom, then collapsed onto her bed.

"That was nice," she said as they both lay on their backs staring up at the ceiling.

Tucker rolled over on his side and smoothed his hand over her breasts. Her breath caught.

"Just nice? Not phenomenal or earth-shattering?"

She rolled over to face him. "Oh, the earth definitely moved for me. It always does when I'm with you."

He didn't smile or make another joke. Instead, he kissed her, this time a soft, gentle kiss that made those flutters in her heart go a little crazy.

When he pulled back, she said, "I didn't get a chance to ask you about Leo's game earlier. How did he do?"

"They won by four runs."

"That's great. I'm so happy for him."

He kept touching her, this time tracing the outline of her hip with his fingers. So distracting, in the best possible way.

"How was work today?" he asked.

"Busy day, like all of them are. Nothing eventful."

"Good. But not easy, either, I'll bet."

She liked that he understood her job, that he knew just because it was a regular day didn't make it easy.

"I'm used to it."

"And now I've kept you up late."

She laughed. "Hey, I'm the one who showed up at your game."

His hand lingered at her hip. "So you're saying you had ulterior motives other than checking out my pitching prowess?"

"I admit to nothing."

"Smart woman."

She was putting this off, but if she was going to do this, the time was now. "I checked out your upcoming schedule and I see you have some away games coming up."

"Yeah. I'll be gone for the next week. Why? Are you trying to get rid of me?"

"After great sex like that, you think I'd want to get rid of you? You're crazy. No, I was wondering if you're free when you're back in town."

He paused and she could tell he was thinking. "My next day off is the Tuesday after we get back. Then I have a Wednesday afternoon game the next day, but I'm free that night." He smiled at her. "Are you asking me out on a date?"

She let out a soft laugh. "Sort of. I'd like to invite you to dinner at my parents' house."

He looked at her and his brows rose. "Huh. Now that is some serious business. Your dad doesn't know about us, does he?"

"Not yet. But after we all have dinner together he will. Is that a problem?"

"Not for me it isn't."

She liked that he didn't hesitate before answering. "Great.

Then it's a date. Let's say Tuesday? I have an early day, so I'd be available for dinner that night."

"Tuesday it is. In the meantime, touching you has made my dick hard."

She looked down at his erection. "Oh, that is a problem, isn't it?"

"It is. Do you have a remedy for that, doctor?"

She wrapped her fingers around his cock and stroked him. "I have the cure for you."

He rolled her over and kissed her, and any thoughts besides Tucker, his mouth and his body fled her mind.

THIRTY

AFTER A GRUELING LOSS TO CINCINNATI, TUCKER SAT in a private room in the hotel with several of his teammates. Since they were barred from alcohol while on road trips, he nursed an iced tea and thought about how great a beer would taste right now.

He'd pitched tonight's game, and once again his curve had been off. He couldn't put his finger on what was going wrong. If he couldn't depend on his curveball, his career was in trouble. The problem wasn't consistent, though. And that was the goddamn problem.

They'd been sailing along up by two runs through the first seven innings. Tucker had been in a groove; his pitches had looked good. Then at the top of the eighth, he'd gotten rocked for four runs, including back-to-back homers. And every single one of those hits had come off his curve.

Shit.

Garrett Scott came and sat next to him, not saying a word.

"This really needs to be a shot of tequila," Tucker said, staring at his iced tea.

Garrett nodded. "We all need a shot tonight."

Gavin Riley slapped Tucker on the back. "This loss isn't entirely on you. We couldn't come up with more runs to help you out."

Tucker looked up at Gavin. "Two should have been enough. I had that goddamn game. Sorry, guys."

"Nothing to be sorry about," Garrett said. "Sometimes shit happens and the game gets away from you. We've all been there."

Gavin nodded. "There isn't one of us here who hasn't blown a game either by losing their pitching mojo, or making an error, or with cold bats that can't manufacture runs. So don't take this loss on yourself."

"Gavin's right," Garrett said. "It's always the team who wins or loses. Not one player."

Tucker had heard the pep talk before. He appreciated it, but it didn't make him feel better. "I'll try to remember that. But this would be a lot easier with tequila."

Gavin laughed. "I'll drink to that. Unfortunately, I'll be drinking to that with tea."

Losing was part of the game and Tucker knew it. The wins were enormous highs, especially in front of the home crowd. The losses? Those sucked, no matter what stadium you played at, but they were especially bad on the road, when the crowd roared every time you screwed up.

It was still hard for Tucker to deal with, even after five years in the majors. But he normally handled the losses with a shrug. This time he wasn't handling it well, because something was wrong with his pitching and he knew it.

He was going to have to figure it out and soon.

He eventually ordered another iced tea and wandered off to the food table to grab some snacks and look out the window. He took out his phone. It was ten thirty and he knew Aubry had the late shift tonight so he couldn't call her. But, man, he really wanted to. Hearing her voice would help somehow.

Instead, he typed out a text: *Thinking about you.*

His fingers hovered on the keypad. The text felt unfinished, like there was something else he wanted to add to the message.

A moment later he sent the text and shoved his phone in his pocket.

Quit overthinking everything, dumbass.

He'd been thinking a lot about her invitation to her parents' house for dinner, about what that meant.

A guy typically didn't get invited to a girl's parents unless she was invested in the relationship. They'd never talked about their relationship. It had just . . .

Progressed, he supposed.

Hell if he knew. He hadn't really had many relationships, and never one that had progressed to a meet-the-parents point. And this one? Yeah, this one had the potential to be a disaster, since he already knew her parents, especially her dad.

Somehow he didn't think her father was going to be too damn happy that she was dating him. Or that he was dating her.

He popped some bruschetta in his mouth and pondered it some more.

"Planning world domination over here, Cassidy?"

He turned to look at Trevor Shay. "More like personal shit."

"Oh."

"Aubry invited me to have dinner with her parents."

Trevor arched a brow. "Like in Clyde Ross?"

"Yeah."

Trevor leaned against the windowsill. "That could get complicated. He doesn't know about the two of you yet, does he?"

"No. I mean, for a while, we were light and uncomplicated, not even really dating, I guess. And now . . ."

"And now, what? It's more than that?"

"I guess. I don't know." Tucker looked out the window and sipped his tea, still wishing like hell he had a whiskey or a shot of tequila. This was way too much deep thinking for iced tea.

"So if you're not into her, don't go to dinner with her parents. Seems a simple enough solution."

If only it were that easy. "Yeah, I'm into her. That's the problem."

Trevor laughed. "That's always the problem. The ones we're not into are the easy ones. The ones we fall in love with? That's where it gets complicated."

Tucker looked at him. "I didn't say I was in love with her."

Trevor patted his shoulder. "You didn't have to. If you weren't in love with her, you'd have said no."

Shit. Trevor was right. He hadn't even realized it. He'd never potentially jeopardize his job unless he had true, serious feelings for Aubry. He looked over at Trevor. "Well, hell."

Trevor laughed. "Good luck, Cassidy. You're gonna need it."

THIRTY-ONE

AUBRY SHOULDN'T BE NERVOUS ABOUT HAVING Tucker at her parents' house for dinner. It was just dinner. And her parents had both met Tucker before, of course. So it wasn't like they were going to grill him about what he did for a living or anything. They knew him.

But still, she knew her father and his stance on her dating . . . anyone. This was going to be a hard sell. She hoped he would go easy on Tucker because he was part of the Rivers team, he was responsible and a really nice guy.

She had planned to prepare her dad in advance by telling him about Tucker, but he'd been stuck in meetings all day and her mom told her he wouldn't be home until late. If she'd known that, she'd have told him about Tucker sooner. As it was, it was possible both her father and Tucker might arrive at the same time.

She was just going to have to hope it all went as she expected it should—no big deal.

To keep her mind occupied, she busied herself in the kitchen with her mom, who was making one of Aubry's favorite dishes—lasagna. Aubry made the salad while her mom baked bread. The smells emanating in the kitchen were to die for. Her stomach was growling.

"You're awfully quiet, Aubry," her mother said. "Did you have a bad day at work?"

Aubry took a sip from the glass of wine she'd poured earlier, trying to calm her nerves. "Work was fine today."

"Then it's something else. What is it? Are you nervous about your father meeting Tucker?"

She sat at the island. "Yes. You know how Dad is about me and relationships."

Her mom looked at the oven timer, then poured herself a glass of wine. "It's all going to be fine. He's not the ogre you think he is."

"I know he isn't. It's just—I don't know what it is, honestly."

Her mother graced her with one of her calming smiles. "You haven't brought a man over here before. Not since high school."

"I know. I guess this is kind of a big deal to me."

"Which means that Tucker is a big deal to you?"

Leave it to her mom to get to the root of her angst. "Yes, he is."

Her mother's lips tipped up. "This makes me very happy."

"Don't get too excited or start planning a wedding yet, Mom. We're just dating. It's not serious."

Except it kind of was. Otherwise, Tucker wouldn't be coming over here.

"Which is more than you've done with any man for quite some time, honey. It's been school and work and nothing else. I'm just happy to see you happy and enjoying yourself."

Aubry couldn't help her own smile. "Thanks. I'm kind of happy as well. Now we just have to hope Dad feels the same way."

The doorbell rang, which meant it was Tucker and not her father.

"I'll get that." Aubry went to the door and opened it, her heart skipping a beat when she saw Tucker dressed in black jeans and white button-down shirt. He looked so handsome he took her breath away.

"You look amazing," she said. "Come on in."

He had a bottle in his hand, but he looked around, then swept his arm around her. "And you are gorgeous."

He brushed his lips across hers for an all-too-brief kiss. "Just in case we don't have a chance to do that. I've missed you."

And there went her skipping heart again. She inhaled, then took his hand in hers. "Come on into the kitchen."

Her mom was just pulling the bread from the oven.

"Wow. It smells good in here," Tucker said. "Can I move in?"

Her mother turned around and smiled. "It depends. Do you mow?"

Tucker grinned. "I can mow, milk cows and even take out the trash."

"Well, we don't have cows, but the other two mean you're in. Hello, Tucker."

"Evening, Mrs. Ross. Thank you for having me over."

"Please. Call me Helen. Clyde is running a little late. What can I get you to drink?"

"I'll have a beer."

"We have several different kinds. What would you prefer?"

Aubry was impressed with Tucker's ability to sit at the island and relax with her mother. Before long, the two of them were talking about beer of all things, since both of them were fond of dark brews. Her mother told them about the trip she and Dad had taken to Germany a couple of years ago, and all the types of beers they'd tasted there.

"I've never been to Germany, but it's on the top of my list now," Tucker said.

Mom gave him a list of beer pubs to stop at in Berlin. Aubry listened with interest, since it was somewhere she'd love to go someday as well.

She heard the front door open, and her anxiety level increased.

"Sorry I'm late," her dad said as he came into the room. "Meeting lasted longer than I expected."

He kissed her mom, then turned to Aubry and smiled. "Hi, sweetheart."

"Hi, Dad. I believe you know Tucker Cassidy."

If her father was disappointed or angry, he didn't show it. He gave Tucker a big smile and a handshake.

"Hey, Tucker. It's great to see you."

Tucker had stood when her father came into the room, and, if possible, looked more nervous than she was. "Evening, Mr. Ross."

"I've been telling Tucker about our trip to Germany two years ago," her mom said. "He's a big fan of beer and he wants to take a trip there, so I told him about the best places to visit."

"Is that right?" Her dad looked over at Tucker's glass. "Looks like she gave you a dark ale. I think I'll have one of those myself."

Her mother poured a beer for him. "Dinner will be ready shortly, but in the meantime, let's move into the living room so we can chat."

TUCKER WAS USUALLY AT EASE WITH PEOPLE, BUT damn if this wasn't an anxiety-producing evening. He knew spending time with her parents was important to Aubry, and getting approval from her dad was even more important.

At first glance, it didn't look like her dad was too upset. That was a good sign.

"The road trip ended up decently," Clyde said. "I was happy to see the Rivers won three out of six against two very tough teams. Especially having to pick up a doubleheader due to the rainout. That's always tough on the road."

"Yes, sir. We had some issues but we're addressing them."

Clyde leaned back in his chair. "Yeah? What kinds of issues?"

This was a conversation Tucker knew Clyde should be having with the coaches, not him, so he was treading very treacherous waters. "Pitching was a little off and bats got cold when they should have been hot. But we have a stretch of home games coming up, and I expect we'll do really well."

Clyde took a sip of his beer. "That's good to hear."

It was nothing he wouldn't say to the media, so he figured his ass was safe there.

"And what did your coaches say about some of the issues?"

"Clyde. You're grilling the poor boy," Helen said. "Less shop talk at home, okay?"

Clyde instantly relaxed his demeanor and smiled. "You're right. Baseball's in my blood, so you'll have to forgive me for getting so intense about it. I love that team and want what's best for them."

"I understand," Tucker said. "I love the team, too. I'd like us to win every game."

"And that's the kind of competitive spirit I like all our players to have."

"And on that note," Helen said, "I'm going to go check on the lasagna, which I'm sure is done."

Aubry stood as well. "I'll help you."

"Clyde, Tucker, why don't you two make your way to the dining room?"

Tucker lifted the bottle he'd brought. "Uh, I brought wine in case anyone is interested. I'm sure it's not as good as the awesome stuff you have in the wine cellar."

Clyde frowned. "How do you know about the wine cellar?"

Shit. Tucker realized as soon as the words left his mouth that he'd made a critical mistake. He shot a quick glance over to Aubry.

"I took him down there that night of the team party," Aubry said. "I'd run into him when we were restocking the chardonnay and I needed an extra set of hands, so he followed me down and helped me carry the bottles upstairs."

"Oh," Helen said. "Well, thank you for bringing a bottle, Tucker. We'll open it and have it with dinner."

Clyde didn't say anything, but didn't seem suspicious, either, which to Tucker's way of thinking was a very good thing.

Thank God for Aubry's quick thinking. He needed to remember to engage his brain before he opened his mouth.

He followed Aubry's father to the dining room, certain he was going to get grilled about his intentions toward his daughter. But by the time they took their seats, Aubry had come in with the salad and bread, and Helen followed shortly thereafter with the lasagna, leaving them no time alone.

Tucker had to admit he wasn't sorry for that. The man intimidated the hell out of him, not because he was Aubry's father—though there was that—but mainly because he was the boss.

Fortunately, conversation at dinner was fairly innocuous. They discussed Clyde and Helen's travels, Clyde's upcoming business deals, which had nothing to do with baseball, and Aubry's work. Tucker was glad to be kept out of the equation. He finally relaxed enough to enjoy the amazing dinner Helen had fixed.

"So how long have the two of you been dating?" Helen asked after she brought out dessert, a spectacular looking cheesecake.

Damn. And things had been going so well. Tucker looked over at Aubry.

"Almost two months," she said.

"What? And I knew nothing about it. You are very good at keeping secrets, Aubry," Helen said.

"How are you juggling dating with your work?" Clyde asked.

"Just fine, Dad."

"But you're so busy. You work a tremendous amount of hours. I just don't see how you manage to have a social life with everything else you have going on."

Tucker so wanted to say something, but this wasn't his argument to have.

"Well, as you know, Tucker is busy as well. He's on the road a lot, and when he's in town he has games, too." Aubry looked over at Tucker and smiled. "But we carve out time to see each other."

Tucker figured Aubry could handle her father.

"And you two have obviously made it work, since it's been two months and you've brought Tucker over for dinner. So is this serious?"

Aubry shot her mother a look. "Mom."

"I'm sorry. But you know I get anxious about these things."

"I'd say for both of us, considering the stage of our careers, it's serious."

Aubry looked over at Tucker, probably as surprised at what he'd said as he was.

Helen beamed. "That's great to hear. Isn't that great, Clyde?"

Clyde nodded, his smile not as pronounced. "Yes. I'm very happy that you've managed to make this work, given both of your hectic schedules."

But Aubry seemed ecstatic. She got up and hugged both her parents. "Thanks, you two."

After they ate cheesecake, Tucker helped Aubry take the dishes to the kitchen. They loaded the dishwasher while Helen put the leftovers away.

Aubry laid her hand over her stomach. "I am so full. I could use a walk. Are you interested, Tucker?"

"Sure."

"Why don't you walk him around the grounds?" her mother suggested. "It'll help your digestion."

"That's a great idea," Aubry said. "It's perfect weather tonight. We'll be back in a little while."

"All right."

Tucker followed her out the back door. He grabbed her hand as they strolled through the gardens.

"Thanks for having my back earlier when I screwed up."

She looked over at him. "Oh, you mean about the wine cellar?"

"Yeah."

She laughed. "Not a problem. I could see the panic on your face when you blurted that out."

"Not my finest moment. I'm glad you can think fast."

"It comes from being grilled by attending physicians. You have to always have an answer on the tip of your tongue."

He squeezed her hand. "And you did tonight. Thankfully."

She looked beautiful tonight in a blue sundress that highlighted her blond hair and gorgeous eyes. Of course, he thought anything she wore made her look beautiful, but tonight, he couldn't keep his eyes off of her. Or her legs as they strolled past the pool house he'd checked out for her the night of the party.

"Did you ever find your uncle that night?"

She frowned. "My . . . oh, right. Yes. He was upstairs in one of the guest rooms. He'd had a lot to drink and had wandered up there to lie down and had fallen asleep."

"Alone, I assume?"

"Yes, fortunately."

"I'm sure that made your aunt happy."

She nodded. "Very. At least that night, anyway."

He put his arm around her. "I'm sorry you have a straying uncle."

"Not much I can do about their relationship if my aunt's the one who insists on staying with him. If it were me, I'd have kicked him to the curb a long time ago."

He stopped and pulled her against him. "You can rest assured there hasn't been anyone but you for me ever since I met you."

She cocked her head to the side. "Really?"

"Well, yeah. Like you told your dad inside, we both have really heavy schedules. It's not like I have a lot of time to date a bunch of women."

Her lips curved. "I see. So it's not that you were all that interested in me. It's just that you're too busy to date more than one woman."

Shit. "That's not what I meant, Aubry. Let me rephrase. I was so blinded by your intelligence and your beauty that no other woman could compare."

"Much better."

They started walking again.

"Plus, you have a great ass."

She laughed. "You always say the sweetest things."

They wandered around the gardens for a few minutes, until Aubry started back to the house. He assumed she was taking him back inside, but she surprised him by going toward a set of stairs that led down.

"Is this where the millions are hidden?" he asked.

She laughed. "Actually, kind of."

She pulled a set of keys out of the pocket of her dress and unlocked the heavy wood door, then gave it a hard push.

"No one really uses this entrance since you can get in here through the back stairs from the kitchen. But I used to sneak in this way, because I know where the keys are hidden." With a secret smile, she led him through a chilly, dark passageway.

That led right into the wine cellar. As soon as they made their way into the room where he'd been that first night he met Aubry, his balls quivered. He could still visualize Laura's knee-to-the-balls reaction to his refusal to move in together.

"This room pains me."

She laughed and cupped his crotch. "Well, that's not a good thing. We need to replace your awful memories of the wine cellar with something a little more . . . pleasant."

His cock sprung to life, hardening as she rubbed back and forth. "You've got my attention now."

"Good attention, I hope."

"Definitely the good kind."

She unzipped his pants and pulled his cock out. "I promise to be gentle. No harm will come to your cock down here."

"Are you sure this is a good idea?"

She paused, her brows lifting. "My hand on your cock is not a good idea?"

"I mean, your parents are upstairs. What if—"

She brushed her lips over his. "Don't worry about it. They have no reason to come down here, and they won't hear us." She stroked him until his breath rasped. "Unless of course—you're afraid?"

He swung his arm around her waist and lifted her, taking her over to the table in the middle of the room. "Now you've laid down the gauntlet, Dr. Ross. And you know I don't back down from a challenge."

She let out a soft laugh. "I was hoping you wouldn't."

He slid his fingers in her hair and kissed her, a hot, deep kiss that obliterated the cold of the wine cellar and turned everything hot. He pulled the straps of her sundress down, drawing back the cups of her bra so he could get to her breasts. The cool air made her nipples pucker, so he took a few seconds to admire the view.

"Suck," she said.

He had to admit he enjoyed the command, and her sense of urgency. He raised his gaze to hers, saw the desire shimmering in her eyes.

He fit a nipple into his mouth and she wove her fingers into his hair, holding his head in place while he flicked his tongue over the velvety soft bud. She responded with a low moan, and his dick twitched, aching to be inside of her.

His dick could wait, because tasting her was all he needed right now. He reached under her dress and slid his hand into her panties to cup her sex.

"You're wet, babe. Are you ready for me?"

"Yes," she said. "Oh, God, yes."

He wanted to make her come first. He crouched down to pull her underwear off, then spread her legs, lifted her dress over her hips and put his mouth on her. She was salty sweet and when she whimpered, he covered her clit with his mouth and sucked her, then used his tongue to lave over the softness of her sex until she lifted her hips, writhing against him.

The sounds she made, the way she moved her body, all made his dick pound. And when she cried out as she came, he planted his tongue on her clit, giving her what she needed as the orgasm rolled through her. He held on to her hips while she quivered underneath him, and when she settled, he rose up, grabbed the condom he was so thankful he'd stuck in his pants pocket and put it on.

He was inside of her in seconds, burying himself in all of her sweet, wet heat. Her pussy gripped him, the aftereffects of her orgasm vibrating around his cock.

Aubry wrapped her leg around his hips and rose up against him while he thrust into her. He cupped her butt, shielding her from the metal table as he drove harder and harder into her, listening to her cries of pleasure.

It was sweet hell, making him want to spill hard and fast, but he held back, gentling his movements as he pressed his forehead to hers.

"What you do to me, Aubry," he whispered, easing into her, then out. "I can't explain it."

She reached up to rub her fingertip against his bottom lip. "I know. I know. For me, too."

It was an emotional connection he'd never felt with any other woman. It shattered him in ways he couldn't fathom. This woman had the capacity to destroy him.

He was in love with her and he wanted to tell her. But when they were alone. Not here. Not now. Instead, he gave in to the sensation, to the rhythm of their bodies moving in unison. He ground against her and she tightened around him. He saw it in the way her eyes widened, and knew she was going to come again. He waited for her, gave her the friction she needed, and when she gasped and came, he thrust hard, releasing the spurts of come that exploded from him.

It was all he could do to stay upright as he released, as everything around him seemed to go black for a few seconds. He held on to Aubry and planted his mouth on hers, fusing the two of them together in this raw passion that seemed to have no end.

But finally, he took a deep breath and gripped the table. Aubry released her leg and let it slowly slide to the floor.

"Now that is a much better memory of the wine cellar than I had previously."

She smiled and kissed him. "I'm glad to hear that. Although if you recall I had my hand on your cock that night as well."

He laughed. "Yeah, but it didn't feel as good that night as it did tonight."

"I'm sure that's true."

They disentangled and righted their clothes. "Uh, I'm going to need to get rid of this condom. And I don't think there's a bathroom down here."

"Come on. There's a bathroom right off the kitchen."

They left the wine cellar the way they came in, then quietly entered the kitchen. Music was playing in the living room, so they snuck into the bathroom and tidied themselves up before reentering the living room.

Aubry's mother was reading, so she looked up. "How was the walk?"

"Invigorating," Aubry said as they both took a seat on the sofa across from her parents. "I feel a lot better now."

"Me, too," Tucker said. "Your property is amazing, Mr. and Mrs. Ross."

"Thanks," Clyde said, setting down his phone. "We've always liked this house."

"Oh, Aubry, I forgot to give you that recipe you asked for. Before I forget again, why don't you come into the kitchen with me and you can copy it down?"

"Yes, let's do that." She stood and looked down at Tucker. "I'll be right back."

"Would you two like some coffee?" Helen asked.

"I'd love some," Clyde asked.

"If it's not too much trouble," Tucker said.

"Not at all." Helen smiled at him before leaving the room.

"Where did you all walk to?" Clyde asked after the women left the room.

Fortunately, Tucker had walked the grounds before. "We went past the pool house to the statuary gardens, then over to the azalea garden. It's coming along nicely there. Everything seems to be in bloom. Really pretty."

Clyde nodded. "Helen loves all her flowers. She makes me get out there all the time and take walks."

Tucker could picture that.

"So, about Aubry. Is this a serious thing?"

Tucker was prepared for this conversation, knew it was coming eventually. "Yes, sir. From my standpoint it is."

"I'm glad you're not taking it lightly. That means something." Clyde leaned forward. "My daughter worked her ass off as an undergraduate, then in medical school, and now her residency. She has a clear plan for her future, and I know you do as well."

"Yes, sir."

"I think you're an outstanding ballplayer, Tucker. I've watched you play and I'm impressed with your talent. I think the Rivers were damn lucky to sign you, and I believe you're going to have an amazing career as a pitcher."

High praise coming from someone like Clyde Ross. "Thank you, Mr. Ross."

"But here's the thing. Aubry's not ready to settle down yet. She's got a year left in residency and she'll need to take her tests after that, then apply to a fellowship. She has to think about her career, not love or romance. The last thing she needs right now is a distraction from a hotshot athlete like you, or God forbid, to fall in love."

Tucker didn't like where this was going, and he wholeheartedly disagreed. "But sir—"

"Let me finish. I've worked my whole life to give Aubry the life I feel she deserves. And she's worked hard as well. I won't let you take that away from her. So you break this off with her, or you'll fall asleep one night playing for the Rivers and wake up the next morning pitching for the goddamn Triple-A team again. Don't think I'm joking here, Cassidy. I will trade you or I will send you down to the minors. You understand me?"

"Coffee for everyone." Helen came in with a carafe and cups, a smiling Aubry trailing behind her, which effectively cut off the conversation between Tucker and Mr. Ross.

Clyde offered up a friendly smile as if he hadn't just upended

Tucker's whole world. "Great. I'm ready for some coffee. How about you, Tucker?"

Still barely able to form a coherent thought, let alone words, Tucker nodded and tried for what he hoped was a smile.

Clyde might be able to play the part of doting husband and happy father, but Tucker had gotten the message loud and clear.

He'd just been told to break up with Aubry. Like . . . right now.

No, he hadn't been told. He'd been threatened. His job—his career—had been threatened. Clyde Ross had made it very clear that if he wanted to keep the job he loved, he had to end things with Aubry.

He just didn't know what the hell he was going to do about it.

THIRTY-TWO

"YOU'RE IN A GOOD MOOD," KATIE SAID TO AUBRY, frowning at her.

They'd decided to go out to dinner after their shift ended. Aubry dipped her chip in salsa, grinned, then ate it, following up with a sip of her margarita.

"Is that a bad thing?"

"No. But usually these after-work dinners are bitchfests and we're both grouchy and grumbly. You are neither grouchy nor grumbling about anything. Instead, you've got a goofy-ass smile on your face. What's up with that?"

Aubry shrugged and took another drink. "I'm just . . . happy."

Katie grabbed her drink and leaned back in her seat. "Okay, what's going on?"

"Nothing," Aubry said with a laugh. "Can't I be happy?"

"Of course you can. But we had a shit day today and we barely had time for a break to pee, yet you're sitting here all smiles. So spill."

"Fine. It's Tucker."

"Ohh, so he's the one putting a smile on your face. That makes sense. What's going on with you two?"

Aubry hadn't seen him for several days, since that night he'd had dinner with her parents. He'd left after coffee, saying he had an early call at the ballpark the next day, and she knew he had back-to-back-to-back games. But still, her parents had loved him, and so did she.

Things were working out.

"He met my parents."

"Really. And how did that go?"

"It went really well. I was afraid my dad was going to have a fit about it. One, because you know how my father is, and two, because Tucker plays for the Rivers."

"And he was okay?"

Aubry smiled. "He was okay. After Tucker left he told me that Tucker was a really nice young man, a professional, and he could see how much I liked him."

"That's great. So things between you and Tucker must be getting serious."

"I think so. Maybe. I don't know. It's hard to say how serious either of us can get with the careers we have. We're both just so busy."

Katie placed her drink on the table and leaned forward. "Oh, bullshit, Aubry. Stop making everything in your life about your work and take your career out of the equation. How do you feel about Tucker?"

She hadn't said the words out loud to anyone yet, but she had to. She just had to. "I'm in love with him."

Katie squealed with joy, got up and came around to Aubry's side of the table, pulled her out of her chair and hugged her. "I'm so happy for you. Does he love you, too?"

Aubry laughed at Katie's exuberance. They both sat down and Aubry moved her drink toward the chair next to Katie's so she could be closer. "I don't know. We haven't said the words to each other yet. But I feel it, you know? I think he does."

"If he agreed to the dinner-with-the-parents routine, trust me, he's in love with you. It's only a matter of time before he says the words."

That was how she felt as well. "So now you know why I'm smiling."

"And now you know why I'm going to glare daggers of hate and jealousy at you the rest of the night." Katie lifted her glass toward Aubry.

Aubry laughed and lifted her glass, clinking it with Katie's. "You will not because you're my best friend and you love me."

"Fine. Here's to love and the lucky ones who manage to land the hot men."

"I'll definitely drink to that."

TUCKER SAT IN HIS CAR IN FRONT OF VICTORIA BALD-win's office, almost too afraid to go inside to talk to her.

It had been four days since Clyde Ross had threatened to trade him. Four days since he'd last talked to Aubry. He was afraid to even text her, though he didn't think her father monitored her phone.

He felt like a goddamned coward. But this was his career. What the hell was he supposed to do?

And that was the problem. He didn't know. Right now he needed intel, so he got out of the car and went inside the building where Victoria's spacious office was located. He'd texted her this morning and asked if she had some time to see him before he had to report to the stadium for his game today, and fortunately she did.

The receptionist led him to her office. Victoria looked gorgeous as always in her dark slim pencil skirt, white blouse and high heels that accentuated her killer legs. He had no idea about her age—late thirties or early forties maybe? It didn't matter. She was beautiful, in that classic-beauty kind of way, her brown hair perfectly styled and brushing her shoulders in a wave of curls.

She was also a shark in this business, and that's what he admired the most about her.

"Tucker," she said, smiling as he entered. "I'm so glad you stopped by. Would you like something to drink?"

"I'm fine right now, thanks."

"All right. Take a seat and tell me what brings you by today?"

His stomach jumbled and he didn't want to have this conversation with her, but knowing was better than not knowing. "I was wondering if you'd heard anything about a trade involving me."

Her brow arched. "A trade? No. Why? Have you heard something?"

"No."

She leaned a hip against her desk and crossed her arms. "Okay. Then tell me why you thought there might be a trade in the works."

He wanted to downplay this so she wouldn't ask a lot of questions. "I was just wondering if you'd heard anything. You know, just to be safe."

She pushed off the desk and took a seat in the chair next to his. "I don't think so, Tucker. You're worried about something. Did someone on the staff threaten you with a trade?"

"No. No one on the staff threatened me with a trade." That part, at least, was honest.

"You're obviously upset enough to have come here today to talk to me. Come on, Tucker, tell me what's worrying you."

There was no way in hell he'd tell Victoria about Clyde Ross's threat. He knew Victoria. She was protective of her players. He'd seen her in action when she was negotiating a deal and she was a tigress, giving no ground where the best interests of her clients were concerned. If he told her what Clyde had said to him, she'd march right into his office and threaten *him* with trading Tucker, telling him what a loss it would be for the Rivers, when that was the last thing he wanted. Now that he knew Clyde hadn't started trade talks—at least not yet—he was going to have to finesse his way out of this.

He dragged his fingers through his hair. "I don't know, Victoria. I think it's just all in my head. You know how it is. The pressure of the game, of wanting to do my best for the team. I had a couple of losses recently that I should have won. And my curveball sucks right now. I can do better."

She sighed. "Tucker. You're having a fantastic year. Your pitching is phenomenal, and it's gotten even better since you've been with the Rivers. My guess is you're only going to improve. The Rivers would be morons to trade you, and trust me, that organization isn't moronic, so relax. Your status with the team is fine."

If only she knew. He smiled and nodded. "Yeah, you're probably right."

"I'm more than probably right. I know my players and my teams, and trust me when I tell you that you're right where you're supposed to be."

"Okay."

She studied him for a few seconds. "Unless you're the one who's not happy and this is your not-so-subtle way of telling me you want out."

He leveled his gaze on her, making sure she knew where he stood. "That's the last thing I want. I like where I am. I like this team."

She nodded. "That's what I thought. So focus your energies on your outstanding pitching, and you let me worry about the front office stuff, okay?"

He stood, and so did she. "Okay. And thanks for letting me vent a little."

She patted his shoulder. "Anytime. That's what I'm here for."

He left Victoria's office a little more clearheaded. But he still wasn't sure what he was going to do.

He loved Aubry. But his career was everything to him.

And he still felt like a coward.

A coward with no answers.

THIRTY-THREE

AUBRY KNEW TUCKER HAD A DAY GAME TODAY. SHE also knew, like herself, that he'd been really busy the past week. They'd hardly spoken and he was getting ready to go out on a road trip again, so she wanted to see him before he left.

Fortunately, their schedules actually meshed for a change, and she had gotten off work right about the time his game ended. She dashed home to shower and change into very sexy underwear and a sundress, slipped into her sandals and drove over to his place. She'd sent him a text message right before she left telling him she'd meet him there.

When he opened the door, she threw herself against him, planting her lips on his for a kiss.

"I've missed you," she said, tossing her purse on the table by the door as she walked in. "God, it feels like an eternity since we've been together. Or even talked."

She fell onto his sofa and curled her legs underneath her, smiling up at him as he entered the room. "We should probably have sex first, don't you think?"

He looked gorgeous in his jeans and T-shirt, said T-shirt hugging all his muscles oh so perfectly.

"Uh, actually, I had made plans to hang out with some of the guys from the team tonight. It's one of the guy's birthdays and he arranged a party at a bar. I'm sorry. I texted you back, but I guess you didn't get my message."

"Oh. You did?" She got up and grabbed her purse so she could pull out her phone. She read his message. "You sure did. I was so excited to see you and I figured you'd . . . Well, never mind."

Her cheeks heated. "I'm so sorry, Tucker. I didn't know."

"It's okay. I'm the one who's sorry. I should have called you when you didn't reply to my message."

"No, really. It's on me. I just thought . . ."

She thought he'd want to see her. They'd barely spoken. She texted him and he'd text back, but she sensed a distance. And now . . .

She shouldn't read too much into this. He was just busy. So was she.

She took a deep breath and headed to the door. "Okay, then. Well, you have fun with the guys tonight."

"Really, Aubry. I'm sorry about this. It's just that I said I'd go to this party for him. And it's just all guys, otherwise I'd take you with me."

"No you definitely should go hang out with the team. Have a great time."

"Thanks. I'll text you later, okay?"

"Sure. Bye, Tucker."

He didn't pull her against him for a kiss. He didn't hug her. It was as if he didn't want to get close to her.

She walked out and he shut the door.

Something was wrong. With him. With them. With their relationship.

When she got to her car, she palmed her stomach, feeling the ache of loss all the way down to her toes.

What the hell was going on?

TUCKER LEANED AGAINST THE FRONT DOOR, LISTEN-ing to the sound of Aubry's car starting up and pulling away.

He had no party to go to tonight. When she'd texted that she was coming over, he'd panicked and that was the first thing he'd thought of to tell her. Unfortunately, she'd showed up at his house looking gorgeous and smelling like candy and all he'd wanted to do was pull her into his arms and kiss her and make love to her and tell her he was in love with her.

Instead, he'd sent her away.

Coward.

He closed his eyes and drew in a deep breath, then let it out.

He was hurting her. Hell, he was hurting himself. This wasn't him. He didn't act this way, didn't skulk around avoiding a woman because he'd been threatened by her father. He'd always addressed uncomfortable issues head-on. Even that night in the wine cellar with Laura, he'd told her up front and honestly that he didn't see their relationship continuing. He'd taken a knee to the balls for it, but he'd been honest with her.

And now? With the woman he loved, he was avoiding and being completely dishonest. It was the most cowardly thing he'd ever done.

And he still didn't know what the hell to do about it.

He needed to talk to someone, and he knew who. He had a road trip coming up, and it would end in Houston, with a day off in between.

He needed to go home and talk to his family.

THIRTY-FOUR

AUBRY DID NOT WANT TO BE AT THIS DINNER TO CELebrate her aunt and uncle's anniversary.

Love was a crock of shit, and who better to represent that than a philandering uncle and the woman who foolishly stood by him despite his constant affairs.

But her mother would have been offended had she not showed up, and since she was off work, she was here. For her mother, and for no other reason.

And okay, also for her Aunt Farrah, who looked beautiful tonight in a gold dress, her hair worn down in gorgeous red waves. She was the bangle bracelet queen, and she was definitely clanging those bracelets with fervor tonight. At least her uncle would be attentive tonight. He kind of had to, since the party was in their honor. Why Uncle Davis felt he could do better than her treasure of an aunt was beyond her ability to understand.

Then again, she didn't understand anything about men these days, including the one she'd been dating. The one who was currently all but ignoring her.

She had a feeling she was being dumped, and if Tucker would just come out and say he didn't want to see her anymore—like a man with balls would—then she'd at least know and she could move on with her life. But this cat-and-mouse game he'd been playing with her where he'd answer her texts and they'd talk like they were still in a relationship, but he couldn't make time to see her?

That was confusing as hell.

She decided not to think about Tucker tonight, so she hung out with her parents and her aunt and uncle, though she tended to avoid her uncle because she thought he was a miserable asshole. She merely tolerated his presence because of her aunt. And tonight, Aunt Farrah was the center of attention, and Uncle Davis was lavishing her with compliments and telling the entire crowd how much he loved his wife.

It was kind of gag worthy, but at least Aunt Farrah seemed to enjoy it. After a while, Aubry had had enough, so she went into the den to pour herself a glass of whiskey. This night called for hard liquor.

Her dad was in there.

"Avoiding the party?" she asked.

He turned to her and smiled. "I needed a break."

"I'll drink to that." She walked over and her father poured a whiskey for her, then handed her a glass while he poured one for himself.

She took a sip, letting the liquid burn its way down. Mmm, so good. Maybe she should get blitzed tonight so she wouldn't have to think about Tucker.

Then again, since she had to report to work early tomorrow, maybe that wasn't such a good idea.

She sat on one of the leather chairs across from her dad. "The party's nice."

"It is. I can't believe Davis and Farrah have been married forty years."

"You and mom aren't too far behind them. Only a couple more years."

Her father smiled. "I know. I think I'll take her to Europe for our fortieth. Do a month-long trip and see Scotland, Ireland, England, France, Germany, Portugal and a few others. She's talked for a lot of years about doing that."

Aubry beamed a smile at her father. "Oh, Dad. She'd love that."

"Good. Don't tell her. I'll surprise her."

Now this was love, and her father constantly surprised her with how thoughtful he was, especially when it came to her mom. He could be a ruthless businessman one minute, and a sweet, considerate husband and father the next.

She really loved him.

"Where's Tucker tonight? Since the party started late, I thought maybe he'd show up after the game."

Her smile died. "I . . . don't know."

"Problems between the two of you?"

"Again. I don't really know, Dad. He's been distant lately. We'll talk or text, but we haven't seen each other. Like at all. And he keeps making excuses as to why we can't be together. I think we might be breaking up."

Her father was silent for a moment, studying his glass of whiskey before answering. Then he looked up at her. "I'm sorry, honey. But maybe it's for the best."

She frowned. "Why would it be for the best?"

"Oh, you know. Your career is so important. You should focus your attention on work and studies. And the possibilities of a fellowship. Not on romance. Plenty of time for that later."

"You and I have always fundamentally disagreed on that, Dad. Do you know a lot of doctors are married before they even enter medical school? Or they get married during their internship? Or residency? People can actually juggle a medical career and a personal life."

"People can, yes. But it's not easy. I just don't want you diverting your attention away from what's important—your career. And honestly, did you really think this thing with Tucker would have lasted? Him on the road half the season, you with your heavy schedule? When would you even see each other? It had to end sooner or later."

A niggling suspicion hit her. Surely he wouldn't. Well, yeah, he definitely would. She thought back to the timing of Tucker's sudden disinterest, and it fit. She had to ask. "Dad, did you say something to Tucker that night he was over for dinner?"

Her father shrugged. "I might have. But only in your best interests, Aubry."

"What did you say to him?"

"I might have, jokingly, of course, said that if he didn't break up with you I'd send him back down to Triple-A ball or trade him."

Icy-cold anger dropped like an anchor into the pit of her stomach. She laid her glass on the side table and stood. "How could you do that? And you know damn well that Tucker respects you as the owner of the Rivers. He would have never taken what you said as a joke."

Her father stood and approached her. "I only want what's best for you, Aubry. I always have."

She backed away. "Don't touch me. Don't . . . God, Dad, how could you do this? How could you manipulate my life this way?"

Her mother came in. "What's going on?"

She turned to her mother. "Dad threatened to trade Tucker unless he broke up with me."

Her mother's look was furious as she looked over at Aubry's father. "You did not."

"I thought it best the two of them not continue the relationship. You know how important her career as a physician is."

Disgusted with her father, Aubry raised her hands in the air. "I cannot be here right now." She walked across the room, kissed her mother on the cheek and left the room. She found her purse, grabbed her keys and said her good-byes to her aunt and uncle, claiming she had to get up extra early for her shift in the morning, then headed out the door.

She made it to the car and down to the end of the driveway before she had to stop and take several deep breaths. She raised her hands off the steering wheel and realized they were shaking. She had to get it under control before she got on the highway.

But how could she do that when her mind was filled with all the betrayal?

Her father, manipulating her life that way.

And Tucker, who hadn't once told her what her father had said, but had obviously made his choice. He'd chosen his career over her.

Of course he did. His career was important to him.

But why wasn't she?

And more importantly, why hadn't he told her?

Maybe because she just didn't matter to him as much as she'd thought. Maybe all these . . . feelings . . . had been one-sided. So his decision had been easier than she'd thought.

Tears pricked her eyes, one escaping to slide down her cheek.

"Oh, hell no." She swiped the tear away. She was going to get angry, not pitiful and sad. She would not feel sorry for herself. And she absolutely would not cry.

She gripped the steering wheel, took several cleansing breaths, determined to be strong about this.

Men were pricks and she was a survivor of idiot men. She pressed calmly on the gas pedal and headed for home.

Or at least she thought she was going home. For some reason her car ended up in the parking lot of Tucker's condo. It was late enough that he should be back home from the game. And lights were on.

There was no way she was going to let this rest, no way she was going to continue to let him avoid her. Not until she said what she needed to say to him.

She got out of the car and went to his door, her heart pounding with a combination of hurt, anger and just a little bit of trepidation.

She didn't know what kind of response she'd get from him.

Maybe her dad's ultimatum had been a relief. Maybe he'd wanted out, and that was why he'd been so easily avoiding her.

She shook her head and rang the bell. Tucker answered the door, his expression grim as he saw her.

"Aubry."

"I need to talk to you."

He raked his fingers through his hair. "Yeah, uh . . ."

She didn't let him finish, just pushed past him and walked into his living room.

He shut the door and turned to face her. "Aubry, look—"

"Don't bother," she said. "My father told me he threatened to trade you or send you down to the minors unless you dumped me."

"He did?"

"Yes. It was an awful thing for him to do. Why didn't you come and talk to me about it right away?"

He cocked his head to the side. "Come on, Aubry. Did you really think I was going to run and cry to you because your daddy was mean to me?"

"So instead you've been avoiding me? You think that's the better solution?"

"I was . . . thinking."

She let out a derisive laugh. "Oh. You were thinking. About what? How best to break up with me? You're an asshole, Tucker. I thought you were someone completely different—a man with honor and integrity, and someone who would never lie to me. I was so wrong about you—about us and what I thought we had together."

"Aubry, I'm sorry. I just didn't know what to do."

"Of course you didn't, because you're a coward. I'm so disappointed in you, Tucker. You could have at least had the balls to be honest with me. Or at least faced me and told me you'd chosen your career over me. That, at least, I'd have understood. Instead, you ran and hid from me. I don't want a man who'd do that, so guess what, Tucker? You're off the hook. We're done."

She headed for the door but Tucker was right there.

"Don't do this. Let's talk."

She laughed. "Oh, so *now* you want to talk? Too late." She stared at the door, then at him, demanding without words that he get the hell out of her way—out of her life.

He moved and she opened the door and stalked out, barely breathing as she made her way to her car. She shut the door and took several deep breaths.

She'd done what she needed to do. It was over now. She should feel better, clearer headed.

She didn't. Seeing him again just made her miss him even more. What they'd had together had been amazing. Why had he thrown it all away?

She sighed, gripped the steering wheel and forced herself to take several more calming breaths.

It was just another failed relationship. She'd get over it just like she'd gotten over the others.

Except this wasn't like the others. She'd never loved anyone before.

Her mind swept back to the look of utter misery she'd seen on Tucker's face while she'd been railing at him.

She shook her head. No. It wasn't possible that Tucker was hurting. The man couldn't possibly have a heart.

Otherwise, he wouldn't have broken hers.

THIRTY-FIVE

THERE WAS NOTHING LIKE THE FEELING OF SETTING
your boots on the front porch of your home. For Tucker, home
would always be the family ranch in Texas where his parents lived.
He stood outside in the early-morning hours watching the golden
sunrise over the tops of the trees, breathing in the Texas air.

It was the first time he'd felt good in weeks.

He might not be a football player like the rest of his brothers,
or like his father, but the Cassidy athletic dynasty was what made
him into the athlete he'd become. And he owed all of that to his
father, Easton. The man was a sports legend, had played football
in college and spent his entire career in Green Bay. He'd been one
hell of a quarterback, and he was one hell of a dad.

It was always good to come home and feel the energy his dad
still emanated.

Tucker needed some of that feel-good fire right now. Because
right now he felt broken.

Coward.

That word hovered incessantly in the back of his head like it had been branded there for all eternity. And he goddamn didn't like that feeling.

He heard the front door open and the sound of boots approaching. He knew without looking those were the sounds of his father's footsteps.

"You're up early. I would have thought you might have slept in."

Tucker looked over at his dad, who, even in his mid-fifties, still looked as robust and healthy as he'd been the last time he'd played a game for Green Bay. Working the ranch kept him active and Tucker was grateful for that.

"Haven't been sleeping much."

"I figured you didn't make this stopover because you wanted to spend a day helping me rebuild fence on the northeast side of the property."

Tucker laughed. "Yeah, not so much."

"Okay. What's going on?"

Tucker looked out over the front of the property. Dogs were playing and scrub blew across in the breeze. But it was calm and peaceful.

Not inside Tucker, though. Inside there was turmoil, a twister of emotions he needed to get out. "I'm in love with Aubry Ross. She's Clyde Ross's daughter."

"Clyde Ross being the owner of the Rivers?"

"Yeah."

"Is that a problem?"

"It wasn't until she brought me to her parents' house for dinner. Clyde pulled me aside and told me that Aubry's career in medicine has to take precedence in her life, and if I didn't stop seeing her he'd send me back down to Triple-A ball or trade me."

"Bastard." His dad took a sip of his coffee, then took a seat on one of the chairs on the porch, propping his feet up on the porch rail. "So what are you gonna do about it?"

"I don't know. If it was any other guy telling me to stop seeing his daughter or else, I'd tell him to fuck off. No one tells me what to do. But Clyde Ross owns the Rivers. He could do anything he wants to me, from trading me to sending me back to Triple-A ball."

Tucker sat on the top step, turning to face his dad. "Instead, I took a step back from the relationship, keeping my distance from Aubry."

"Understandable knee-jerk reaction to having your job threatened. What did Aubry say when you told her what her father said?"

"I didn't tell her. I didn't want to pit her between me and her dad."

His father took another few swallows of his coffee before answering. "Okay. I can kind of see your point there. But now I guess you're gonna have to choose."

The door opened. "Choose what?"

Tucker's mom came outside. A former lawyer, she was smart, savvy and had managed to raise five unruly children without killing any of them.

"Kid's got a problem with a woman and her dad," his father said. "Tucker, fill your mom in on what happened."

While his mom took a seat next to his dad, Tucker told her what had happened with Aubry and with Aubry's father.

"Well, hell," his mom said. "That's unfair. To you and to Aubry. She's not a child and she's old enough to make her own decisions regarding her personal life. But to threaten your career like that? That's below the belt, Tucker."

"Yeah. The worst thing is that I immediately backed away from Aubry. I deliberately avoided her. Deep inside, I knew it was the wrong choice, but I got scared."

"How do you know it's the wrong thing?" his mother asked, her lips curving as if she already knew the answer.

"Because I feel miserable. Every damn day I wake up feeling awful, and I go to bed feeling awful. I miss her. I miss talking to her and I miss seeing her. And even worse, she found out about her father's threat. She came to my condo and read me the riot act. Then she dumped me."

"Ouch." His mother sipped her coffee. "I don't blame her for being angry with you, Tucker. We women don't like it when men keep secrets."

"This is true," his dad said.

"You should have been honest with her from the beginning," his mother said.

Tucker grimaced. "That would have felt like running to Aubry to fix my issue with her dad. That didn't feel right to me. I don't know, none of this feels right."

"But is she worth losing your job over?" his dad asked. "Because if you continue this relationship with her, her father might make good on his promise."

"Yes. She is worth it." That's when he realized he should have told Aubry right from the beginning. He should have stood up to Clyde and told him he could do whatever he wanted to him, but that it wouldn't matter.

"I guess you've got your answer, then, Son," his father said. "But you've got to be prepared to live with the consequences."

"Yeah, I know. I guess I just needed the time to think this through. Or maybe I never needed any time to think it through. Hell, I don't know what I needed. I feel shitty now that I've let all this time go by. Aubry thinks I abandoned her, that I chose my career over her. She probably hates me."

"Oh, I don't know," his mother said, laying her hand on his dad's knee. "We women are very forgiving. We have to be, because you men are often idiots."

"Hey," his dad said, frowning at her.

She laughed, then rubbed her shoulder against his.

He looked at his parents, at the obvious love they had for each other even after all these years. He knew they'd had their squabbles over the years, had seen them argue, then make up. It was true love between the two of them.

That's what he wanted. What he wanted to have forever.

With Aubry.

Now he just had to get back home and see her after his game tomorrow night.

And make things right.

THIRTY-SIX

THE LAST PERSON AUBRY EXPECTED TO SEE AT THE hospital during her shift was her mother. When Marie buzzed her and told her that her mother was in the waiting area, Aubry's heart clenched. She quickly grabbed her phone, wondering if she'd missed an urgent call or text telling her something awful had happened.

Nothing.

She hurried out to the waiting room.

"Mom, what's up?"

"I'm sorry to bother you at work. I know you're busy."

"It's actually a fairly light day today, so don't worry. Is everything okay?"

Her mother grasped her arm. "Everything's fine. Do you have . . . a minute to get some coffee?"

"Sure. Let me tell them I'm taking a break."

She dashed in to tell Marie she'd be off for a short while to take her lunch, then met her mom. They left the hospital and walked down the street to a deli. Aubry ordered a sandwich with iced tea, and her mother got a coffee. They grabbed a table in the corner.

"How are you?" her mother asked. "I haven't seen you since—"

"The night I stormed out of the house? I'm sorry about that."

Her mom grasped her hand. "Do not be sorry about that. Your father was an ass. I'm still not speaking to him."

Her lips curved. She could imagine her mom giving her dad a really hard time. Her mother was sweet and warm and kind. And when she was angry—usually with her dad, the house could get very frosty.

That, at least, made her happy.

"I'm so sorry your father did that, sweetheart. He had no right to interfere in your life that way. I have had many conversations with him about this. Many. Conversations."

Aubry laughed. "I'm sure Dad has really enjoyed those conversations."

Her mother smiled over the rim of her coffee cup, then set the cup down. "He hasn't enjoyed them at all. But you can rest assured that he will never, ever again bother you about your work, or your personal life. And he will not be trading Tucker."

Aubry shrugged. "That part doesn't matter since it seems Tucker made his decision. He chose the Rivers."

"What does that mean?"

"It means he stopped seeing me. Not that I blame him. Career is everything, and I'm sure Dad scared the hell out of him by threatening to ruin his career. I'm just so mad at Dad. Hell, I'm mad at both of them."

Her mother sighed. "This just makes me angry with your father all over again. Maybe we should have hit up a bar instead. I could use a cocktail."

Aubry laughed. "It's not Dad's fault that Tucker chose baseball over me. Obviously our relationship isn't meant to be."

"Give the boy some time, Aubry. Your father can be more than a little intimidating. Heaven only knows what he said to Tucker. It might take him a while to come around. But based on what I saw of the two of you together, I don't believe for one second that Tucker plans to walk away from you forever."

She wished she had as much confidence in Tucker as her mother did. Unfortunately, she had all the proof she needed. He hadn't stood up to her father, and he'd deliberately backed away from her.

It was over.

She only wished she was over him. Unfortunately, her heart hurt, she was crushingly disappointed in him and she couldn't sleep at night. She wanted to lay all the blame at Tucker's feet, but she couldn't.

The worst part of it all was he'd never once talked to her about any of this. Other than the night she'd showed up at his place to vent her feelings, and that conversation had been decidedly one-sided. She'd walked out and they hadn't really talked things through. So she had no closure.

Not that it would help if she did. It was still going to hurt, but maybe they needed to have a sit-down, rational, two-sided conversation. An official end to their relationship.

Then, maybe, she could start to heal.

THIRTY-SEVEN

TUCKER SAT IN HIS LOCKER AT THE BALLPARK, THINK-
ing more about Aubry than about pitching tonight.

He'd spent as much time as he could with his parents, because
he didn't see them often enough. He left for the airport early this
morning to catch his flight back to St. Louis, giving him plenty of
time to make it to the ballpark for warm-ups.

But before he went out there, he needed to make contact with
Aubry. He sent a text message.

*I'd really like to see you. I'm pitching tonight. Can you come to the
game?*

He figured she was probably at work, so he didn't expect an
answer.

Except his phone buzzed.

I don't know.

He stared at his phone for a while, at the answer she'd given him.

Yeah, he deserved that. He deserved worse than that.

He typed a response.

Please.

He waited, and she responded right away.

I'll think about it. Gotta get back to work now.

It was the best he could hope for, but at least it wasn't an outright no. And that gave him some hope, which was a lot more than he expected.

He'd hang on to that and hope like hell she showed up for the game.

If not, he'd go over to her place after the game tonight and beg her to take him back. On his knees, if necessary.

After he told her he loved her.

But for now, he needed to get his head—and his pitching arm—ready for tonight's game. His curve still hadn't been working like he wanted it to, and that needed to be his number one priority. He'd been working on it with the pitching coach, and he was hoping to get the kinks out of whatever it was in his curve that had been kinked lately.

It was bad enough he'd totally fucked up his personal life. He at least needed to get his professional one back on track.

Grant had texted and told him that he and Katrina and the kids were coming to the game, so he'd at least have family in his corner tonight.

And right now, that counted for something.

AUBRY REFUSED TO LOOK AT THE CLOCK. THEY'D HAD several emergencies come in, she'd been running from room to room, and time had gotten away from her. She and Katie barely had time to exchange looks of utter agony as their hands were filled with broken bones, cuts and abrasions from a multi-vehicle accident.

Fortunately, there were no fatalities. By the time they had everyone either discharged or admitted, she was exhausted. She grabbed something to drink and stepped into the break room, where a couple of the attendings and some of the residents had tonight's baseball game on television.

Tucker was pitching. It was the top of the fifth inning. She was still torn about going to the game.

What was he going to say to her that hadn't already been said?

Or, rather, not said? He'd made his feelings and his choices abundantly clear to her. And despite the pain in her heart, deep down she understood.

Career came first. It had to. He was building his career, and she had gotten in the way.

Of course she first and foremost blamed her father for interfering in her life, but when push came to shove, the decision had been Tucker's.

But then again, she wanted closure, and maybe that's what Tucker was looking to give her.

The official breakup conversation.

No. He wouldn't do that at the stadium. He'd come to her house to break up with her. She might not understand a lot of things about him, but she knew him well enough to know he wouldn't officially break up with her at the Rivers' stadium.

Which made her wonder why he wanted her to come to the game? What did he want to talk about that couldn't wait?

She tried to sit in one of the corner chairs just to catch a breath and hydrate, but the announcer talked about the pitches Tucker was throwing, how every one of his curveballs was hitting the mark. Part of her tuned it out, but another part of her glanced at the score and realized the Rivers were up by two runs.

And they were in the top of the fifth inning, and the other team hadn't had a hit yet.

She stood, slowly making her way toward the television.

"What do you think, Aubry?" David asked her. "Do you think it's possible that Cassidy will throw a—"

She stopped him before he could get the words out. "Oh, my God, David. Don't say it. It's bad luck."

"You don't really believe in that, do you?" Dr. Chen asked.

He'd barely acknowledged her outside of their interactions during the workday. And she'd certainly never stood side by side with him watching a baseball game.

"In medicine? No. In baseball? Absolutely. So if you'd like Tucker to . . . you know, then no one say a word about it. You can think it and hope for it in your minds, but for God's sake, don't say it out loud."

And for the very first time in—ever—Dr. Chen smiled at her.

She started toward the other room where the lockers were located, but stopped at the doorway. "I'm out for the night."

"Headed to the ballpark to catch the rest of the game?" one of the residents asked.

She didn't even try to hide it. "Absolutely. I wouldn't want to miss this."

She and Tucker might be on the outs. They might even be over. But if there was even a chance he would . . . you know . . . there was no way she wouldn't be there to support him.

She hurriedly changed clothes and dashed to her car, grateful the hospital wasn't too far from the stadium and that she had a pass for VIP parking. She showed her pass to the gate attendant, then went downstairs instead of up. There were always extra seats available where the staff and wives sat above the batter's box. That's where she wanted to sit tonight.

She didn't want to sit in the owner's box. One, because her father was there. Two, because she wanted to sit with the crowd, to feel that anticipation, that level of excitement with everyone in the stadium, instead of being removed from it.

She said a quick hello to everyone, then found herself a vacant seat in between Liz Riley and Shawnelle Coleman.

"I thought you'd be in the owner's box with my dad," she said to Liz.

"The action's better down here. And . . . you know," she said, motioning to the field with her head. "There's some exciting action going on out there."

"Yes, I saw it from the lounge at the hospital. I got here as fast as I could."

"You're here at the best time," Shawnelle said. "It's getting really good now. He's given up a few walks so far tonight, but not . . . the other thing."

She'd missed an inning and the other team still hadn't had a hit. She swallowed hard as she felt the anticipation and excitement of the crowd, but there was also a kind of revered hush, as if the crowd didn't want to do anything to mess up Tucker's concentration. Baseball fans knew what was happening—what could happen—but they also knew not to say the words out loud, not even to each other in the stands. No one wanted to jinx Tucker.

Tucker took the mound at the top of the seventh and Aubry tried to gauge his mood as he warmed up, wondering if he was tense or if there was anything else on his mind. She recalled their text conversation before the game, actually pulled out her phone to look it over, hoping she hadn't said anything to upset him.

She could have been friendlier, but he'd caught her off guard. She hadn't expected to hear from him and didn't know what to make of his request to see her. She had hoped he'd had a change of heart and wanted to see her to tell her he loved her, but she refused to give in to that hope. But either way, she had to know.

She'd brushed it to the back of her mind with everything going on at work, and then she'd stumbled upon the . . . thing happening here at the ballpark, and no matter what went on between the two of them, she had to be here to support him.

She found herself holding her breath with every pitch and, along with the crowd, cheering wildly with every strike. When the first batter grounded out to first base, she stood and clapped. The second batter took two balls, then hit a pop fly to center field that was caught. Aubry had barely breathed as the ball sailed into the fielder's glove for the out.

Tucker threw two strikes in a row to the third batter, then three balls. The batter fouled off the next three pitches, battling the full count. When the batter hit a long ball to left field, Aubry stood, along with everyone else in the stadium. When the ball was caught by the fielder, the stadium erupted in wild cheers.

It was still on, and the Rivers were going to bat next.

"Oh, my God," Liz whispered, then turned to her. "Do you think?"

Aubry grinned. "I hope so. I really hope so."

"But you know we can't hope too hard. There are still two innings left."

"I know," Aubry said. "Anything can happen in two innings."

She'd seen it time and time again. A pitcher could take a . . . you know . . . into later innings, and all it took was one hit, and then it was over.

But still, she hoped. For Tucker's sake, she really hoped.

Plus, he was throwing so well.

She and Liz linked hands.

She couldn't imagine the pressure Tucker must be feeling right now, but she sent him every bit of mental good luck she could right now.

She had a very good feeling about the . . . thing.

This was Tucker's night. She just knew it.

TUCKER SLIPPED ON HIS JACKET AND SAT ALONE IN
the corner of the dugout. No one spoke to him, and he knew why.
Everyone knew why.

He didn't want to think about it. It was just another game, like
any other game, and he intended to approach his pitches the same
way he always did. Face each batter the same way as usual. Every
inning was just an inning that he wanted to keep run free.

And that was all he was gonna think about.

Right now he concentrated on the Rivers batting. They had a
man on first and third with one out in the bottom of the eighth
inning. When Dedrick Coleman slammed a long ball that went
over the left field fence, Tucker breathed a sigh of relief, then stood
to clap with his teammates.

They were up five to nothing. That was a great cushion for the
team in case he gave up some runs.

He had to focus only on that. The team. Winning the game.

Nothing else mattered.

When the Rivers finished the inning, he shrugged out of his
jacket and took the mound for the top of the ninth, appreciating
the roar of the home crowd. He drew in their energy, hoping like
hell he could finish this game with a win for them.

He refused to think about the other thing. That was a pipe
dream, a rarity for a pitcher. All he wanted to do was finish the
game. A shutout would be great. He'd aim for that.

He threw his warm-up pitches, then waited for the first batter
to come to the plate. Top of the order was up, so this wasn't going
to be easy.

His arm still felt good, though. He was within his comfort zone as far as total pitch count.

He was ready.

He took the pitch call from Sanchez.

A curve. His curve was on fire tonight—thank God—so he nodded, wound up and threw.

A strike.

His next two pitches were fastballs, and the batter bit on one that he grounded to the shortstop.

One out, and the crowd went crazy.

Two outs to go. Energy and nervousness sizzled down his spine. He pulled the energy forth and batted down the nervousness.

Just another game, and a game he needed to finish.

He walked around behind the mound, took the ball and rubbed it in his hands, focusing his concentration only on the next batter.

His first pitch was a ball, high and outside.

Shit.

Focus, Tucker.

He leaned in, took the sign from Sanchez, then threw the curve. It sailed perfectly and the batter swung and missed for a strike.

Tucker fed on the cheers of the crowd, the noise almost deafening. Focusing, he threw the next pitch, the batter swung and the ball sailed toward right field. For a second, Tucker didn't breathe—not until the ball landed in Trevor Shay's glove for out number two. Tucker exhaled, taking in the ever-increasing decibel level from the crowd.

He had to admit he dug it. A lot. It wasn't distracting to him at all, because his focus was on the prize now.

He absorbed the crowd noise and what was just beyond his grasp. He had this. One batter left. He could feel the win, and the win was all he was going for, was all he thought about. Not the other thing.

The batter came to the plate and Tucker was ready for him. He zinged a curveball and the batter didn't swing.

The ump called a strike.

The crowd was on their feet now, stomping and cheering as Tucker threw the second, another curve. This time the batter swung.

And missed.

Strike two.

Sweat poured down Tucker's face, down his back. He pulled off his ball cap to swipe his face with his arm, tucked his cap back on, then stared down the batter while waiting for the call sign.

This game was his. He had the batter and he knew it.

He took the sign from Sanchez, nodded, wound up and threw the pitch.

Curveball.

Called strike three.

Holy shit. He'd just thrown a no-hitter.

Holy shit.

The stadium erupted. Tucker threw his glove down and jumped up and down like a kid. He didn't care. It was a career maker. Sanchez came running to the mound and so did the infield guys. He was surrounded and tackled and he'd never laughed so hard.

He'd never been so elated, so goddamn relieved a game was over.

"You did it," Sanchez yelled at him.

The rest of the guys slammed him on the back and Tucker felt tears prick his eyes. He didn't even try to hold them back as the whole team surrounded him. He looked around at all his teammates, and despite the wild roar of the crowd, he thanked them all, because without their hot bats and their amazing defense, this wouldn't have happened for him tonight. He owed them everything.

He loved this team. He loved these guys.

The fans were still roaring as he made his way to the dugout.

"You gotta go back out there," Trevor Shay said.

He did, and lifted his cap to the crowd, making a full-circle turn to acknowledge the entire stadium. They roared even louder. He couldn't hold back his grin, unable to believe this had happened.

He'd thrown a no-hitter. It was still so surreal. He wasn't sure when this was going to really sink in.

Wow. Wow. It was something every pitcher dreamed of doing. It was something Tucker had dreamed about since Little League, but never in his wildest imaginings did he think it would ever happen to him in the big leagues.

His coach threw an arm around him.

"Goddamn fine job out there, Cassidy," Manny said. "One of the best games I've ever been a part of."

Tucker couldn't hold back his grin. "Thanks, Coach."

"You've got the whole team wanting to hug you and shake your hand, and about a billion press ready to talk to you. It's your night kid. Enjoy every minute of it."

"Thanks."

His pitching coach came over. "I think you can quit worrying about your curveball now, Tucker."

He laughed. "At least for tonight. Thanks for all your help, Bobby. I couldn't have done this without you."

Bobby shook his hand, squeezing his arm. "The talent is all yours, kid. I had nothing to do with it."

He still couldn't believe it had happened. He couldn't wait to talk to his parents and his brothers.

Grant. Grant had come tonight. He hoped he and Katrina and the kids would come down to the locker room. He couldn't wait to see his brother, and was so damn glad he'd been here for this tonight.

He turned to Manny. "My brother was here for the game tonight. Can you make sure he gets through to the locker room?"

"Which one?"

"Grant. And his girlfriend and her brother and sister."

"Sure. I'll take care of it. You just go enjoy the moment."

"Thanks, Manny." He couldn't get this stupid grin off his face. He could imagine his phone was blowing up with calls and texts right now.

But he sure as hell wished Aubry had been here to share it with him.

He was going to see her later. An even brighter spot than this win.

They'd talk. And he'd apologize like crazy to her.

But first . . . all this.

THIRTY-EIGHT

AUBRY SAT IN THE STANDS AND CRIED.

First, she'd cheered like a madwoman, screamed until she was hoarse and hugged both Liz and Shawnelle, all of them jumping up and down like kids. The whole stadium had rocked. She'd been thrilled to be a part of it.

And then she'd cried with utter happiness for Tucker. She couldn't even imagine what it must feel like for him.

She'd been around baseball her entire life, understood the nuances of the game probably more than she ever wanted to, thanks to her father. She'd watched a few no-hitters on television, and had even been present at the stadium for one before this, when she was a child. She knew what they meant to a pitcher. She knew what it meant for Tucker. It was a lifetime achievement that not a lot of pitchers ever realized. This was so momentous for Tucker. It was a game he'd never forget.

She was so grateful to have been here to see it happen.

She rubbed her arms, amazed to feel the chill bumps there.

For Tucker. She was so happy for him.

After spending some time chatting with Liz and Shawnelle, they made their way down to the locker room, which was an utter madhouse of players and press.

"We'll never get inside," she said.

"Ha. Think again," Liz said, pushing her way past the throng with her agent credentials.

Champagne was flowing. Or spraying. And Tucker was the recipient. He was drenched, as was everyone else within close range. Aubry stood back and absorbed the happiness running rampant through the room. It was a night for celebration, television crews were in there along with print press, and she couldn't be more excited for Tucker.

She hung back to watch it all.

When she saw her father walk in, he said hello to the press, then went over to talk to Tucker.

Aubry chewed on her bottom lip, wondering how that exchange was going to go.

She eased a little closer so she could hear what they were saying.

"You did a remarkable job tonight, Tucker. I'm so impressed." Her dad held out his hand.

"Thank you, sir." Tucker shook his hand.

Cameras caught it all, the two of them smiling at each other. She knew it was all for show.

"I need a break for a second, guys," Tucker said. "Mr. Ross, can I have a minute?"

"Sure."

Aubry ducked behind the lockers as Tucker pulled her dad away from the cameras.

The two of them ended up right where she was hiding.

"You can trade me," Tucker said.

"Excuse me?"

"I'm in love with Aubry, and I don't intend to stop seeing her. So send me back down to Triple-A ball or trade me. Whatever you want to do."

Aubry's heart squeezed.

He loved her. Tears filled her eyes.

He loved her. And he'd just thrown down the gauntlet to her father. Right there, in the locker room, with all those reporters standing five feet away.

Wow.

"Oh," her father said. "That. Well, I don't intend to do either."

Tucker shrugged. "Whatever. Just know that you can threaten me with anything you want to, but it's not going to stop me from loving your daughter."

Tucker started to walk away, then saw her leaning against the lockers.

Her dad saw her as well. "I'll let you two talk."

Her father walked away and she stepped out from between the lockers. She didn't want to ruin this moment for him, so she smiled and hugged him. "Congratulations on the no-hitter, Tucker. I am so happy for you."

He pulled back, his expression a mix of worry and utter elation. "You saw the game?"

She nodded. "I had to work late, but I got here. I saw some of it before I got here on the TV in the hospital lounge. As soon as I saw what was happening I raced over. I needed to be at the stadium to see it. For you."

Someone called his name. He looked back and nodded, then turned back to her. "I've gotta do this."

"I know."

He grasped her hand. "I still really want to talk to you, Aubry."

"I heard what you said to my father."

"I meant it. And I'm sorry. Those words don't seem adequate."

She let go of his hand. "We'll talk when you're done here. Come over to my place."

He looked over at his grinning teammates, at the field of reporters. "This might take a while."

She laughed. "I'm so keyed up I won't sleep anyway. Call me when you're done."

"Okay."

With a long, lingering look at her, he turned, wandered into the throng and disappeared.

Her father came over.

"Aubry."

She was still so angry with him, but he was her father, so she'd stand and listen.

"I've gotten an earful from your mother, and obviously you heard what Tucker said."

"I did."

"I'm so very sorry. Sometimes I let my concern for you outweigh my good sense. And I interfered in your life when I shouldn't have."

"You hurt me, Dad. And you hurt Tucker, too."

"I know. I love you, Aubry. It would kill me to lose you. Please tell me you'll forgive me."

She saw the pain in his eyes, and knew without a doubt his apology was sincere.

"I love you, too, Dad. But you have to start trusting in me. My career is important to me. I'm not going to do anything to jeopardize it."

"I realize that now. I also know you have a fine young man there, who's willing to change his career to be with you. That says a lot about his character."

She looked over to where Tucker was answering questions from the press. "Yes. And you owe him an apology as well."

"He'll get one from me, but not tonight. Tonight is his night and I intend to give him space to enjoy it. I'll talk to him tomorrow."

"You do that."

Her father stepped forward and grasped her hand in his. "From the time you were a baby I felt it was my responsibility to look out for you, to make sure you stayed on the right path. I guess I need to let you go now."

He looked so sad it broke her heart. "You never have to let me go, Daddy. You just have to give me the freedom to let me grow."

He pulled her close and hugged her. She wrapped her arms around him, knowing that the two of them were going to be fine.

"Now you go talk to the reporters and revel in your superstar pitcher," she said. "A pitcher you were almost stupid enough to let go."

Her father cocked his head to the side. "I can't believe you called me stupid."

"If the stupid hat fits . . ." she said with a smile.

Her dad smiled. "Okay, you're right. I own the stupid hat and I'll wear it with all the shame I deserve."

She laughed. "I'll talk to you later, Dad."

She headed out to her car, checking her text messages on the way. Several from her fellow residents all cheering Tucker's win.

One from Katie that just said, *Omgomgomg. A no-hitter! O.M.G. Hope you celebrate appropriately with your stud tonight.*

She smiled and shook her head, and hoped they'd get to the point where they could celebrate—appropriately.

She got in her car and headed home.

THIRTY-NINE

THAT HAD BEEN EXHAUSTING. EXHILARATING BUT also exhausting. Fortunately he'd worn more champagne than he'd had to drink, celebrating with Grant and Katrina and Leo and Anya, who'd all been thrilled to be at the ballpark for the no-hitter.

Tucker had gotten a huge hug from Grant, and finally kudos from the superstar quarterback who'd told him it was the best damn pitching he'd ever seen.

And Leo had been in awe to be in the locker room, so Tucker had introduced him to all the players and had told them all that Leo had just won his high school team's state championship. They all congratulated him, and Leo was probably grinning as much as Tucker.

He'd given a ton of interviews, so he drank a lot of water, and showered off all the champagne and sweat before getting in his car to drive to Aubry's.

He'd talked to his parents and his brothers and sister. He'd never heard his brothers more animated, or more excited about baseball. After all these years he'd gotten his brothers to admit that he was good at this baseball thing. The perfect part of this was he had text messages from all of them celebrating his no-hitter and telling him he was a damn good pitcher.

He intended to save those to throw it in their faces the next time they tried to make fun of him for choosing baseball over football.

It was a good night.

But now was the hard part—facing Aubry.

She'd come to his game tonight. He grinned as he pulled off the highway, unable to believe she'd actually showed up to the game. When he pulled into the parking lot of her condo complex, he was still smiling.

Hell, he might smile for days. He was running on a high that might not ever go away.

At least not until his next loss, which was inevitable.

He hoped it wasn't too late. Celebrations and interviews had lasted a lot longer than he'd expected them to. But her lights were on, so he knocked lightly at the door.

She answered right away. Her hair was straight, and she wore capris and a T-shirt, so it looked like she'd showered, too.

"Long night," she asked as she stood aside for him to come in.

"The longest."

She closed the door. "But the best, right?"

He shoved his hands in his pockets. "Yeah, it was pretty good."

She motioned toward the sofa, so he took a seat. She sat next to him. "Come on, Tucker. It was more than pretty good. It was amazing. You were amazing. And being a part of it—I can't even explain what that felt like."

He so wanted to touch her, to lay his hand on her knee, to tug her close so he could feel her body against his. But he had no right. Not anymore. Not after what he'd done. "I felt the electricity of the crowd while I was pitching. It really helped."

Her face was lit up with excitement. "I'm so glad. I was wondering if it would be too noisy for you there at the end. But we were all so caught up in the moment."

"No, it really did help. It was like a supercharged environment, and I really think it was all the positive vibes that helped me win."

She laughed. "No, it was your talent that propelled you toward that no-hitter tonight. Your curveball was on fire. It was like a perfect storm of pitches. You could do no wrong."

She was saying all the right things—about his game. "Thanks. It's a game I'll remember throughout my entire career. But you know, that's not why I'm here."

She took a deep breath, then let it out. "About my dad. I was so pissed at him. My mother is so angry with him. And he's very sorry. He said he's going to talk to you about that tomorrow. He owes you a big apology."

"Well, it happened. The worst part is I didn't do anything about it. It shocked me at first and I just kind of took a moment—a really long moment, unfortunately, to think about what that meant. Like, was he really serious? And if so, what would that mean for my career?"

She nodded. "Understandable. I mean, really, Tucker, I understand. You've worked your ass off to get where you are. Once I found out what my father did, I understood the choice you made."

She was letting him off the hook, and that wasn't acceptable. He shook his head. "No, it wasn't okay, Aubry. I didn't want to tell you what he said because I didn't want to put you in the middle between me and your father, forcing you to have to make a choice between us. Second, I should have chosen you. Right away, I should have chosen you. Because without you, this career means nothing to me."

Aubry's heart did that squeezing thing again, like it always did since she'd fallen in love with Tucker. She swallowed, her throat gone dry as she struggled for a response. "I . . . your career is everything to you."

"Yeah, it is. But when I tried to keep my distance from you, baseball didn't have the same spark. So while I love the game, I love you more. And I'm so sorry that I didn't realize that right away. Please forgive me for hurting you."

Now the tears fell, and she blinked them back. "Tucker. I love you, too."

He pulled her into his arms and kissed her, and it was like an explosion of warmth and love and the passion that had always been there with him. It was as if everything in her world was right as long as he was holding her.

"I've missed you," he said, rubbing his lips against hers.

She felt the heaviness of his hard cock pressing against her hip. "I've missed you, too. Make love to me."

He picked her up and carried her into her bedroom, then set her on the bed. He stood next to the bed and pulled off his T-shirt, then unzipped his pants, kicked off his shoes and let his jeans drop to the floor.

Aubry arched a brow. "Commando, huh?"

"I was in a hurry."

She reached for his cock. "Works for me."

She stroked him, tipping her head back to watch his face as she wound her hand around him, then put her mouth on him. His loud groans were her undoing, making her dampen and quiver with need.

He pulled his cock from between her lips and pushed her back on the bed.

"I need my cock inside of you."

He tugged on her capris and pulled them off, along with her underwear, then dragged her shirt over her head and made quick work of taking off her bra. Once naked, he swept his hands over her body.

"I've missed you like this. Naked, with my hands on you."

She shivered under his touch, those amazing goose bumps she got whenever he touched her. "Yes. Touch me."

He cupped the globes of her breasts, then rubbed his thumbs back and forth over her nipples, making her ache. As he snaked his hands down over her ribs, she parted her legs, giving him access to her sex. He cupped her, rubbed her clit and slipped his fingers inside of her, making her gasp at the shattering sensations he could evoke so quickly.

She hadn't made herself come since the last time they were together. It had been too long, and she was so ready she could go off right now. But, like Tucker, she wanted to come with him inside her.

"Now," she said. "I want you inside me now, making me come."

He got a condom and put it on, then pulled her to the edge of the bed and bent one of her legs, wedging it between his arm and body to hold her in place while he entered her. Then he leaned forward, thrusting into her with slow, deliberate strokes.

"This is where I belong, Aubry," he said as he moved within her. "This is where you belong."

"Yes." She arched her hips, giving him deeper access.

He bent and stretched lengthwise across her body, cradling her head between his hands, and kissed her. She was lost in him, drawn into the mix of love and sex, of emotion and powerful physical sensation.

"I can feel you tightening around me," Tucker said as he withdrew, then pushed into her. "Can you feel my cock swelling?"

She swept her hands over his shoulders, raking her nails down his arms. "I feel everything."

And when he ground against her, she splintered, unable to hold back her wild cry as she released. Tucker took her mouth, groaning against her lips as he came. She held tight to him as she rode out the waves of her shattering orgasm that left her limp, but oh so satisfied.

"Mmm," was all she could say afterward.

"Yeah." He pulled away and disappeared to deal with the condom, then came back. He sprawled on his side next to her and played with her hair.

"Do you work tomorrow?" he asked.

"No, I'm off."

"Good. We can stay up the rest of the night having sex."

She laughed. "Are you sure you have the energy for that? You've had kind of a busy night."

He toyed with her nipple, watching as it perked to a tight point. "Babe. I've got stamina to spare."

She looked over at him. "You're running on adrenaline. Eventually you'll crash."

"Maybe." He bent and licked her nipple, then blew on it, making her laugh. "We'll see how long I last then. I give it four or five more times."

She rolled her eyes. "I'm not sure I'll last for four or five more times."

"Lightweight."

This really was perfect. She wondered, though . . .

"Tucker."

"Yeah?"

"Can we really make this work? We both have crazy schedules."

He smiled and smoothed her hair away from her face. "I think that's what'll make our relationship work so well. Not despite our atypical jobs, but because of them. I won't have to worry about you being lonely while I'm on the road, because you have a career that keeps you busy and satisfied."

She rolled over on her side to face him. "And I won't have to worry about you being pissed off that I'm working so many hours, because you spend so much time on the road. And when we're together, it'll be quality time."

"Exactly. Face it, Aubry, we're perfect for each other."

"You're right. We are. Like tonight. Whenever we're together it's like we've been apart for months. Every time will be like this."

"Like the very first time." He swept his hand over her hip. "Explosive. Romantic. I promise."

"I believe you."

"I love you, Aubry."

Her heart flipped. "I love you, too, Tucker."

He pushed her back onto the bed and covered her lips with his, making her sigh with renewed arousal. He had always swept her away, had always wound her up with his words and his body and the way he had captured her attention from that very first night she'd found him in her parents' wine cellar.

Would it always be like this? So wild and crazy and filled with excitement. She didn't know, and even if it wasn't, she was in this relationship wholeheartedly with him.

Forever.

Dear Reader,

Thank you for reading *All Wound Up*. There will be more Play-by-Play books coming up. *Unexpected Rush*, book eleven of the Play-by-Play series, will be Barrett's story, releasing in February 2016. While you're waiting, I've included a first-chapter excerpt of *Unexpected Rush* for you to enjoy.

Coming up in December 2015 is *Make Me Stay*, book five of my Hope series. This is a small-town contemporary romance series with characters who all live in the same town, who all know one another and whose love for one another can get them through any of life's difficulties. I hope you enjoy the first-chapter excerpt included for *Make Me Stay*.

Happy reading,
Jaci

TURN THE PAGE TO READ A PREVIEW OF THE
NEXT BOOK IN THE PLAY-BY-PLAY SERIES

UNEXPECTED RUSH

COMING IN FEBRUARY 2016 FROM BERKLEY BOOKS

"MEN SUCK."

Harmony Evans tossed her purse on the kitchen table of her grandmother's house and sat next to her best friend, Alyssa. It was Thursday night—family dinner night at Granny's house. Everyone was coming over, just like every Thursday at Granny's. Right now she'd prefer to be sitting in the corner of a dark bar, nursing a dirty martini. She was going to have to settle for sweet tea because, short of death, you did not miss Thursday night dinner at Granny's.

She'd already come in and kissed Granny, who was holding court in the living room with Harmony's brother Drake and some of his friends, giving her time to catch up with Alyssa.

Alyssa laid her hand over Harmony's and cast a look of concern. "And why do you hate men? Is it Levon?"

Harmony wrinkled her nose, preferring never to hear the name of her now ex-boyfriend again. "Yes."

"Did you two break up?"

"I did not break up with him. He gave me the classic, "It's not you, it's me" speech. He's doing so much international travel with the law firm, and he just can't devote enough time to the relationship, so it wouldn't be fair to me to lead me on when he knows he can't commit. He went on with more excuses but it was all blah blah blah after that." She waved her hand back and forth.

Alyssa's gaze narrowed. "What a prick. Why is it so damn hard to find a man of value, one who will respect a woman and give her honesty?"

"I have no idea." Harmony pulled one of the empty glasses forward and poured from the pitcher that sat in the middle of the table, already filled with tea and ice and loaded with so much sugar she'd likely be awake all night. At this point, she didn't care. She'd work it off in a gym session tomorrow. "All I know is I'm glad to be rid of him. It was bad enough his bathroom counter had more product on it than mine did."

Alyssa laughed. "There you go. What does a man need on his counter besides a toothbrush, soap, deodorant and a razor?"

"According to Levon, there was stuff for his beard, trimming devices, facial scrub, moisturizer—separate ones for his face and his body. An entire manicure set for his nails, for use when he wasn't off getting mani-pedis of course."

"Of course," Alyssa said, then giggled.

"Oh, and the scents. Let's not forget his entire rack of colognes."

Alyssa nodded. "The man did reek, honey."

"I think he owned more perfume than I do."

"Never a good sign. See? You dodged a bullet."

"I did."

Alyssa lifted her glass. "Let's toast to that."

They clinked glasses. "To men we're lucky to have not ended up with," Harmony said.

"What are we toasting to?"

Harmony looked up to find Barrett Cassidy standing at the kitchen table. He was her brother Drake's best friend and teammate, and since the guys both played for the Tampa Hawks football team and they were in football season, Thursday nights meant Drake would drag his friends over to the house for dinner.

One of the nicest things about living in Tampa, as a matter of fact. She'd often thought it had been fortuitous that her brother had been drafted by the hometown team. It had kept him close to home all these years, and of course, one couldn't beat the awesome eye candy her brother brought home now and then.

Especially Barrett. Most especially Barrett.

"We're toasting the end of Harmony's relationship with a man who was absolutely not right for her," Alyssa said.

Barrett arched a brow, then gave Harmony a sympathetic look. "Really. Sorry about that."

Harmony shrugged. "Nothing to be sorry about. Alyssa's right. He wasn't the man for me."

"Then I guess I'm . . . happy for you?"

She laughed, and she could tell this was uncomfortable for him. "Come on. Sit down and have a glass of iced tea with us."

"I'm not sure I want to wade into these waters. Breakups are not my territory."

"Oh, come on, Barrett. Surely you've dumped a woman before," Harmony said, pouring him a glass. "Or you've been dumped."

He pulled out a chair and sat. She'd never realized before how utterly . . . big he was. He'd always kept his distance from her, preferring to hang with Drake, so this was the closest she'd ever been to him. Both he and Drake played defense for the Hawks. Barrett was absolutely pure muscle. Just watching the way his muscles flexed as he moved was like watching liquid art. She could stare at his arms for hours, but she tried not to ogle. Too much, anyway.

"I've been dumped before, sure," Barrett said. "And maybe I've broken up with a woman or two."

Alyssa leaned close to Harmony. "He's downplaying being the one who dumped the woman."

"I heard that, Alyssa."

"I meant for you to hear me, Barrett. You're just trying to be the good guy right now because we're roasting the not-so-good guys."

Barrett narrowed his gaze. "See, I told you I shouldn't be sitting here. If you're gonna want to bad-mouth my species—which you have a right to, since some asshole broke up with you, Harmony—then I should leave. Also, I'd suggest something stronger than iced tea. It helps."

So maybe he had been dumped before. It sounded like he knew how to get through it.

"It's okay, Barrett," Harmony said. "Me getting dumped is definitely not your fault. I'm not as pissed off about it as I probably should be, all things considered. So you're safe here."

Besides, looking at Barrett could definitely make her forget all about Levon and his prissy bathroom counter. She wondered how many items Barrett had on *his* bathroom counter? She'd just bet not many.

She turned her chair toward him, determined to find out. "Actually, I have a ridiculous question for you, Barrett."

He turned his gorgeous blue eyes on her and smiled. "Shoot."

"How many items currently reside on your bathroom counter?"

Barrett cocked a brow. "Huh?"

Alyssa laughed. "Very good question."

"I don't get it," Barrett said.

"We're conducting a poll about men and their bathrooms," Alyssa said. "Indulge us."

Barrett finally shrugged. "Okay, fine. Uh . . . soap, of course. Toothpaste and toothbrush. Deodorant. Maybe a comb?"

Harmony smiled when Barrett struggled to come up with anything else. She knew he was an absolute male of the not-so-fussy-about-his-grooming variety.

He finally cast her a helpless look. "I don't know. I've got nothin' else. Did I fail?"

"Oh, no," Harmony said. "You most definitely passed."

"You should go out with Barrett," Alyssa suggested. "He's a nice guy, and he obviously doesn't keep thirty-seven things on his bathroom counter."

Barrett laughed. "Yeah, and Drake would kill us both. Well, he'd definitely kill me."

The idea of it appealed, though. She'd had such a crush on Barrett when Drake had first introduced them all those years ago. And now? Hmmm. Yeah, definitely appealing.

"What my brother doesn't know won't hurt him—or you. What do you say, Barrett? Care to take me out?"

BARRETT WAS AT A LOSS FOR WORDS. HARMONY WAS his best friend's little sister.

Only she wasn't so little anymore. When he'd first been drafted by Tampa, he and Drake had bonded. Both of them played defense, they'd been roommates and they'd become friends. It had been that way for the past five years.

He'd been coming here to Granny's house ever since that first year, back when Harmony had been in college. Now she was a woman, with a career of her own, and she'd just been dumped by some guy obviously too stupid to know what a treasure he'd had.

She was beautiful, with light brown skin, long, dark curly hair and those amazing amber eyes. She had the kind of body any man would want to get his hands on, curves in all the right places . . .

And he had no business thinking about Harmony at all, because there was a code—no messing with your best friend's sister.

Absolutely not. No. Wasn't going to happen.

He pushed back his chair and stood, looking down at Harmony as if she was Eve in the Garden and she'd just offered him the forbidden apple. "I know the rule, Harmony, and so do you. I think I'll go check out what Granny made for dinner tonight."

He might be tempted, but there was too much at stake. He was going to step away from the sweet fruit in front of him before he decided to do something really stupid and take a taste.

Because going down that road would spell nothing but doom.

TURN THE PAGE TO READ A PREVIEW OF THE
NEXT BOOK IN THE HOPE SERIES

MAKE ME STAY

COMING IN DECEMBER 2015 FROM JOVE BOOKS

REID MCCORMACK STUDIED THE BLUEPRINTS FOR THE old mercantile he'd agreed to renovate in downtown Hope. He still had no idea what he was doing back in his hometown, or why he'd agreed to this job.

It was a big project, and he had plenty of projects with his company in Boston. Shifting responsibilities over had been a giant pain in the ass, as was taking a leave of absence and putting his company—his baby—in the hands of his associates. He'd sweated blood and risked a hell of a lot of money to get his architectural firm up and running, and with numerous late nights and damn good work, he'd made a success of McCormack Architectural Designs.

The thought of not being in Boston overseeing the business sent a shot of nervousness straight to his gut. But, he had to admit, when he'd come to town for his brother Logan's wedding in the spring, and they'd taken a look at this old place, it had been the childhood memories, plus the challenge of restoring the mercantile to its former glory, that had been too hard to resist.

He had ideas for the mercantile. A lot of them. And now that he and his brothers had bought the old building back from the town, it was their responsibility to do right by it. Though Logan and Luke's contribution was limited to providing their part of the capital. As the architect in charge of the project, Reid was going to be the one to put the actual work into it.

He intended to do it justice.

And when the job was done he'd head back to Boston, where he belonged.

Because while Hope would always be home to him, it wasn't his home anymore.

So now he stood in the middle of a pile of crap covering the main floor of the old mercantile, his boots kicking around years' worth of dust and debris. He might be the youngest McCormack brother, but he had great memories of this old place.

His lips ticked up as he remembered the old building in its glory days. One particular day, Dad was walking them past, trying to corral three rambunctious boys on their way to the ice cream store. Reid was always the best behaved, so he'd stayed by Dad's side while Logan and Luke ran off ahead, getting into one thing or another. But he and Dad had stopped to look inside. At the time, there had been offices, with busy people doing their jobs. Even at age five, Reid had been fascinated by the old brick building. Dad had been, too. Reid could still remember the people inside stopping to smile and wave at him. And he'd waved back.

Mom hadn't been with them that day. She often wasn't. Raising kids hadn't been her favorite thing.

Had she ever come to town with them? She'd often gone into

Tulsa by herself to shop. But she'd never brought him or his brothers along. She'd said they were too rowdy and she needed her space.

Yeah, she'd needed a lot of space. So much space that as soon as Reid had turned eighteen, she'd taken a hike.

Forever.

He heard a knock on the front door, dissipating the cloud of memories.

Figuring it was the general contractor he'd hired—or maybe his brothers, who were also supposed to meet him here today, he went to the door and pulled it open.

It wasn't the contractor or his brothers. It was Samantha Reasor, the owner of the flower shop around the corner. Sam was the one who'd pushed hard for them to take on this project. Or rather, for him to take it on. She was as passionate about the mercantile as anyone in Hope.

Today she wore skinny dark jeans that showcased her slender frame. Her blond hair was pulled high on top of her head, and she had on a short-sleeved polo shirt that bore the name "Reasor's Flower Shop." And she had the prettiest damn smile he'd ever seen, with full lips painted a kissable shade of pink.

Not that he was thinking about kissing her or anything. He was back in Hope to work.

"Hi, Reid. I heard you were in town and getting ready to start the project. I couldn't wait to get inside here again. I hope I'm not bothering you or anything. If I am, I can take off."

"Hey, Sam. You're not a bother. Come on in. Though the place is still as dusty as it was when we did the walk-through in the spring. Are you sure you want to get dirty?"

She waved her hand as she stepped in. "I don't mind. I've been arranging flower baskets all day for an event. There are probably leaves in my hair."

As she walked by, he inhaled the fresh scent of—what was that? Freesia? Roses? Hell if he knew since he didn't know jack about flowers, only that Sam smelled damn good. And there were no leaves in her hair.

She turned in a circle, surveying both up and down the main room. "It's amazing, isn't it?"

He laughed. "Right now it's a dump."

Her gaze settled on him. "Oh, come on. Surely you can see beyond the trash and the layers of dust to what it can be. Do you have ideas yet? I mean, of course you do, because you're here to renovate." She spied the rolled-up documents in his hand. "Do you have blueprints?"

"Yeah."

"Care to share? I'd love to see the plans you've worked up."

"Actually, the general contractor is due to show up here shortly, along with Luke and Logan. You're welcome to hang out while we go over them."

She pulled her phone out of her back pocket. "Unfortunately, I can't. I have a delivery to make in about thirty minutes. But I'd really like to see the blueprints. Are you busy for dinner tonight?"

"Uh, dinner?"

"Sure. Why don't you come over to my place? I make a mean plate of spaghetti. If you're not busy with your family. I know you'd like to get reacquainted with them, so I don't want to step all over that."

"No, it's not that. I've been here a couple days already, so we've done the reacquainted stuff." He didn't know what the hell was going on. Was she asking him out, or was she just interested in seeing the blueprints?

"Perfect. Give me your phone and I'll put my address and cell number in it."

He handed his phone over and Sam typed in her info.

"Is seven okay?" she asked. "That'll give me time to close up the shop and get things going."

"Sure."

"Great." She grasped his arm. "I'm so glad you're here, Reid. I'll see you later. You and your blueprints."

She breezed out the door and he found himself staring at the closed door, wondering what the hell had just happened.

Sam probably just wanted to get a good look at the blueprints when they'd have more time. She was interested in the old building. Not in him.

And he wasn't interested in her. Or any woman. He was in town to refurbish the mercantile, and nothing more.

But at least he'd get to enjoy her company and a home-cooked meal tonight.

SAM WENT BACK TO THE SHOP, WISHING SHE'D HAD more time to check out Reid—check out the blueprints. Not that Reid wasn't some awesome eye candy. Today he'd worn loose jeans, boots and a short-sleeved T-shirt that showed off his tanned, well-muscled arms.

It had taken everything in her to walk out of the mercantile. Fortunately, she had a job and a timeline, and that always came first. She loaded up the flowers that Georgia Burnett had ordered for the chamber of commerce luncheon today, put them in her van and drove them over to the offices. Georgia, who'd had a terrible fall last year and had spent several months laid up, was back to her old cheery, mobile self again. And since she was the mother of two of Sam's friends, Emma and Molly, Georgia was like a mother to Sam as well. Which was so nice since the only family Sam had left was her Grammy Claire.

And family was a big deal to Sam.

"Hello, Georgia, how are you?"

"Doing wonderfully, Samantha. And you?"

"Great." She pressed a kiss to Georgia's cheek while simultaneously juggling two baskets of flowers.

"The baskets are gorgeous, honey," Georgia said. "The tables are already set up inside, so you can place them in the center of each one."

"Will do."

Sam went about her business, and once she finished, she said good-bye to Georgia and headed back to the shop. She had several individual flower orders to prepare and deliver, which took up the remainder of her day.

Which suited her just fine. Busy was good for business, and business had been great lately. She had two weddings coming up, including Georgia's daughter Molly's.

When her phone buzzed, she smiled. Speaking of the bride-to-be . . .

"Hey, Molly," she said, putting her phone on speaker so she could continue to work.

"Are you sure the peach roses are going to come in on time?" Molly asked.

"Yup."

"And how about the lilies? Oh, and the corsages for my mom and for Carter's mom?"

"All under control, honey."

Molly paused. "I'm being a neurotic mess, aren't I?"

"Nope. You're being a bride. This is normal."

"I have a checklist of items; and then I came across flowers, and I know we've gone over this a hundred times, but you know, I just had to check."

Sam was used to this. Brides called her all the time, even if everything was perfect. "Of course you had to check. Call anytime. But Molly? I've got this. Trust me."

"Okay. Thanks, Sam."

"You're welcome. I'll talk to you soon." She hung up, figuring Molly would call her again tomorrow.

Which didn't bother her at all, because as a florist, her job was to keep her customers happy. And when one of her customers was also one of her closest friends, that counted double.

She delivered the afternoon flowers, then came back to clean up the shop and prep things for tomorrow morning. By then it was closing time, and she made a quick grocery list so she could dash in and get what she needed for dinner tonight.

She had no idea why she'd invited Reid over for dinner. First she had to go in and start blabbering at him like she had some kind of motormouth disease.

Ugh. What was wrong with her, anyway? She was normally calm and in control of herself.

Except around Reid for some reason. Ever since that night at Logan and Des's wedding when she'd sat next to him and felt an instant ping of attraction.

And once it was there, she'd been ridiculously shy around him.

Normally when a woman was shy, she'd be quiet, right?

But not Samantha. No, she had run-of-the-mouth issues when she was around a man she was attracted to.

So what did she do with Reid? She invited him to dinner. An impulse suggestion, for sure, and only because she really wanted to see the blueprints. But was that the only reason? When he'd been in town in the spring for the wedding, she'd definitely felt that tug of . . . something.

Then he'd gone back to Boston and she'd ignored it then, figuring it was nothing more than a passing mutual interest in the mercantile, but seeing him today, that tug had been something entirely different, and totally biological.

She chewed on her bottom lip and decided to call her best friend,

Megan, for some advice. She punched in Megan's number on her phone.

"What's up, Sam?" Megan asked when she answered.

"Reid McCormack is back in town."

"Oh, great. So he's going to start work on the mercantile."

"Yes. I popped over there today when I saw him go in. And then I invited him to dinner."

Megan paused. "That's interesting. Why?"

Sam pulled up the stool behind the counter and took a seat. "I don't know. Impulse. And, you know, I got to talking to him. I might have overtalked."

"You babbled."

Leave it to her best friend to know her so well. "Yes, I babbled. I guess I babbled my way into inviting him over for dinner. We were chatting about the building and he had the blueprints, which I was really interested in, and I could tell he was busy, so it was an impulse thing."

"Always go with your impulses, Sam. You're obviously attracted to him. Did he say yes?"

"He did. And why do you think I'm attracted to him?"

"Everyone saw the way the two of you hung out at the mercantile in the spring."

Sam frowned. "What do you mean, everyone saw? What did they see?"

"Oh, you know. Heads together, wandering around checking the place out. And when you climbed up the ladder to look at the tin ceiling? He checked out your butt."

Sam leaned her arms on the counter. "He did not. He did? Really?"

"He did. Chelsea and I were watching. And he was not looking at the ceiling. He was looking at your butt."

"Now that *is* interesting."

"I know. So enjoy dinner. And see what happens for dessert."

"I will. But you know, I didn't invite him for dinner to have . . . dessert with him."

Megan laughed. "Sure you didn't."

"Megan, I'm serious. I just wanted to see his blueprints."

"Is that what we're calling it now?"

Sam rolled her eyes. "You're so funny."

"I know I am. Call me tomorrow with all the details."

"Okay."

She hung up, grabbed her purse and locked up the shop, then headed out to her car. Once inside, she looked at her phone to double-check her grocery list.

She was going to cook a spaghetti dinner for Reid McCormack tonight, and then she was going to look over his blueprints. And by blueprints, she really meant actual blueprints. Nothing involving "dessert."

But if he checked out her butt again, dessert might be back on the menu. And she wasn't talking sweets.